WHEN A STRANGER CALLS

JEN TALTY

This is a work of fiction. Names, characters, places, and incidents either are the product of the author's imagination or are used fictitiously, and any resemblance to actual persons living or dead, business establishments, events, or locales is entirely coincidental.

WHEN A STRANGER CALLS: New York State Troopers Series, Book Six

COPYRIGHT © 2017 Jen Talty

All rights reserved. No part of this book may be used or reproduced in any manner whatsoever without written permission from the author or Cool Gus Publishing except in the case of brief quotations embodied in critical articles or reviews.

Jupiter Press

A very special thank you to THE TALTY CREW! Without your support and feedback I wouldn't have been able to step out of my comfort zone and write this book!

To Casey Hagen…Thanks for making me laugh.

To all the men and women who serve in law enforcement. You are greatly appreciated!

NOTE FROM THE AUTHOR

This, for now, is the last book in the *NY STATE TROOPER SERIES*. I have loved writing this series and sharing it with you.

However, please check out *THE BUTTERFLY MURDERS*, which is set in my native town of Rochester, NY.

Sign up for my Newsletter (https://dl.bookfunnel.com/6atcf7g1be) where I often give away free books before publication.

Join my private Facebook group (https://www.facebook.com/groups/191706547909047/) where she posts exclusive excerpts and discuss all things murder and love!

Never miss a new release. Follow me on
Amazon:amazon.com/author/jentalty
And on Bookbub: bookbub.com/authors/jen-talty

PROLOGUE

Fifty years ago...

Rusty Fowler stared at the infant suckling at his wife's breast, his little fisted hand resting against her chest.

"He's beautiful," he whispered as he ran his hand across the baby's bald head. "And so are you."

Ashley looked up at him with a bright smile and tears in her eyes. "Are you sure you want to keep up with this charade?"

"It's not a charade and I've never been surer of anything in my life." He sat on the edge of the hospital bed. "I told you seven months ago that I loved you and can't live without you." He'd met *his* Ashley at the local corner store. She'd been shopping for the family she cooked for and he'd been on his way home after a double shift in a factory in the next town over. It didn't bother him that she'd already been pregnant. He loved her at first sight and she loved him back.

"But the baby isn't yours."

He stroked the baby boy's cheek with his index finger. Rusty would have been crazy not to worry about resenting this child, considering he couldn't have any of his own, but the moment he laid eyes on the boy, he knew that somehow, he'd make this trio a family. "I am this boy's father. The only father he will ever know."

Ashley let out a guttural sob.

"Don't cry, baby."

"I don't deserve you."

"It's me who doesn't deserve you." He kissed *his* Ashley on the lips. "What shall we name our son?"

"Our son," she whispered. "Russell, after you of course."

"And his middle name?"

"You pick."

He thought about it for a long moment. "Merriman. Your maiden name."

"Russell Merriman Fowler. It's perfect."

"Just like his mother."

She smiled, staring at her son, tears gliding down her cheek. "I want to quit my job and stay home with our son. I was thinking I could start a catering business."

"Sounds wonderful."

Rusty leaned over and kissed *his* son. No one could take that away from him now.

CHAPTER 1

BROOKE FOWLER STARED at her late grandfather's will, which left everything to her. Everything included a rundown house in Lake George, fifty-thousand dollars, and an old brass key with an illegible note. She wiped a single tear that had rolled down her cheek, swallowing the primal need for revenge.

In less than two weeks, she'd lost all she'd held dear.

Finding out her live-in boyfriend had been cheating on her with *her* own assistant sent her over a cliff she wasn't sure she could ever recover from. She balled her fists just thinking about it. She should regret having tossed an expensive one-of-a-kind painting at Debbie, her assistant, but she didn't. She didn't even regret trashing her office, then storming off to the eighth floor where all the VP offices were located, trashing her boyfriend's office, along with tossing a mug at him, though the bastard ducked and she missed.

Getting fired and arrested? Yeah, that sucked. Big time.

The worst, though, had been finding out her grandfather had died. He was all she had in the world and now he was gone. She never got a chance to say good-bye and tell him how much he'd meant to her, even when she didn't always show it. She, of all people, should know how precious life was and how quickly it could be taken away.

"Sorry to have kept you waiting," her grandfather's attorney said.

"I kept my grandpa waiting and he died."

"Excuse me?"

Brooke blinked and looked around the lawyer's office decorated in modern white furniture with wall to wall bookcases, which held, old, thick law books. Whoever decorated this place should be shot.

"I cancelled a visit with him to go to a stupid party with my boyfriend, only I didn't even get to go to the party." She thought about continuing the ugly story, but what would be the point? Instead of going to the one person she could always turn to in times of need, she spent the night in county lock-up. No amount of mascara would make any mug shot look good.

"Mr. Fowler was eighty."

Brooke narrowed her eyes. "A spry eighty, thank you very much." Though, she'd been begging him to go to the doctor for a physical. Turned out he had a heart condition. The doctors told her that even if the condition had been caught a few months ago, he still might have had a massive coronary anyway. That didn't make her feel any better.

And now she was alone.

Really alone.

"Is there any reason I'd have to leave the house?" She'd only arrived in Lake George two days ago. When she reached the house after identifying her grandfather's body, the front door had been wide open. She thought maybe the paramedics had left it that way. That was until she walked into her grandpa's guest bedroom, which had also been his office, and all his desk drawers had been pulled out, files everywhere.

But the kicker had been the next morning when she walked into the kitchen and the back door had been ajar and she knew damn well she hadn't left it unlocked. She called 9-1-1 for a second time. The cops had been nice enough, but couldn't really do anything except talk to a few of the neighbors.

"No reason why you can't live at the house," the attorney said.

"What about the money?" God, she sounded like a cold-hearted bitch. She wanted to scream *I loved my grandpa. He was the best man in the world!* But again, what would be the point? Both her parents and her grandparents had taught her to be practical. Chin up and face the world head on, no matter what.

Being jobless also required her to be practical.

Facing a misdemeanor charge of assault and a civil lawsuit *required* her to be balanced and level headed, which certainly wasn't an easy task in her current state of mind.

"There are various legalities we need to jump through, but this is a simple estate, so I suspect two months, three at the most."

Brooke did a mental calculation of her bank accounts and current bills, the biggest one being the Camaro convertible she'd splurged on when she'd been promoted to Regional Sales Manager. She could sell the car and buy a Hyundai. Easy peasy.

Not.

Acid bubbled up her esophagus. She loved that damn car.

"What about my pending legal situation?"

"It could slow things up, but not by much." The attorney handed her a business card. "I don't handle those kinds of cases, but this woman does and she's very good. If you don't have a lawyer for that situation, call her. I'll tell her you're a client of mine and I'm sure she'll cut you a break."

Brooke took the card. *Jillian White-Sutten, Attorney at Law.* "I will call her. Thanks." Another thing she couldn't afford.

"I need a few signatures on these papers." The lawyer pushed a couple of documents across the desk.

Brooke scanned the papers, which were all requests for probate court, and signed them.

"I'll be in touch," the attorney said.

Brooke nodded as she gathered up her belongings. The lawyer's secretary walked her to the front door.

She stepped onto the sidewalk, her brand new black Camaro, parked in front of the building, taunted her. Her grandfather had been so proud of her accomplishments, always reminding her that her parents and grandmother were smiling down at her. She looked to the sky and waved. "Sorry. Seems I've developed a temper."

People walked by, giving her weird looks. She shrugged it off. Let people think she was nuts. Her mind had fractured in a million directions. Her heart shattered. The combination sent her into a rage she thought would take over her life if she didn't find a way to push it down, controlling it, until she found the time to fall apart. She hopped in the car, revved the engine while the top folded down, before slamming it into drive and pulling out onto the street, heading for the main drag off Lake George Village.

By the time she turned off Beach Road on to East Shore drive, tears burned the sides of her face, probably taking thick clumps of mascara with them. With no cars in sight, she pressed down hard on the gas. Her trembling fingers curled around the steering wheel at ten and two. The wind whipped her hair across her face. She blinked, picturing the forty-five-degree turn coming up, followed by a few lesser curves, but still harrowing at higher speeds. Foot to the floor, she wanted to feel the car lean on its edge, taking the turn fast, hard, and out of control.

Fire flew from her skin as it did when she'd gone bat-shit crazy in her office. 'Ballistic Brooke', that's what her ex-coworkers called her as she'd been escorted out of the building…in handcuffs.

She sucked in a breath, lifting her foot of off the pedal, tapping the brakes.

Her heart skipped a beat and her body trembled. She'd never been an adrenaline junkie, so why did she all of a sudden want to test her own limits?

The next five miles she did her best to control her breathing and clear her brain. She should be thinking about her grandfather's funeral arrangements, not what it would be like to start a new career as the female version of Evil Kneivel.

She pulled into the country store at the corner of Cleverdale and Route 9. When she'd been little, her grandparents would give her a dollar and she'd go to this very store and buy an ice cream, skipping the entire way. Glancing around the parking lot, she realized how much it had changed, yet stayed the same. Another line of gas pumps and an addition to the building were the most notable changes.

She leaned forward and cleaned up her face. She really wasn't a vain woman, but her grandmother taught her that a little style and grace made a powerful woman less intimidating.

The bell rung above the store door, just like it always had. The pimpled-faced kid behind the register didn't even look up, his fingers tapping away on a smartphone. She made a beeline for the freezer and snagged three boxes of Éclair's ice cream on a stick. The chocolate ones. Her father's favorite. After that, she stopped in the beer section and picked up a case of her parent's favorite beer.

The kid looked up at her when she dropped the case on the counter.

"I.D., please."

She laughed, though it sounded more like a snooty grunt. At almost thirty, getting proofed didn't happen often. "Thanks." She signed the credit card receipt and picked up her groceries, turning on her heels, nearly walking right into Mrs. Georgina Ramsworth. "Excuse me," Brooke muttered, adjusting her bag and her beer.

"I would say so." Stuffy Mrs. Ramsworth lowered her gaze to Brooke's feet, then followed it up to her face with a scowl. "I'm sorry for your loss. We were very grateful to your grandfather for being our driver and taking care of the house during the winter these last few years." The words might be kind, but the woman giving them was anything but. "He will be missed."

"Thank you. I appreciate it."

Mrs. Ramsworth reached out toward Brooke's chest, but yanked her hand back as if she'd been burned. "Such an exquisite pendant. Where did you get it?"

"It was my grandmother's," Brooke said as she tried to scoot around the unpleasant lady so she could make a beeline to her car, before she told her to screw off.

"It looks like an antique. And quite expensive, dear."

Brook chomped down on her tongue. "It belonged to my grandmother."

"I see." Mrs. Ramsworth frowned. "When will the funeral

arrangements be announced?" Mrs. Ramsworth always reminded Brooke of Cruella Deville with the way she constantly looked down at anyone who wasn't from the same stock as her.

"I'm working on them." She wanted to add it would be private, but her grandfather would have a hissy fit right there in heaven. He wanted people to celebrate his life.

"If you need anything, we are right down the street."

Right, like she'd let Brooke through the front gate. Her husband, the original Wendell Ramsworth, however might. He'd always been sort of nice to people, but his wife certainly wore the pants in that family. "Nice to see you again." *Not.* "I need to get going."

Mrs. Ramsworth pointed at the case of beer. "That isn't going to solve anything, dear. I know you're hurting, but it's really not the way to deal with it."

Why? Because it's not a five-hundred-dollar bottle of wine?

"I have a friend dropping by, so it's not all for me." Wow. She just resorted to lying to a woman who would judge her no matter what she did.

Brooke scooted around the snobby socialite and ran for her car, dumping her ice cream and beer into the passenger seat. When she turned, she caught the ugly gaze of the younger Wendell Ramsworth, the eldest and only grandson. Great. Just what she needed.

"Hello, Brooke," he said as he leaned against the hood of her car. "I'm real sorry about your grandfather. He'd been very supportive this last year with my situation, so, if there is there anything you need, just let me know."

"Really?" She gritted her teeth. "It's one thing for your grandmother to be fake nice to me, but you?"

"There's no reason for me not to be nice and I know Michelle would love to see you." He reached out and squeezed her shoulder. "You know how to reach us if there is anything we can help you with."

"Thanks to you, Michelle and I haven't talked in years, so, don't go acting like we're all hunky-dory." Wendell didn't care about anyone else but himself. He acted all nice and sweet, but deep down he was a ruthless, self-serving bastard, and he proved that the day he made her out to be a liar in the eyes of her best friend.

He laughed. "I'll tell Michelle you said hello."

"Whatever." She hopped into her car. Heat bristled off her finger tips as she slammed the gearshift into drive, gravel peppering the air in the wake of her spinning tires, causing the back end of the car to fishtail. She didn't care about anything other than the pounding of her heart against her chest. Tears once again stung at her eyes. Holding the pedal down, the engine roared like a lion, drowning out the million thoughts crushing her brain.

Sirens bleeped behind her.

She jumped, easing her foot off the gas, slowing the car down. She blinked a few times, trying to pull herself back to reality from wherever she'd just gone. Her hands quivered as she rolled the car to a stop on the side of the road, shifting it back into park. Her heart beat so fast it smacked the back of her throat.

What the fuck was she doing? Had she lost her ever lovin' mind?

She checked the rear-view mirror and did her best to rub away the black smudges under her puffy, bloodshot eyes.

The State Trooper stepped from his vehicle, looking around as if he didn't have a care in the world as he adjusted his hat and hooked his sunglasses into his pocket.

She turned around, clutching her chest, wondering if she should get her license and registration out. She'd been pulled over before. Most cops were nice enough, even if they did give you a ticket, but since her night behind bars, all cops gave her heartburn.

"Ma'am," the trooper said, resting his hand on the door.

She blinked, mustering up the courage to look at him.

"Do you know why I pulled you over?"

She nodded, gripping the steering wheel, prying her eyelids open. "Sorry, I've had a bad day," she whispered as she turned her head, opening her eyes. She gasped at the deep color of his eyes. Intense, dark chocolate eyes.

"Are you okay?" He arched a brow, leaning a little closer.

She blinked a few times, mesmerized by the richness of his stare. "Ma'am?"

"Umm…yeah, I'm okay."

He cleared his throat. "Not to be rude, but you look like you've been crying. Did something happen back at the store?"

"What?"

"I noticed you talking with a gentleman before peeling out of the parking lot. Did he upset you? Hurt you?"

She shook her head, shifting her gaze, making damn sure she didn't focus on his pupils, which was like staring into the eyes of a cobra, but one that didn't want to strike. Or maybe he did. "No. I was upset before I ran into that ass…Mr. Ramsworth." She wiped her cheeks.

He cracked a smile, which annoyed her, but hopefully he didn't notice her scowl.

"Is there something I can help you with? Did someone cause these tears that might need a visit from a Trooper?"

Biting down on her tongue, she kept herself from crying…or knowing her, it would come out as a laugh. "I'm fine, really." She snagged her purse, pulling out her wallet. "I've honestly had one of the worst weeks of my life."

"Where are you headed?"

She leaned across the car, flipping open the glove box, contemplating on how to answer. Was it home? Her grandfathers? "Home," she said.

"You live on Cleverdale?"

"Side street by the marina."

He placed his hand on the side of the car. "Is there something I can help you with?"

She shook her head. "I just need to get home." She held up her license and registration papers.

He looked between her face and her hand. "Drive home without peeling out or going over the speed limit." He tipped his hat. "I hope you start having a better week."

"Yes, sir…um…thank you." She stared at the trooper while he sauntered away as casually as he'd arrived. He took his hat off, put his shades on, and slid into his car. When he drove past her, he nodded.

Sucking in a few deep cleansing breaths, she put the car in gear and looked over her shoulder before easing out on to the road and drove exactly one mile under the speed limit, half excepting the trooper car to be tucked behind a group of trees somewhere.

As she passed Ramsworth Manor, a chill prickled her skin. Turning onto Mason Road, she told herself she'd gotten over everything that had happened between her and Michelle. That the rush of anger and hurt was a combination of grief…about a lot of things.

She pulled into the gravel driveway and parked under the car port, forcing her mind to think beyond the last few days.

Looking around, she saw so much potential to her grandparent's place. It had never been a thing of beauty, but since her grandma had passed, it had become too much for her grandpa and things had gotten run down. She'd begged him to sell it, even offered for him to come live with her and Larry, though Larry told her 'over my dead body.' That should have been the first sign, but sadly, she ignored it, like she ignored so many tell-tale signs of the pending doom of her relationship.

Fumbling with her keys, trying to hold the case of beer and ice cream in her hands, she gave the door a good hip check and stumbled in, tripping over something. "Crap," she muttered doing her best to stop from falling on her face. She looked around the small family room and a new level of indignation filled her already bottomless pit of sorrow. The cushions from her grandparent's antique sofa had been tossed haphazardly on the floor. Her grandmother would have a fit if she saw the armoire desk drawers hanging open, while personal papers littered the chair.

"Again!?"

She kicked one of the cushions and stomped off to the kitchen, putting the ice cream in a small cooler with some ice. She cracked open a fresh beer, enjoying crack-sizzle as the metal separated. The bubbles tickled the back of her throat as she guzzled half the can, then coughed, some of it coming back up.

She put the other eleven cans in the cooler, closing the lid tight and leaned against the counter, contemplating if she should even bother to call the cops again. They'd probably think she was one of those women who called regularly because either she was nuts or needed attention, which was crazy in another way.

A discolored corkboard her grandmother used to keep track of important things, but her grandfather used for absolutely nothing, held a single business card, tacked at an angle, taunting her. She racked her brain, trying to remember if it had been there the last time she had visited and seen her grandfather.

Two months ago.

How could she have let that much time pass without seeing him? The fact that she talked to him every week via FaceTime wouldn't make up for the lost moments she could have spent with him had she not been so wrapped up in making a name for herself, and trying to get her now ex-boyfriend, to marry her. What a waste of precious time.

She chugged the rest of the first beer, the bitter bubbles smacked her throat. She'd never been much of a beer drinker, preferring a mixed drink or a glass of wine. But tonight wasn't about her, but honoring tradition. She eased her way across the kitchen, squinting, trying to make out the name on the card. It wasn't until she stood two feet away that she could read the words: Sergeant Tristan Reid, New York State Police. Also imprinted on the card was a local station address, phone number, and cell number.

She glided her fingers across the stock paper with raised letters. A clear tack held it up at the center, something her grandmother would have lost her mind over. *Always....Always tack papers upper center, or at both corners. Never....Never in the middle.* Brooke twirled the pendant hanging from her neck.

Holding the card in her hands, she wondered why her grandfather had kept it, much less tacked it to the board. The day after his beloved bride died, he took down all her business cards, putting the information into his smartphone, but he refused to take down *her* board.

So, it made no sense that her grandfather tacked any card on it, unless it was something very important.

"All right Tristan Reid, Mr. State Trooper. Why does my grandfather have your card on his board and will you help me?"

Tristan shed his uniform for a pair of jean shorts, a white T-Shirt, and a well-deserved beer. He stepped from his double-wide, though everyone else called it a modular home. Whatever you called his rental didn't matter. Nestled between a large home on the right, two more modular whatever's on the left, and a fantastic view of Harris Bay with his sporty new fishing boat parked at the dock fifty feet away, he chose to call *it* home.

He sipped his beer, staring at the boats racing across the lake, thinking about the chick in the convertible.

Brooke Fowler.

Rusty had shown him dozens of pictures of the beautiful Brooke, his pride and joy.

Mentally, Tristan slapped himself upside the head for not looking at her driver's license so he could have given his condolences without looking like a stalker.

Before he knew who he'd pulled over, he had every intention of not only writing her a ticket, but giving her a really hard time. Until he saw those whiskey-colored eyes with flecks of pain. He'd seen that kind of misery in his own eyes fifteen years ago when his sister died.

Out of respect for Rusty, he let her go with a warning. He'd also make a point to stop by in the morning and give his condolences and hope he'd be able to act like he had no idea who she was when he'd pulled her over.

How would he explain that her grandfather thought Tristan was the only man suitable for his grandbaby? He shook his head.

Tristan appreciated the sentiment, and based on everything Rusty had told him about Brooke, Tristan wanted to meet her, even if she was way out of his league. If only his sister, Tamara, were here to guide him through the crazy world of a woman's mind.

His neighbor's little girl came barreling up the walk way, waving frantically. He waved back, smiling. For years, he didn't mind not being able to keep a girlfriend for more than a few months, but now that his thirtieth birthday loomed over his head, all he could think about was finding the right woman. The one who wouldn't mind a man who thought it perfectly natural and normal to tell a woman what she cooked for dinner tasted like a stale bag of chips.

His phone vibrated on the table next him. It was a 518-area code, but he didn't recognize the number. If whoever called wanted to talk to him, they'd leave a voice mail. But telemarketers didn't leave messages. What the hell. He might as well have a little fun since he had no plans for the evening and he was still wound up from a double shift.

"Hello?"

"Um…yeah…hi. Is this Tristan Reid?" a female voice echoed out of his speaker.

This telemarketer was off to a bad start, though her voice sounded like ice cream rolling down a cone on a hot summer night. "Yes." He rolled his eyes. Pathetic he'd listen to a pitch about some miracle product that would change his life just so he could hear the sexy voice on the other end of the phone.

"I found your card tacked to a board in my grandfather's kitchen. I was hoping you could help me."

Tristan sat up straighter. "My card?"

"Yeah. It says Sergeant Tristan Reid. I don't know why my grandfather had it, but I could use your help."

"And you are?" Tristan didn't give his cards out often and generally he only gave them to other law enforcement officers, lawyers, judges, and occasionally a hot chick.

"Brooke Fowler."

He paused a moment, sucking in a breath and nearly choking on it. He set his beer on the table. "You're grandfather just died the other day."

"Thanks for the reminder."

Tristan closed his eyes for a moment. "I'm sorry for your loss. Rusty was a kind man. How can I help?"

"Since he died, his house has been broken into three times.

Twice I've called the police and a sheriff shows up. Nice enough, but they didn't really do much."

"Why didn't you call the third time?"

"It just happened and I'm calling you."

He jumped to his feet, knocking the table over, sending his beer to the ground. Thankfully, it had been a can and not a bottle. "Were you in the house when it happened?"

"No. I came home and found the sofa cushions on the floor and the desk drawers open." He noted her casual tone, but also noted a sense of sadness, and perhaps a tinge of resentment.

"Are you alone in the house now?" He ran inside his trailer, snagging his keys and weapon.

"I'm alone, but I'm sitting on the front lawn."

"I'll be there in a couple of minutes." He clipped his weapon on his belt and took off jogging down the road. He figured cutting through the corner empty lot with over-grown grass would be faster than driving. He sneezed twice as his arms and legs brushed against some tall weeds, sending pollen in the air. By the time he came up on the side of the Fowler house, he wished he'd taken the car.

Brooke sat in an old metal chair, back to him, with her black hair pulled up on top of her head in a messy bun, stray stands dangling toward her shoulders. A cooler strategically placed at her side also doubled as a table where two beer cans rested.

He cleared his throat. "Miss Fowler?"

Her body jerked and the chair crumbled, tangling her in a hot mess.

"Shit." He closed the gap, but she managed to untangle herself. She stood, facing him with the look of death.

"You friggin' scared me," she yelled. "You always go sneaking up on people like that? Christ." She brushed some of the hair that had fallen from her face. Her gold eyes glared at him. "Who the hell are…oh, it's you."

He looked around the yard for anything suspicious. "We meet again." He rubbed his jaw, staring at the woman he'd pulled over less than twenty minutes ago. Her eyes not as puffy. Her shirt was wet from the spilled beer. And if he wasn't mistaken, she held one of those chocolate ice cream sticks his boss's kids got from the ice cream truck. "Those don't go with beer."

She cocked her head to the side and narrowed her eyes to tiny slivers. "Don't care." She stuffed half of it in her mouth, before tossing it on a plate that had at least one other wooden stick. Her sad brown eyes turned a fiery orange. "So, you're Tristan."

He nodded. "Can I take a look around? Make sure no one is lurking about and then we can talk."

She shrugged, then downed her beer in one gulp. "Be my guest."

He bit his tongue when she reached into the cooler and grabbed another one. "Why don't you come with me?"

She nodded and followed him into the house, still chugging away on the beer.

He'd been in this house a few times and knew Rusty Fowler to be a bit of a neat freak, so to see papers on the floor, a lamp knocked over, among other things, indicated a break-in. He leaned in, taking a close look at the door and the doorjamb. "It doesn't look damaged."

"It was locked when I came home. All the windows closed, so no idea how they got in and out."

"How do you know someone actually broke in?"

"Are you kidding?" She held her hands out. "Do you see this place?"

He nodded and walked through the family room, toward the kitchen and peered in trying to come up with something decent to say, but his brain formed nothing. Perhaps that was a good thing.

He peeked into the two bedrooms, but nothing else seemed out of place.

"What happened the first two times?"

She stepped out of the front door, down the three wooden steps, and leaned against the side of the house. "When I first came here the day after he died, the front door was open. Someone had emptied the contents of the desk in the guest room. My grandfather had to have things perfect, so he'd never go outside to work in grandma's garden with it looking like that."

"Did the cops dust for prints?"

She nodded. "They did everything they were suppose to do, I think. The second time they came, however, they just thought I left the back door open since nothing was disturbed."

"Have you changed the locks?"

"On my list of things to do, but I really need to formalize my grandfather's funeral. I know he wants to be with grandma and my parents." She shrugged. "I need another beer. Would you like one?"

"Sure." He grabbed his cell phone out of his back pocket. "I've got a buddy who owns a construction company. I'm sure he can get someone out here today or tomorrow to change the locks."

"You don't have to do that." She straightened out her chair, easing herself into it and cracked open two more beers. "You were already nice enough not to give me a ticket."

"All in a day's work." He texted Doug, copying Stacey on it. "Your grandfather was well liked and respected. I can't think of anyone who would want to hurt him or have a grudge. What about you? Any enemies?"

"Not really."

He adjusted the other metal chair and looked in her direction, catching her gaze. Her eyes calmer than before, but he wondered if anything could fill the hole that seemed to dive into her soul.

"How'd you know my grandfather?"

"Just from being neighbors. I'd wave when I drove by and he was outside. One day he walked by my trailer around the corner—"

"Next to the Wallen house?"

He nodded.

"That's a modular home, not a trailer. It's a big difference."

"That's what everyone keeps telling me." He watched her guzzle another beer, so he set his down, figuring she might need someone to protect her from herself. "Anyway, I was outside planting some flowers."

"You garden?"

"Can I finish the story or are you going to interrupt me every sentence?"

She pursed her lips as she reached into the cooler and pulled out another cold one and an ice cream.

He wanted to tell her to slow down, but by the way she scowled at him, he thought better of it. "Rusty stopped by and introduced himself. Said if I was going to drive by every day, we should be on a first name basis. We ended up going down to the Mason Jug and had a few beers together."

"Nice of you to be kind to an old man."

Tristan laughed, remembering the conversation about how it wasn't healthy for a young, viral man such as Tristan, not to have a girlfriend, much less any prospects for a girlfriend. "It was the other way around. He took pity on me. I'm going to miss him."

"But why did he have your card?"

"I had the honor of arresting Wendell Ramsworth the III, for a DUI. I found out later, your grandfather worked for them."

A loud crushing sound echoed as she smashed her beer can into the armrest of her chair. Impressive and scary.

"Sorry." She tossed the empty into the tin trash can on the other side of her chair. "I'm not normally like this, but really, I had the worst friggin week ever."

"I understand, but I think you might consider slowing down? Pacing yourself?"

"Might be right." She held up the can, then took a smaller sip, though he sensed her sarcasm. "I wanted to shoot my grandpa when he said he was going back to work, especially for them."

"He told me he'd gotten bored and needed something to do after his wife passed."

"That's what he told me. He always had to be doing something. I still don't understand why he had your card or why it was the only thing tacked to his kitchen board."

"I broke up a fight between Wendell and some guy at the Mason Jug. Wendell decided it would be fine to sucker punch me after I broke it up, so I hauled his ass in for a second time. Rusty had to pick him up, and by the way Wendell went off on me, I worried he might be a prick to your grandfather, so I gave him my card and told him to call me if Wendell ever made a dipshit move."

"Wendell always makes asshat decisions."

"Do you know him well?" Tristan asked.

"More than I'd care too." She tapped her fingernails on the metal arm rests. "I've never lived up here, not even for the summers, but we came often to visit my grandparents."

"Where did…do you live?" Tristan glanced down Mason Road, which ended at Ramsworth Manor, though the only thing you could see were two sections of the house. Everyone referred to them as the 'twin peaks'. One located at the north end of the property, the other on the south side.

"Born and raised in Plattsburg."

"Did you go to school there?"

She shook her head. "I went to NYU and then moved to Albany for my job."

"Your grandfather talked about you all the time and how successful you'd become. He said you worked for PMT Corp?"

She gave him a sideways glance. "Grandpa was my biggest fan."

"But he wasn't a fan of that boyfriend of yours. Larry, I think he said his name was. Where is he, anyway?"

Her jaw dropped open. "How do you know about my boyfriend?"

Tristan cringed, reminding himself that he should always think before he speaks, especially around women, even women well on their way to being drunk. Though, he didn't blame her. He'd be doing the same thing if his grandparents had died. "Rusty might have mentioned your boyfriend and the fact that he wasn't overly fond of him."

"Nope. Grandpa hated him."

"May I ask when the funeral will be? I'd really like to pay my respects." Huh. That sounded almost normal.

"I'm hoping Sunday."

"That's in four days. Anything I can do to help?"

"Be careful, I just might take you up on that offer. If I remember in the morning."

"I'll remind you."

"You do that." Her tone definitely had a sarcastic ring to it, but he still planned on reminding her.

He scratched his head. "Can I ask you a question?"

"I hate it when people do that." She waved the ice cream in the air. "What are you going to do if I say no?"

"Not ask the question."

"Okay, ask. I might not answer."

He laughed, though when she glared at him, he decided that might not have been the appropriate response. "Why ice cream and beer? The thought of mixing the two seems gross. I mean red wine and ice cream works, but this is like using mustard as sauce for noodles or—"

"No need to go on and on, geez. To answer the question, this is a tradition and it started when my parents died. My grandfather would expect me to do it for him." She fingered her grandmother's pendant. A few weeks after she died, Brooke had spent a couple of days going through the family photo albums and not one picture showed her grandma wearing the necklace. "I supposed he'd be okay with me sharing it with you."

He snagged an ice cream from the cooler and chowed down before taking a swig of his beer, gagging.

She laughed. "It's kind of gross and it's not like he ate these." She pointed to the ice cream. "And drank this at the same." She held up her can, raised it to the sky. "Regularly. The last time we did it was when my grandma died."

"That's fucked up to have lost so many people." He closed his eyes taking a long breath, remembering the day his twin died. Fucked up had been the only way to describe it, but the world thought to say, 'fucked up' wasn't an inappropriate response. "I didn't mean it the way it sounded."

"But it's the truth."

"So, really, where is the boyfriend? I'm shocked he's not here with you." Rude did not cover what just came out of his mouth.

"Talk about fucked up, but I don't want to bore you with the dirty details."

"I promise. I won't be bored."

She shrugged. "I dumped his cheating ass before my grandfather died. Unfortunately, the girl he was banging was my assistant. She'd left her phone in my office and it was blowing up." Brooke covered her mouth and belched. "Excuse me."

He looked at her, wondering if he should offer some sort of condolences, or words of wisdom. His experience with relationships were more like ships passing in the night.

"I picked it up to bring it to her and noticed my boyfriend's number. The stupid bitch hadn't locked it, so when I tapped on the message I got a nice view of my boyfriend's dick. Scrolled some more, and there was her crotch. I went ballistic right there in the office. Lost my job, my boyfriend, my apartment and—"

"You win on having the worst week ever."

"Gee thanks."

He really needed to shut the fuck up. "I'm sorry about your grandfather. He was a class act."

"Thanks." She tipped her beer.

He clanked his against hers. "My buddy just texted. He'll be here in fifteen minutes to put new locks on your doors."

"Wow. That was fast."

"He and his wife are down the street at my boss's house."

"Tell me something." She twisted in her chair, tucking some stray strands of her hair behind her ears. "When was the last time you talked to my grandfather?" She hiccupped.

"A couple days before he died. He stopped by my place and asked if I wanted to go for a bite and a drink at the Mason Jug."

"What did you talk about?"

"After he got me all caught up with you."

"He did what?" her voice screeched. "Caught up how? Did he know I had lost my job? What that asshole Larry had done?"

"No." Tristan wanted to reach out and hold her, but figured she'd slap him. "At least I don't think so. He mentioned a new promotion. Showed off a few pictures. He always beamed with happiness when he talked about you. But that was about it."

"So, you knew who I was when you pulled me over." She tossed a wooden stick in the trash can. "And you didn't say a single word to me?"

"I thought it would sound creepy if said anything without having looked at your driver's license."

"That sounds creepy considering you knew who I was when I called." Her face tightened and heat exuded from her body. "What else did you talk about?"

He couldn't come up with a quick lie, so he opted for partial truths. "Mostly about my job and the fact that everyone I work with is married or getting married and has kids or thinking of having kids and I'm helplessly single."

"I bet he tried to set you up with the first young girl that walked through the bar door. My grandfather tended to be a bit of a romantic."

Tristan smiled, remembering the way Rusty's face light up like a Christmas tree every time he talked about *his* Ashley and their great love of all times. Epic, he'd call it. "Nope. He said he was saving me for someone special."

"Really? Who?"

"You." He swallowed his breath. "That's really why he had my card, so if you ever dumped the dumbass he planned on calling me up, or maybe the next time you came to visit, he'd have me over for dinner. He did call a few times, but he always managed to get me when I was on patrol." He really should learn how to lie.

"Good Lord," she muttered, shaking her head. "On that note, I'm going to get drunk, if you don't mind."

"You're already drunk," he said.

"No. I'm. Not."

"Try to stand up." He arched a brow.

She pushed her hands against the armrests and rose too quickly as she stumbled over into his lap.

He groaned.

She held up her index finger and thumb making a sign for small. "Maybe a little."

"I'd say a lot." He pointed to the sky, wanting to hold her for just a minute. "See that?"

"See what?" She hiccupped.

"Orion's belt. Right there." The stars aligned themselves perfectly in the dark night.

"I've never been able to figure that shit out." She shifted, making it perfectly clear he needed to get her off his lap.

He eased her back in her own chair, eyeing how many beers were left, and taking a couple out as if he were going to drink them. "I think I need to spend the night with you." He cringed at how bad that sounded.

"That was a creeper statement."

"Not how I meant it. Really, I'm a gentleman, but not so good with my words. Probably why I'm still single." He mentally slapped himself. No point in telling her what a moron he was since he'd already shown her.

"Maybe you're not dating the right women, or trying too hard to be something you're not."

He shrugged. "Being single isn't the worst thing in the world."

"It's not the best either." She opened another ice cream. "I'm going to be sick before this night is over."

"I'll hold your hair back."

She burst out laughing. "That's actually kind of sweet."

He cracked a smile.

"Will you help me find out who is breaking in?"

"I don't know what more I can do outside of putting on new locks and maybe installing security cameras."

"Do you know how to do that?"

"I'm pretty good with my hands and have installed more than one video camera."

She burped, then laughed. "If I wasn't a smidgen drunk, I'd be kicking your ass off my property."

He stared at her with his hands wide. "What? Why? All I said was that I'm good with my hands and know how to…huh, together they do sound perverted."

She laughed. "I like your honestly, but I'm kind of glad I won't remember this in the morning."

"Just don't ever ask me if you look fat in something that you actually look fat in."

She lowered her chin and arched a brow. "Any woman who asks if they look fat are fishing for a compliment and the only right answer is the one they expect, which is they look fucking fantastic."

"Wouldn't you want to know the truth?"

"Me?" she paused, making a face as she went from the ice cream to the beer. "I wouldn't ask the question in the first place."

"Smart woman," he said.

"I have one other favor to ask of you."

"Yeah, what's that?"

"My grandfather left me a brass key with a note that is illegible. Can you help me find what the key goes to and maybe figure out what the note says?"

Tristan pondered her request as Doug's pickup rolled to a stop in front of the driveway. Stacey, his fellow trooper, and her son waved. He glanced between the road, and Brooke. She sat sideways in the chair, one foot under her ass, a beer in one hand, and ice cream in the other.

How could he say no.

"I'll help you, but you have to help me with something."

"Name it."

"Help me understand women and why I can't keep a girlfriend."

"I might not be the best person for that, but sure, what the hell." She reached into the cooler. "Damn, only a couple left. Guess I'm drunker than I thought. Thanks for coming by. I'll call you when I'm sober."

"I'm gonna stay right here with you."

"Not necessary. Besides, this isn't going to be pretty."

"Don't care. I'm not leaving, so deal with it."

"You're sounding like a creeper again."

"I might sound like a creeper, but this creeper is still a gentleman, and I'm not going to leave a drunk woman alone in a house that has been broken into three times. So, think of me as your personal guardian stalker creeper."

"You really are a weird one."

CHAPTER 2

Brooke lifted her head an inch off the pillow and groaned as a sharp pain ripped through her brain. She tried to swallow, but her dry mouth caused by dehydration prevented her throat from working properly. Rolling to her back, she pried her eyes open. It took many blinks and a good minute before the room came into focus. Well, not focus, but enough clarity to realize she'd slept in her grandfather's room. The taste of vomit lingered on her lips as she licked them.

"Say it ain't so," she whispered as a memory of leaning over the toilet while a combination of chocolate, beer, and a few other flavors she couldn't pinpoint, erupted from her mouth and the sexy, hot trooper stood behind her, holding her hair…just like he said he would.

No. She'd dreamt that.

Only, when the scent of hazelnut coffee filled her nostrils, she knew Tristan had seen her at her very worst. She could only imagine what she'd said to the poor guy.

She forced herself to a sitting position, squeezing her eyes closed until the room stopped swaying back and forth. Hang-over food. That's all she needed.

Her feet hit the floor with a heavy thud. She pushed herself to a standing position on shaky legs, her clothes from the other night tossed over the chair in the corner, her bra displayed prominently at the top. She grabbed her breasts, looking down at herself. Thankfully she had on shorts and a tank top, but terrified as to how she got in them. She brought her fingers to her temples and rubbed while she tried to gather her last memory…all she came up with was puking and Tristan telling her he'd take care of her.

She stepped from her grandfather's room, peering around the corner, hoping he'd made coffee and just left. But, no. There he sat at the kitchen table, the morning newspaper spread wide, his large hand wrapped around a mug.

"Good morning." He flipped the page of the paper, keeping his focus on the black and white pages instead of her.

"Nothing good about it," she muttered, adjusting her ponytail. *Screw it. He saw me make love to the porcelain God.* If he thought her attractive before, it ended with that scene. "So, what's going on in the world this morning?"

"Just reading about a murder that could have ties to one that happened here."

"What a way to start your morning."

"Goes with the badge," he said.

She poured herself a cup of joe, then went about getting all the ingredients she needed to make a breakfast sandwich, trying to ignore the cute cop with bed hair in her kitchen. A wave of nausea rose from her gut to her throat. She gripped the counters, taking in deep breaths. In through the nose, and out her mouth in a loud swoosh.

"Sit down." Strong, tender hands gripped her shoulders, guiding her to a chair. He set a mug in front of her. "Are you sure you want to eat?"

"Egg, cheese, and bacon sandwich is the best hang-over food ever created."

"Last night you called it drunk food."

"Can we never bring up last night again, please?" She cupped the mug, raising it to her nose and inhaled sharply. The bitter hazelnut calming her stomach. Thankfully, she didn't have the shakes.

He laughed. "I have so many questions and some of your statements need clarifying."

"No. They. Don't."

"Yeah. They. Do." The egg sandwich machine sizzled as he sprayed it with Pam and added the ingredients before shutting it closed. "Some of them might help me with my problem with women."

She'd forgotten that part of the deal.

Five more minutes and she'd be cured. Well, not cured, but she wouldn't feel like her stomach had been pulled inside out through her mouth. "I need water and then I'll give you some pearls of wisdom."

"I'll get you a glass, but you have to answer one question for me, okay?"

She closed her eyes. "What?"

"Do you really want to flip this house?"

She sighed, relieved it wasn't something crazy, like admitting she peed in her ex-boyfriend's shampoo before collecting her stuff. "I do, but it will be a few months before I can start the project and even then, I don't know if I have enough money. I'm also am unemployed, making it difficult to get a loan."

He set a plate in the center of the table with two large sandwiches. "My friend that was here last night."

"You mean tall, dark, and dreamy with the beautiful pregnant wife, and perfect little boy with manners of a saint?"

Tristan nodded as he sat down, taking one of the sandwiches. "He and his father-in-law own a construction company and they take on projects like this all the time. When you rambled on last night, I called Doug and he's definitely interested in talking to you about it."

"I'm so far from doing anything, but I appreciate it."

He set a business card on the table, but the letters all blurred together. She held it at arm's length, then brought it back and forth toward her face. Nothing.

"Just talk to him. If nothing else, he'll have a lot of information and ideas. He's a good guy. Plus, he might be able to give us some ideas about that key."

"Thanks." She took a sandwich and pulled it apart. The thick, melted cheese stretched as she set it on a small plate and cut through the layers with her knife. She took tiny bites, keeping her stomach from lurching forward, while he stared at her. Amusement glowing from his eyes.

"What?"

He grinned like a little boy catching his first fish. "Your boobs are not too small, nor are they too far apart."

"What the hell?" She dropped her fork. "Why would you say that to me? I thought you weren't the kind of guy who took advantage of drunk women?"

He tossed his hands in the air, leaning back. "Trust me, I didn't take advantage. I didn't even touch you when you begged me too."

She opened her mouth, her hand ready to slap him when a vivid image popped into her mind. "I didn't beg," she whispered, remembering him delicately helping her into her pajamas and into bed, most definitely keeping his hands to himself. "What you said is why you don't keep girlfriends."

"It was a compliment."

"It was a backward compliment, so it doesn't work."

"You said it to me when ripping your ex a new one. And by the way, your ex-boyfriend is blind because you're hot. I mean smoking hot. He's a moron to trade you in for a slut."

"Oy. I get you're trying to make me feel better, but really, do you hear yourself?"

"Okay, so maybe I could have said it differently."

"Ya, think?"

"You've been handed a shit load of crap in a short period of time. Don't let assholes like that make it worse. You've got a lot going for you and it's not just nice breasts."

Immediately, her nipples puckered against the thin fabric of her tank top, reminding her she didn't have a bra on, wondering what, other than her boobs, he'd noticed. She should be furious, but she found herself turned on and amused. "Instead of commenting on my breasts, maybe you could have actually told me what attributes I have going for me, because otherwise all I heard was 'nice boobies'."

He laughed. "But they are really..."

She tilted her head and gave him her best scowl. While she found him endearing, other women wouldn't.

"Okay. You're smart. You're funny. You can laugh at yourself and I get the impression you don't take shit from anyone. I admire that. Also—"

"Stop there. No need to risk putting your foot in your mouth again."

"Okay, but I'm confused. Women like it when men complement their bodies."

She shook her head and quickly regretted it when the pain ricocheted off her teeth. "Who has been giving you dating advice? Yeah, we like to be told we look beautiful in a little black dress, or that our hair looks nice. But that's all you focus on."

"Women are complicated." He tapped her plate. "Eat your breakfast. I've got to head out in a few minutes. I need to return the patrol car and I have a meeting, but I'll be back around lunch time with a couple of security cameras. You have internet, right."

"I sure do."

He stood, clearing his plate and putting it in the dishwasher. She nibbled at her food, while watching him go about cleaning up the kitchen, putting the eggs and bacon away, wiping down the countertops, washing the egg machine. Other than he having no filter, he had to be one of the sweetest men she'd ever met.

Awkwardly sweet. Only way to describe it.

"I've got to go." He touched her shoulder, before dropping his hand to his side. "See you later."

"I'll walk you to the door."

She followed him through the family room, admiring his trim, but muscular frame. His biceps tightened as he opened the front door. She lifted her head as he turned.

"I know it's summer and everyone leaves the door unlocked during the day, but I think you should keep yours locked."

"Because of the break-ins? They seem to be looking for something of value, not hurting me."

"It's not just that. The case I was reading this morning didn't sit well with me, so humor me and lock the door, especially when doing things like showering."

"Great. Now I'll be thinking of the movie Psycho." She raised her hand and made a stabbing motion while trying to recreate the music from the movie, though it sounded more like a pig being castrated. Out of the corner of her eye, she saw Wendell slow from a jog to a walk as he rounded the corner. "Jerk," she muttered.

"Excuse me?" Tristan questioned with a contorted face.

"Not you. Wendell. He walks up and down this stretch of road every day after his run. He's been doing it for years."

"Oh." Tristan glanced over his shoulder.

"Brooke." Wendell waved, then scowled. "Tristan, what are you doing here?" Wendell had the nerve to step onto her property.

"None of your business," Tristan said, hands clenched to his sides.

"I hope he didn't force you into anything just to get out of a ticket." Wendell stretched his arms up over his head.

"You're not going to bait me," Tristan said.

"Interesting how you'll let a woman off the hook, but a rich white boy? Tisk Tisk." Wendell waved his finger. "Piece of advice, Brooke. Stay away from him. He's a dirty cop and—"

"Don't make me arrest you again." Tristan tensed and Brook grabbed him by the shoulders, holding him steady.

"Arrest me again, and I'll have you fired for brutality and harassment." Wendell drew his lips in a tight line. "I'm warning you, Brooke, he's bad news."

"I can pick my own friends. Now if you don't mind, Tristan and I have a few more things to discuss."

Wendell backed up a few steps. "Michelle really wants to see you and I hope you'll be nice to her. My grandparents and parents would like to know when the service will be."

"Tell Michelle not to bother." She leaned forward, letting her hands run down Tristan's muscular chest. "I'll put a notice in the newspaper."

Wendell shook his head as he waltzed down the street, taking baby steps, constantly looking over his shoulder.

"You two have some history." Tristan turned and wrapped his arms around her waist.

"So, do you."

"Wendell had tried to buy his way out of his DUI, which wasn't just alcohol, since I also found a small amount of cocaine on him. He tried to use his influence to get out of doing a little community service. After that, it had been an all-out battle to find ways to make my life miserable, including filing a harassment charge. It was tossed, but only after I'd been put on administrative duty for a month while the review board followed up on the bogus complaints."

"That sucks, but Wendell is a spoiled child who has always thought money could buy his way out of trouble"

"I feel bad for his wife, she seems like a nice girl." His fingers grazed the sensitive skin at the small of her back. "He's looking at us, isn't he?"

"Yes." Her heart fluttered in a mix of toxic anger toward the memory of her best friend thinking she tried to get Wendell into bed.

"By the way he looks at you, I suspect he's got the hots for you. So, it seems like a moral imperative we suck face in front of him."

"We're going to need to work on your terminology. Saying that doesn't make me, or any woman, want to kiss you."

"But you're going to do it anyway, right?" He grinned, which she found to be oddly boyish and cute.

"This isn't because I like you or anything." She tilted her head, closing her eyes, and brushed her lips against his, barely touching them, not wanting to get too personal. Just enough to get under Wendell's skin.

He pulled her tighter, thrusting his tongue into her mouth and swirled it around in a smoldering, erotic dance. Any trace she had of her hang-over disappeared and was replaced with hot tingles across her skin. She moaned, wrapping her arms tighter around him, stroking his shoulders and back, trying to climb inside him, if that were possible.

So much for an impersonal kiss.

His hands slid down her back, cupping her ass. All she could think about was wrapping her legs around him and letting him carry her off to bed. She'd let him take advantage of her at least five different ways.

He squeezed her hips, pulling away.

She shivered.

"That could easily get carried away," he said, pressing his forehead against hers. "Not only do you have great breasts, but your ass—"

She pressed her finger against hir lips. "While it's nice to have my body appreciated, for future reference, this would have been a good time to say something romantic. Perhaps tell me that the way I kiss reminds you of a warm summer breeze. I mean for when you're with someone else."

"Right now, I don't want to be with anyone else."

She smiled. "You're learning."

"I actually meant that."

"Oh." She stared into his dark, smoldering eyes wondering what it was about him that made her want to tell him everything there was to know about her and find out what made him tick.

"I really need to get going." He released his grip. "I will be back around one."

"You don't have to do this today."

"But I want to. Now please go inside. You're not wearing a bra," he whispered.

"Oh." She crossed her arms, suddenly aware of her aroused body.

She stepped back inside and closed the front door, moving to the window and watched as Tristan walked down the street and disappeared around the corner. Tristan was like no one she'd ever met before. Kind, considerate, and awkward, which on him managed to be sexy.

But she had no idea what to make o...
importantly, why she'd agreed to it. Giving W...
humiliate her would only lead to more embarrassm...
came to Mr. and Mrs. Wendell Knoll Ramsworth, ...
preferred to fly under the radar.

Then again, considering recent events, she wouldn't mind...
Michelle thought she had a hunky trooper as a boyfriend.

She shook her head. Michelle knew about the last boyfriend, so this would just make her look like a slut, all over again.

The tile floor cooled her feet as she made her way to the bedroom, regretting kissing Tristan, but not regretting the actual kiss, if that made any sense. Just as she pulled her pajama top over her head, the doorbell rang. She let out a long sigh as she scrambled to put some clothes on before racing back to the front door.

Her eyes narrowed and her blood turned cold as she stared at Wendell and Michelle. "What do you want?"

"We wanted to give you this." Michelle held out a card. "I also want to know if there is anything I can…can… do for you." She touched her neck with her thumb and forefinger.

"Not a thing." She went to close the door, but Wendell shoved his arm through the opening.

"My wife is trying to be kind, which I told her it was useless."

"Your point?" Her lungs screamed to take a deep breath as her body erupted into an inferno of flames. The same dizziness she'd experienced the day she went bonkers at Debbie and Larry filled her heart with a desperate need to hurt someone else.

Wendell shoved another envelope in her face. "Take her card and this."

"What is it?" She stared at a manila envelope with her name on it. Visions of getting a knife to open it with, but instead slitting his throat, filled her mind.

She swallowed the thought, shoving it so far down she prayed she'd forget she had it.

"A very generous offer for the house and all the land that goes with it."

33

She laughed. "You've got to be kidding me? You want me to sell? To you?"

"I know you've never really liked it up here and—"

She interrupted Wendell. "You don't know shit about me or my life. Take your offer and get the fuck out of my house."

Wendell tossed the envelope and card inside before stepping away, looping an arm around his wife, her protruding belly enhanced when she turned sideways.

"I guess congratulations are in order," Brooke said with a tinge of disgust and a fraction of jealousy. Not that she was ready or wanted a baby, but it just reminded her that she'd spent the last four years on a man no better than Wendell.

"You've turned into a mean girl," Michelle said, shaking her head. "Can't believe I thought we could be friends again."

Brooke's body radiated a wrath so intense her fingers twitched to lace them around Wendell's neck. She slammed the door shut, turning the lock. Her body trembled as she slid to the ground, tugging her knees to her chest. Tears burned the corners of her eyes. Michelle had made her choice six years ago when she chose to believe a lying cheat over her best friend since the first grade. It had taken Brooke a while to get over the betrayal, so it alarmed her now that seeing them sent her into an irrational state of panic.

Tristan pulled his convertible Range Rover into the gravel driveway, parking next to Brooke's Camaro. He strolled up the broken concrete walkway, looking east, eyeing the 'twin peeks' of Ramsworth Manor. He'd never been inside the gate, but Rusty had a few stories to tell about the place. Rusty told him that every five years, Mrs. Ramsworth would gut the kitchen, making sure they had the latest and greatest. After that, they'd sell their furniture at an auction house, their way of 'giving back', and replace it with the latest trends.

The only good thing Rusty had to say about the family was that they paid a decent salary to their employees, though they still had a high turnover rate, which Rusty had decided was based on their lack of empathy toward those that worked for them.

One of the things Tristan valued so much about his parents was that they, for their wealth, lived a much more modest lifestyle, though still lavish enough, but they didn't have a staff of people running around, doing things for them. His mother did laundry and cooked all the meals. She had a cleaning crew that came twice a week, but only once a month to clean the children's bathrooms and bedrooms, forcing them to do it themselves, along with other chores. The Reid family motto had always been, no one, or no job, is beneath you.

He rang the bell to Brooke's house, happy she'd locked the front door.

The door creaked open an inch as she peered through the crack. "Oh," she said, swinging the door all the way open. "Come in."

"I didn't mean to scare you into hiding."

"You didn't." Her long-wet hair clung to her back. Her white tank top accentuated her tanned, toned skin, and the cut off jean shorts clinging to her hips heightened her curvy, but firm ass. "Reliving the music from Psycho in the shower did."

"Sorry about that." His fingers twitched. "My buddy Doug wants to come over to do some measurements. He'd love the opportunity to renovate this place." Tristan followed her back to the kitchen. A portable filing case had been tipped over on the table and papers covered the top. "And he said to send him an image of the key, which might help him in his search."

She reached into a bag and pulled out a key and a note. "Go ahead and send him an image, and if he wants to give me a free estimate, that's fine." She plopped her butt on a chair. "Looks like you didn't get the security camera."

"Back ordered, so I opted for one day shipping from Amazon. They will be here by ten tomorrow morning and since I don't work again until tomorrow at 4pm, I'll be able to install it for you."

"Okay, well thanks for stopping by." She lifted a few papers, twirling her hair with her free hand, dismissing him.

He cocked his head back "You're in a bad mood. What happened?"

She pointed to a large envelope with her name on it. "That happened."

He reached out and lifted it into his hands, holding it up to the light, though it would be impossible to see through this kind of thick envelope lined with bubble wrap. "What is it?"

"An offer for the house."

"From who and how much?"

She rested her elbows on the table, her hands cradling her face. "Wendell, and I have no idea how much. I haven't opened it."

"What the hell does he want with this property? It's not on the water."

"Probably wants to build a small strip mall or something."

"It's zoned residential."

"Only part of the property. The back portion that butts up to the Marina is all zoned commercial."

Tristan shook his head. "A strip mall would destroy his property value."

"The Manor isn't his, yet. Why are rich people such asshats?"

He swallowed, doing his best not to furrow his brow. "Not all rich people are jerks." He regretted bringing his convertible. He knew what hers cost, and his was more than double that. "My boss is rich and he and his wife are really great people."

"Your boss is in the minority."

So is my family.

Tristan pulled out a chair and sat down, holding up the envelope. "Are you going to open this?"

She shook her head.

"Why not? Don't you want to know what he's offering?"

She glared at him. "I'm not selling to him."

"Okay, but don't you—"

"You want to know, go ahead. Be my guest." She tossed a card sized envelope at him, the corner hitting him in the chest before dropping to his lap.

He ignored the temper tantrum and unsealed the large

envelope, pulling out a legal document. He flipped the page and stared at the offer. "Seventy-five grand."

"What!?" She shoved her chair back, racing around the table, putting her hands on his shoulders. Her damp hair fell over his head.

"That's a horrible offer." He brushed her silky hair from his face, but not before taking a lingering whiff of her tropical shampoo.

"It's insulting, is what it is."

He rubbed the back of his neck, twisting his head left and right, trying to work out the knots, as well as the sexual tension.

"What do you think this place is worth?" she asked.

"I don't know. I rent my place, but I'm paying twice as much as I would in the village and the modular next to me is for sale for three-twenty-nine."

His muscles tightened as her hands slid up his arms, squeezing his biceps before shoving his hand away and digging her fingers into his shoulders. "Wendell doesn't do anything without a motive."

"I would have to agree with you." He tried to keep from groaning, but the way her hands moved across his aching muscles sent his mind and body into the pleasure realm.

"The question is: why does he want this land?"

"No idea." He moaned the words. "But all the more reason to talk to my friend Doug. He knows the property around here and what it's worth." He reached back and curled his fingers behind her knee.

Her body went rigid.

He dropped his hand.

"That was awkward," she whispered. "Sorry."

"Don't be. Best massage ever. All it needs is a happy—"

She covered his mouth. "And that's why you're single."

"It was meant as a joke." He glanced over his shoulder. "And you're smiling, so you obviously took it as intended." He leaned back in the chair.

"I'm not a woman you're trying to have a relationship with."

He wanted something with her, he just wasn't sure how much of what he was feeling was physical or…he didn't know the or part. "Shall I open the card now?

"Might as well." She leaned against the table, arms crossed, staring down at him.

He ripped the card open in one swoop. "Typical condolence card."

"Don't read the sentiment. Just tell me what she hand wrote, if anything."

"Dear Brooke, sorry for your loss. I always liked your grandfather. Don't you think it's time we move passed what you did?"

"Ha! What I did? Crazy bitch."

Tristan glanced up.

"Keep reading, unless that's it."

"I forgive you. It was a long time ago. I hope you'll pick up the phone and call me. The ball is in your court. All the best, Michelle."

"Well, *honey*, the ball has always been in my court and I did nothing wrong."

"Let's go sit outside with some lunch and you can tell me what the hell went on between you and Wendell's wife."

"Why?"

"I'm nosey and you mentioned something about a fight with her last night."

"Fine." She titled her head and gave him a fake smile. "I don't have much in the way of food."

"You've got plenty." He stood, standing inches from her, heat radiating from her body to his. They stared at each for another uneasy moment. A million inappropriate things came to mind, but he bit his tongue. Ducking his head inside the fridge, he scanned the contents. A loaf of bread. Some eggs and cheese. Bacon and sausage. OJ, and oddly, a bottle of Champagne. He pulled out a drawer and snagged a nice ripe tomato.

"BLT's with mimosas." He pulled out the ingredients, glad the bacon was pre-cooked and all he'd have to do was zap them in the microwave. Easy, no mess.

"You drink mimosas?"

"Some chick I dated drank them all the time. I developed a taste for it."

"What happened to the girl?"

"She dumped me about two months into the relationship."

"Why?"

"Something about me calling her ass fat, among other things."

Brooke glared at him again with those orange fiery eyes. She had nice eyes, but only when they were more gold than fire balls of hell.

"I'm an ass man. I like big butts, so it was meant as a compliment." He shrugged.

"Did you use the word *fat*?"

His pulse beat a little faster as she reached across him, pulling the toaster out. "I didn't mean fat as in ugly fat."

"Fat implies ugly."

"I suppose your right," he muttered, slicing through the tomato and laying it over a few pieces of lettuce while he waited for the microwave to ding.

"Here." She shoved a bottle of soda in front of him. "I'll pass on the alcohol. I really don't need a repeat of last night."

"Neither do…" he stopped himself, not wanting to imply he didn't enjoy himself…well, he didn't enjoy some of last night, but he didn't not enjoy it…Jesus, no wonder he couldn't keep a girl. "It will be nice to sit and get to know each other."

"Well, color me happy. That is what I'm talking about. Say stuff like that, and you'll be saying 'I do' before you know it."

The bottle of soda slid through his fingers as he blinked, staring. Fumbling, he caught the bottle, saving it from landing on the floor and splattering about the kitchen.

"Marriage phobia?" she asked, taking the soda from him and pouring two tall glasses.

"I wouldn't say it's a phobia." But a concept he'd given up on this past year. Being told you're not marriage material a million times by various women will make any man gun shy.

"That might be your problem."

"I'm not afraid of getting married," he snapped. "I actually want to get married. Have kids. The whole nine yards, only it seems impossible because I don't understand women and I can't seem to say the right fucking…shit, sorry."

She patted his biceps. "It's less about saying the right thing and more about being either in tune with the woman you're dating, or more importantly, finding the right woman who finds your flaws adorable."

"That's gibberish to me." He yanked the bread out of the toaster, smothered the slices with mayo, before tossing on the other ingredients. He no longer wanted to learn how to keep *a* woman. He wanted to figure out how to *get* and *keep her*. "I'm done dealing with my shit now." He lifted two plates. "Let's go talk about Michelle and her asshole husband while we eat."

"On one condition."

He rolled his eyes.

She laughed. "I'll tell you the entire ugly story if after I'm done we get pen and paper and make a list of things you want in a woman, things that are deal breakers in a relationship, and what you think are good and bad qualities." Holding the two drinks in her hands, she headed toward the front door. "Deal?"

She kicked open the front door and he walked right into her, shoving her down the three steps. She stumbled, but managed to stay upright and didn't knock over the drinks.

"I'm so sorry." He raced to her side. "Are you okay?"

"Is that thing yours?" She pointed to the Range Rover convertible.

"Mostly the bank's." His white convertible shined under the summer sun. Cars had been the only thing he spent any of his trust fund on. Other than that, he lived inside his current pay scale.

The jury was still out on whether his parents were proud or concerned for his future. His father had scowled when he bought the car, knowing the money came directly from his trust. His mother tried to enjoy hanging out in a double-wide, but it certainly wasn't where she envisioned her oldest son living.

"How does a cop afford that?" She looked between him and the car, her gold eyes wide.

"I live alone. I have no expenses other than my cell phone. I really can't afford it on my salary, but I had to have it." Not really a lie.

"I take it when you go out on a date, you pick the woman up in that?" She raised one of the glasses before turning, her hips swaying as her bare feet glided across the grass to her makeshift patio smack in the middle of the front yard.

"In the summer, yes," he breathed out, trying to keep his thoughts out of the gutter.

"Where do you go on a date?" She set the glasses down on the small table before adjusting both seats, easing back into one, crossing her legs. Legs that went on forever. Her frayed jean shorts barely covering her tight ass.

"Different places. Wherever."

"Please tell me you take them to a nice restaurant or someplace romantic and not the pub down the street."

"What's wrong with the Mason Jug?"

"Good grief. There are ways to wine and dine a lady without spending a lot of money."

"That's what Josh says." Tristan stood there, staring at her like an idiot, holding his plate while she glanced up at him, smiling, then frowned.

"What?" she questioned.

"Nothing," he muttered, moving his chair with his foot before sitting and taking a huge bite of his sandwich, focusing on the aroma of crisp bacon and not the woman who smelled like a big bowl of tropical punch he wanted to go swimming in.

"You look like you're disgusted with me or something."

His mother always told him to never talk with his mouth full of food, so he chewed and swallowed and drank some soda. "The complete opposite of disgust, but the words would have been totally inappropriate, according to you."

"So, something sexual in nature." She poked him in the shoulder. "Now I'm dying to know what you were thinking, partly because your body language is closed and if you act this way around women, well, another reason why you're single."

"I'm frustrated because it's a no-win situation. I say what I was thinking and women act like I'm a pig. I say a tamer version of what I'm thinking and women think I'm only trying to get into their pants." He squared his shoulders, trying to relax. "So, sometimes I clam up and say nothing and then I'm accused of being emotionally distant."

She tucked her hair behind her ears. "Okay, but why did you clam up this time? Because of my comment about marriage?"

"No. Marriage and a family is something I honestly want." He forced himself to look her in the eye and not stare at her gorgeous long, lean legs. "You're an attractive woman."

"Thank you."

He cocked his head.

"That was an appropriate complement for the moment and not over the top, just nice. Is that what you were thinking?"

"No. I was staring at your legs thinking about what it would be like to wrap them around my waist, my hands cupping your ass, and my tongue in your mouth."

She raised her hand to her face, laughing.

"At least you're not calling me a bastard." He dropped his sandwich on the plate and plucked out the large slice of bacon.

"I'm sorry, really." She cleared her throat and the laughing stopped, but she still smiled like the devil. "When you first meet a woman you're attracted to, is it always about her body and sex?"

"That's not the only thing that gets my attention, but it's the first thing, and yeah, I'm sort of focused on getting first kisses out of the way."

"Does being with a woman sexually make you nervous?"

He choked on a piece of bacon. "Not at all, but I know what I like in the bedroom and when talking to a woman, I try to find out what she likes, and if we're compatible, well, that gets me in trouble."

"That might be a conversation saved for the bedroom during the act."

He laughed. "That's where I do it, but it gets interpreted as dirty talk and then I'm a pig because I like that and I have a need for control." He needed to shut the fuck up, and now. Who has this conversation with a woman he actually wants to get into bed…eventually.

"Here's your tip of the hour. Try to avoid dirty talk early on. There are lots of ways to figure a woman out. You can do things like hold her hand, wink, put your arm around her. Simple things that make her feel appreciated and sexy and then get bolder with your actions, but try to follow her lead and push her at the same time."

"You make it sound like I should be coy and play hard to get."

"Not at all." Her lips turned upward and her eyes danced in the sun light. Her black hair curling over her shoulder.

His fingers twitched, the desire to fist her hair, yanking her head back, exposing her neck so strong he raised his hand, but dropped it quickly. Christ. This woman made him crazy.

"I'm suggesting that instead of focusing on the way a woman looks, ask probing questions about her job. Family. You'd be surprised by how much you can find out about a woman both emotionally and sexually by engaging in small talk."

The noise of a car driving by faded into the background as he stared into her brown pools of passion. His mind wandering off to places he'd never thought of. Long romantic walks on the beach. Floating in his boat under the stars, searching for Orion's belt.

A crackling of a twig breaking snapped him out of a trance. He jerked his head to the side as a fox ran across the street.

"Your turn. Tell me about Michelle and your history with her." He watched her as she nibbled on her sandwich. Her pink tongue darted out of her mouth, licking her rosy lips. It was impossible not to think about sex in her presence, but he found himself wanting more of her. Wanting all of her.

"Michelle and I have known each other since grade school. We did everything together. Even went to the same college and were roommates. I introduced her to Wendell."

"You and Wendell used to be friends?"

"No. She'd come with me a lot to visit my grandparents. One night we saw him out in the village and while I slipped away to the bathroom, he swooped in and bought her a drink."

"Technically, you didn't introduce them."

She laughed. "You're right."

"But you're better than being upset with her over who she chose to marry."

"Thank you." She nodded at him with approving eyes.

He shrugged.

"I can't control what she does, but I did warn her that from what I knew he'd been a player, a bit of a drunk, toss in a recreational coke user, and it's a recipe for relationship disaster."

"Wendell is a disaster."

She nodded. "When my grandmother died, I came up here for a week and I was a hot mess. I tried to keep it together for my grandpa, but it wasn't easy. One night, after I put grandpa to bed, I came outside and went for a walk. Wendell was pulling into the manor and stopped. I got in his car and went to the main house. He got me a drink, I cried on his shoulders. I thought he might actually have a decent bone in his body until he tried to feel me up."

"What did you do?"

"Smacked him and let him know I'd be telling Michelle, only he called her that night saying I was all over him and tried to seduce him."

"And she believed him?"

"He got one of his staff to tell her they saw the entire thing, so yeah, she believed him."

"That sucks."

"It gets worse." She set her plate on the ground and stared across the street. "A month later, I came up here to help my grandpa. It was after season, so I certainly didn't expect to see Wendell. Nor did I expect to see him cheating on Michelle."

"You saw?"

"I saw him with his tongue shoved down some other chick's throat after snorting a line of coke."

"He's a dick."

When she turned to face Tristan, a single tear rolled out of the corner of her eye.

He reached over and wiped it away with his thumb, letting his fingers linger on her cheek.

"I told Michelle what I saw, and she didn't believe me. Actually, she told me that Wendell said I threatened to make up stories about him if he didn't sleep with me."

He balled his fist. "That's nuts."

"Well, in the end, she thought I was jealous of her and her happiness. To this day, she believes I wanted Wendell and his millions. But all I wanted was for her to have a good life."

"Does he still cheat?"

"I have no idea and frankly I don't want to know because I'd feel the need to tell her and not because I want to break them up, but because of what happened to me."

He leaned back in his chair, putting his ankle over his knee. "I sense there is more?"

"You're perceptive." She let out a dry chuckle. "The summer between my senior year in high school and my freshman year in college, I spent most of the summer here and dated a guy that worked at Ramsworth Manor. I was young and stupid and we took a bunch of naked selfies together. I didn't realize I hadn't deleted them from the cloud, so years later they show up on a fake Facebook account, but tagging my real one, so showing up on my wall. Michelle was the only person who had seen the images, besides my boyfriend at the time, and she had access to my cloud."

"That's a bitch move."

"I'm sure it was more a dick move, since I doubt she'd actually do it herself, but she's the only one who would have given Wendell access, so there is that. I have no proof of anything." She gripped the armrests of her chair. Her tone growing dark and body rigid. "My grandpa understood I didn't put them out there, but I will never forget the disappointed look he gave me that day. That look was worse than all the perverts and creepers that came out of the woodwork commenting on the images."

Tristan reached out, ready to put a hand over her arm, but he thought better of it when her golden eyes glared at him.

"Were the pictures taken down?" he asked.

She nodded. "I called Michelle and screamed at her for an hour, threatening legal action. Told her we had an IT expert that could verify the account had been set up using Wendell's IP address."

"Did you?"

"We were prepared to hire someone. Grandpa wanted to find a way to have him arrested."

Tristan glanced down the street. Lush, colorful bushes and trees lined Ramsworth Manor like fortress walls. "I would enjoy slapping handcuffs on that asshole for a third time. What he did is criminal."

"My grandpa didn't like that I dropped it so quickly, but I needed to walk away from them. I'd just gotten the job I was fired from and started dating Larry. I needed to focus on my future, not the crap from the past." The words made it sound as though she had been over it, but the intensity of her dark tone told another story.

He knew all too well what it was like to push pain down so deep that it boiled until the pot ran dry and exploded. "I can understand that, but again, what he did is punishable under the law and he should be held accountable."

"He'd buy his way out by paying off cops, judges, lawyers, whoever. It's what all rich people do."

Tristan blinked. "Not all rich people are entitled little pricks like Wendell and not all cops would let him get away with it, much less take a bribe."

"I'm sorry. I didn't mean you." She hugged herself. "It's just seeing them again, and knowing Michelle is pregnant...I feel sorry for their kid."

"Now I feel bad I made you retell the story."

She glanced at him and smiled, though he could tell it was forced by the way the color of her eyes shifted between orange-gold and gold. "I said I would tell you and now it's your turn."

"I was hoping you'd forget."

She laughed. "Nope. I'm going to write out a list of questions and you're going to answer them, bringing them back to me tomorrow when you come and install my security cameras."

"I don't think you should stay here alone, so maybe I should stay with you, or you can crash at my place."

The way she tilted her head with a playful arched brow sent his mind reeling to places he didn't understand. All women affected him. But not like this one. She actually made him want to be a different kind of man and he had no idea why, much less how.

"If I were a random call you came out on as a police officer, would you be offering to be my personal bodyguard?"

"Well, no." He winked. "But since we already slept together."

She laughed. "You on my grandfather's couch is not sleeping together."

"I didn't sleep there. I slept in the bed…with you."

"Stop teasing me." She waved her hand in the air before bending, collecting their plates. "Oh shit." She bolted upright and stared at him. "I asked you to stay until I fell asleep, didn't I?"

He nodded. "Only I fell asleep shortly after and just stayed." He couldn't tell if her narrowed stare came from amusement at the situation, or if he was about to be cut with her razor-sharp tongue. "You drank way too much. You threw up. I was worried it might happen in your sleep." He tossed his hands in the air. "Honestly, the only reason I stayed."

She cocked her head the other way, her lips pursed.

"I woke up at 4 in the morning and went into the family room and stayed there. Swear to God." Why he'd opened this can of worms, he had no idea, other than his sense of humor and that of a lady were two entirely different things. "I don't like the idea of you being here alone without a security system in place, considering three break-ins during a short period of time. Besides, your grandfather would have waggled his finger at me and then scolded me like I was twelve for leaving you alone."

She set the dishes on her chair.

He swallowed as she took two steps and stood in front of him. He braced himself for the slap when she raised her hands, but instead she cupped his cheeks and brushed her lips against his in one very tender, but way too short kiss. "You're oddly sweet." She smiled. "Let's go work on getting you a girlfriend."

"Why don't you be my girlfriend?" he muttered.

"Ha ha. That's funny."

"I'm being serious."

She took his hand, pulling him out of his chair, laughing. "I just broke up with a guy I'd been with for four years, living with for the last two. I haven't even had the chance to deal with how I feel about that. Pile on my grandfather's death, the loss of my job. Honestly, I don't even think I could give you a one-night stand."

"I don't want a one-night stand. I've had enough of those and I wasn't even trying to have them." He followed her into the house, carrying the empty glasses, staring at the back of her head, not ass, wondering how the hell he would get her to actually go out with him on a real date.

Better yet, where would he take her?

He frowned. First dates weren't the problem. It was every date after that where he crashed and burned.

CHAPTER 3

BROOKE PEEKED her head through the door into the family room. The dim morning sun filtered through the glass, landing on Tristan's bare chest. The sheet she'd given him pooled at his waist, showing off his tight six-pack abs. She let her gaze linger down the length of him all the way to his toes. He wasn't broad and his muscles didn't bulge, but it was obvious he worked out regularly since there wasn't an ounce of fat on him…at least that she could see. Sexy was the only word that could describe his body. But it was his awkwardness in certain situations that she found herself the most attracted to, though awkward was the wrong word for it, because he truly had a way about himself that the *right* woman could fall madly in love with.

She wasn't that woman, but she'd make it her mission, along with flipping this house, to find him the right person. Best way to get over a broken heart.

And to control this sudden insanity she'd developed. She hadn't been the kind of woman who resorted to violence, much less lose control of her emotions.

Careful not to make too much noise, she made a full pot of coffee before sitting down at the table, pulling out all her financial information. She held up the lease for the apartment she shared with Larry, staring at her signature, knowing she'd have to pay her half of the lease until it was up, or Larry moved in his new girlfriend.

At this point, she really hoped the lying little bitch moved in so Larry could cheat on her, giving her a taste of her own medicine.

She jotted down her share of the rent, cable, utilities, along with her car payment and insurance numbers, focusing on the task, not the turmoil that tightened her heart. She took out all the expenses for her grandfather's house, including estimates for the funeral, and added them to the expense sheet. She multiplied the monthly expenses by three, just in case she didn't get the money from the estate right away. That reminded her about the estate tax, lowering her bottom line even more.

When all was tallied, she should have felt some relief. She could live off her savings for the next three months. After that, she'd only have the money her grandfather left her, which she needed to invest back into the house and she was sure that wouldn't be enough. Of course, there was the lawsuit that had been filed by her ex-assistant, hence the inability to be confident in flipping the house.

She tossed the pencil across the table and leaned back, gasping as Tristan…bare-chested Tristan…stepped into the kitchen, pulling his T-Shirt over his head.

"What's all this?" he asked.

"Expenses and income." She told herself she shouldn't be confiding in Tristan about most things in her life, but the way she reacted to everything these days, it might not be a bad idea to at least work through this stuff with another person. Not only was he easy to talk to, he was a straight shooter and she admired that. "If I want to flip this place, I've got to make enough money to cover my immediate expenses for the next three months. If I combine my savings with what my grandfather left me, I might have enough, but my bills are over my head."

"May I?" He pointed to the paperwork as he pulled out a chair.

"Please."

There was something odd about having a stranger look over

your personal financial situation. At least she thought it should be peculiar, but as she studied his intent eyes and relaxed demeanor, she realized that she trusted him. She knew that was crazy, but it was the truth, considering what few friends she had right now, what could she do.

If her grandfather liked him enough to tack his business card on the corkboard, it was enough for her.

"It makes sense for you to live here, but based on this you'll need to at least get a part-time job and then you'll need to think about where to live while construction is going on. A friend of mine owns the Heritage Inn. You could probably stay there at a discount. Of course, I have an extra bedroom and I wouldn't charge you rent."

"I'm going to need to get a job regardless." She ignored the offer to be his roommate and rose to refill her mug, pouring some for him. "Not sure what kind of job I could get here, but I'm sure there could be something in Glens Falls or Saratoga. Not a horrible commute."

"I'm sure there's a lot of sales positions you could get." He pushed a few of the papers around until he uncovered the official notice that had come in yesterday's mail. "What's this?" He unfolded the paper. "Who is Debbie Taggard?"

"My ex-assistant. She's suing me, not to mention I was arrested for simple assault. At least the company I worked for only wants me to pay for the damages, which I already pulled from my savings."

"Shit." Tristan rubbed his jaw. "The simple assault, as long as it's your first offense, it will be plea bargained with no time and possibly nothing on your record, but add the civil lawsuit, well, that really sucks."

"Tell me something I don't know." Brooke sat down and stared into the steam swirling up in the air from her coffee. Closing her eyes, she tried to push the memory of that day out of her mind. Rage had never been an emotion she'd experienced before and it came on so fast she had no idea she'd been in the middle of it until she'd been hauled out of the building in restraints. Now, a couple of weeks later, the fire that burned in the pit of her stomach, scorching up to her eyes as they went blind from the emotion that could be recalled in an instant, hadn't subsided. When it came, all she wanted to do was hurt someone.

Anyone.

She inhaled the bitter almond smell from her coffee. If she were being honest with herself, she'd seen the signs of the demise of her relationship during the last year, and she chose to ignore them. That intense wrath was self-directed. Not that she'd brought it on herself, or that Larry's cheating was her fault, but she wasn't stupid, and she knew he'd been screwing around for a while.

A warmth wrapped over her hands.

"Are you okay?" Tristan asked.

She blinked her eyes open, feeling the sting of tears. Her hands trembled between her hot mug and his tender fingers.

"You sort of left the building for a while." He lowered his head, catching her gaze. "What's wrong?"

"Sorry. I'm just annoyed," she said, not wanting to get into the entire mess with anyone, not even the perfect stranger in her kitchen.

"From the tension in your body and face, I'd say it's a hell of a lot more than annoyance."

"I'm overwhelmed with my life right now." She pulled back, removing her hands from his soft grip. It would be easy to curl up in his arms and cry, or take out this aggression on his body in the way of mindless, rough sex. Her body twisted between the need to explode with adrenaline and the desire to disappear into oblivion.

His rich, dark eyes tore into the deepest part of her mind, tearing down her ability to hide those things she kept from the world. She'd built a successful career by locking up those vulnerabilities that could rise up and cripple her ability to be the ruthless, but fair woman she needed to be in business. Her insides trembled as the heat from her belly simmered through the rest of her body.

"I'd say you're more crushed by your life and if you don't let at least some of it out, you're going to lash out at the wrong time, getting yourself into more trouble."

Her muscles tightened as her lungs burned for air.

"What's got you so angry right now?"

"Drop it," she said behind gritted teeth. Her hands gripped the side of the table, stopping her from standing, hurling her chair across the room. Or maybe jumping on his lap, straddling him, taking advantage of him a dozen different ways. Her chest heaved up and down. The sound of blood rushing through her body echoed across the room.

"I'm not going to drop it because something is going to set you off, like it did the day I pulled you over, and you're going to do something you'll regret. I'm concerned it will be far worse than hurling a painting at your assistant."

"Screw you." Her chair screeched as she stood. "You're a cop, not a shrink, so stay the fuck out of my life."

"No." He had the nerve to walk over to her.

She turned, pressing her hands against the counter, taking in deep breaths, trying to calm down. Up until she'd lost it the day she had been escorted from her place of employment, she'd become a master at controlling her feelings and she wasn't going to break down now in front of Tristan. All that showed was weakness, and that wasn't tolerable. The madness over her ex would melt away in time. The pain of her grandfather's death she'd learn to live with.

That's how it worked.

How it always worked.

Powerful hands pressed against her shoulders. She shrugged them off, whipping around.

"You need to leave." She fisted her hands as her pulse pounded in her throat in one continuous beat.

"No," he said, holding his ground.

Her skin prickled with a combination of fire and ice. Spots floated in various colors across her blurring vision. "I need a moment alone."

"You can't bottle this up. Come on, let it out. You'll feel better."

She shoved him so hard he stumbled back, hitting the table.

"If that's how you'll get it out, keep it coming." He held up his hands, waggling his fingers, gesturing her to come forward. "You want to hurt someone? Come on, give me your best shot."

The blood roaring through her body muted all other noises, including her inner voice. She came at him with every intension of slamming her fist in his face, her arm cocked and ready. But instead, she threw her arms around his shoulders and crash landed her lips against his so hard their teeth clanked as his back collided with the wall.

With her mouth still tangled up in his, she grabbed him by his shirt, maneuvering him to the family room, propelling him on the sofa as she straddled him. She wanted to feel his bare chest against her skin, but didn't want to remove her tongue from the inside of his mouth as she swirled it around his.

She clutched his shirt, trying to rip the fabric apart, but to no avail.

His hand slid up her back, across her neck, cupping the back of her head, fisting her hair, gently tugging as he pulled his lips from hers.

She shivered, opening her eyes, searching his for answers. For an awareness of what just happened, because she didn't understand how she went from pure fury to raw passion in less than what it took to get her convertible from zero to sixty.

He cupped her cheek, rubbing the wetness away. She hadn't realized she'd been crying, but the sob that echoed as she sucked in a deep breath gave her pain away.

She wiggled, trying to get away from him, but he held tight, keeping her gaze in a mesmerizing lock, his hand still holding a clump of her hair, pulling her to his chest as he adjusted his body, stretching out on the sofa, tucking her head in the crook of his shoulder. She shuddered as his arms wrapped protectively around her body.

The moment his warm lips pressed against her forehead, a guttural groan of sorrow escaped her mouth. She buried her face, her shoulders shook up and down as she did her best to keep the crying to sniffles, but by the way his embrace tightened, she didn't think she'd been successful.

There was no way to stop this freight train. The last time she'd cried like this was when her parents died, but it was in the arms of the strongest woman she'd ever known: her grandmother. The woman had a heart of gold, but her skin was tough as nails. Nothing could break her, not even the loss of her only son, though she'd never been quite the same. She constantly told Brooke that the dead didn't want the living to die. That giving up and burying your head in the sand, dishonored their memory. She told her to grieve. To get it all out. Then make her parents proud.

Brooke continued to cry. Until a week ago, she was sure they were smiling down at her, but now? All four of them had to be rolling over in their graves at the mess she'd made of her life.

Tristan didn't say a word. He just held her close, letting her body expunge all the negative energy she'd been carrying around.

As soon as she thought the tears were about to stop, they'd start all over again. She had no idea how long she carried on and she supposed it didn't matter. She'd have to remember to thank Tristan for not taking advantage of her for a second time because she wouldn't have stopped and that would have not only been embarrassing, but it wouldn't have helped.

This actually might.

She relaxed her body into his, letting out a long sigh, forgetting about the world around her. As she drifted in and out of sleep, she thought of her grandfather and his desire to fix her up with the man who gave her a safe place to grieve.

After installing the security cameras next to the two doors as well as one on the front of the house facing the street and one on the back facing the lush trees that separated the property from the Marina, Tristan peeked his head into the master bedroom. Brooke faced the door, hands tucked up under her cheek, knees bent to her waist, still sound asleep.

Crying for two hours would exhaust anyone.

At least the puffiness in her eyes subsided and the crinkle in her forehead disappeared. She looked almost peaceful.

It broke his heart that a woman with so much confidence had to endure so much pain throughout her life, causing her to bottle it so deep, she had no idea what she was really crying about. The betrayal she'd suffered would have broken most people. But what saddened him even more was that she thought strength came from shying away from the pain versus tackling it head on. He'd made the same mistake when his twin died in his arms and it nearly cost him his future.

Leaving the door open, he made his way to the kitchen table, sitting down with a soda and her 'dating' questionnaire. She'd hounded him earlier to finish it and he did ask for her help. He needed a lot of help because all he could think about was her and that made him an asshole considering all she'd been through.

He unfolded the paper and stared at the first question.

What physical qualities do you desire in a woman?

"That's easy." He wrote: *Athletic.*

After you're attracted to a woman, what about her makes you want to go out on a second date.

He tapped the pen to his temple. He promised himself he'd be honest with his answers.

Sense of humor, doesn't take herself too seriously, independent, intelligent, and isn't phony. Basically, someone like you. Nope. You.

He leaned in, glancing into the bedroom at sleeping beauty. He needed to erase that answer. Dumb ass.

She stirred, stretching her legs out, her eyes blinking open. "Tristan?" she whispered.

"Right here." He raced from the kitchen to the master and sat on the edge of the bed, careful to keep his hands to himself. He'd always had trouble deciphering attraction and real feelings when it came to women. But with her, his confusion delved deeper. The attraction was undeniable and he was sure he liked her. He figured he liked her before he'd even met her through all the stories her grandfather told. Over the course of the last year, he really hoped he would get the chance to at least have dinner with her.

"Thank you," she whispered, rubbing her eyes. "I'm sorry I dumped all that on you. I'll be better in a few days."

He eased into the bed, fluffing the pillow. "What you're going through will take more than a few days. Have you ever really grieved for your parents? Grandmother?"

She scrunched her eyes, propping herself up on her elbows. "Of course I have. Why would you ask me that?"

He took her pillow, folding it over before putting it behind her back. "What happened in the kitchen wasn't only about what is going on right now with your ex and the passing of your grandfather."

She glared at him. "You have no idea what you're talking about."

He laced his fingers together, resting them over his stomach. "Do you always nearly hit someone when you are upset?"

"I wasn't going to hit you." She folded her arms across her chest. "You egged me on, which just made it worse."

"Maybe, but you were ready to have sex with me to bury all the pain you've been carrying around for years, and I certainly didn't start that."

"A lot of people use sex to get through things." She scooted to the side and jumped off the bed, stomping her way to the bathroom. "Just like getting drunk for a night. It's not like I go around doing either all the time." She slammed the bathroom door.

He let out a long breath putting one hand behind his head, closing his eyes. His own anguish over his twin sister's death still tormented him. He understood rituals. He had his fair share of them for birthdays, holidays, and the day she died. Some he shared with his family, since they all lost a sister and a daughter as well. But others were just for him.

It had taken him two years and a shit load of trips to the police station for acting out before he learned that holding on to that kind of sorrow would only destroy him.

The door to the bathroom squeaked open as Brooke stepped in front of him. "You made me feel like shit for how I acted."

"Wasn't my intention." Knowing how easily he could set her off, he thought carefully about his next words. "I've been where you are with a hurt so deep you go blind to your actions. You might see it coming, but you can't stop it. Next thing you know, you're peeling out of a store in your car. Had I not stopped you, you might not have slowed down at all."

"That's not true. I'm not that reckless."

"I didn't say you were, normally, but if you don't really deal with everything you'll end up with an asshole like Wendell or hundreds of other guys that would gladly take you to bed the moment you straddled them."

She put her hands on her hips. "Are you saying I threw myself at Wendell?" A tiny flame ignited in her eyes.

He needed to find a way to help her get past the need to protect herself from her own heartache. "No. But he did try to take advantage of you while you were vulnerable, knowing people use sex to get through bad things, as you said."

"This is ridiculous. Don't you have to go to work or something?"

"Not for a few hours, so sit down. I'm not finished talking." He should shut his trap. Not his battle. Not his fight. But he couldn't drop it. Or wouldn't.

"I'm done."

He sat up and grabbed her arm as she tried to spin around. "This might have been easier if you'd just hit me because that would have snapped you out of your wrath. That's not you, but it will become you if you don't deal with all this shit."

"I am dealing with it!"

He shook his head. "You think that eventually the pain will ease its way out, only you're shoving it so deep inside that even a two-hour crying session won't scratch the tip of the iceberg."

"Oh, what do you know?" She glared at him.

"I know a little about rage and death. I lived it. My twin died in my arms when we were fifteen. And I know better than most that if you swallow it, telling yourself you'll get over it in time instead of purging it, you'll end up throwing a picture at someone, hit a cop, even if he's egging you on, or have sex with the first man that walks through that front door. You need to expunge it so that when the next tragedy comes, or the memories flood your mind, you'll be ready." He let go of her arm, taking a deep calming breath. Over the years, it had gotten easier to talk about Tamara and what happened without having a surge of uncontrollable grief. It wasn't that he didn't feel it, but he had learned to remember her without all the emptiness her death created.

"I didn't know," Brooke whispered. She pushed his legs and sat on the edge of the bed. "What happened?"

"That's a story for another day." He sat cross legged, leaning against the headboard. "I can't imagine losing my parents or grandparents on top of my sister's death. Or the break-up and betrayal of friendships and lovers. So, I don't pretend to understand exactly what you're going through. I'm sure you think you're dealing—"

"I'm sorry about your sister and I appreciate the fact you care, but—"

"Let me finish." His pulse beat erratically as visions of his sister flashed in his mind like a moving picture. Thankfully, he'd learned to suppress the negative images, most of the time. "Your grandfather talked about you all the time. He probably told me more than he should have."

She opened her mouth, but he pressed his finger to her lips. "He worried about you. He saw you as a strong, vibrant woman who could do anything except take care of herself where it counted."

She batted his hand away. "So, you're basing this assumption that I'm some raging out of control lunatic ready to explode on what my grandfather told you?"

"No." He took her hands in his. "I'm basing it on what I've seen and what I've been through, then adding in the words of a kind old man who would have worried about you no matter what." Not wanting to give her a chance to interrupt him again, he continued. "It's true what they say about twins. Tamara and I had a deep connection. The moment she walked into a room, I knew what she was feeling and thinking. I sensed things with her when we weren't together and she about me. When she took her last breath, I felt that connection snap and a piece of me died with her." He shivered. "It was like talking to someone when you're lost in the darkest forest and your cell dies and you can never recharge it and you're alone in total darkness. Not even a single star to show you the way."

"That's horrible. I'm so sorry."

"After her funeral, I spent two weeks in her room, surrounding myself with all her stuff. I wouldn't leave and I couldn't cry. I let the anger cook inside me until it took me over. I lashed out at my parents. My little brothers. Something would trigger the overwhelming misery and I would do things like drive my car way too fast, almost hoping something bad would happen, wondering what it would be like if I wrapped it around a tree." He arched a brow.

Brooke gasped and covered her mouth.

"Mind you, I didn't want to die, but I was looking for something as intense as the loss I felt, hoping it would make it go away. You know that feeling, don't you?"

"Yes," she whispered.

"You can't numb it away with alcohol and you can't thrill it away with adrenaline. You have to let it become part of who you are now." He reached out and ran his thumb across her cheek, then dropped his hand to his lap. "You're a resilient woman, but I think you misunderstand what strength means in grief. You don't take it on the chin."

"My parents and grandparents would want me to continue my

life and that is exactly what I'm doing. They wouldn't want me to wallow in self-pity."

"But that is exactly what you've been doing for years and it has caught up to you."

"That's not true." She scowled. "I don't wallow in anything. I agree, I'm out of sorts right now, but just about everything that could go wrong has gone wrong in less than two weeks. I'd say you'd be a little bat-shit crazy too."

He curled his fingers around her legs, drawing her closer. "You're allowed to fall apart. Put your fist through a wall. But until you reach deep inside and acknowledge that you feel abandoned by—"

"I wasn't abandoned by anyone."

"You were abandoned in death and the people you loved the most like your boyfriend and Michelle, they betrayed and abandoned you as well. It's triggered a chain reaction. You can't make it go away, so you've got to spend some time allowing all of this to become part of your narrative."

She let out a dry chuckle. "For a guy who thinks it's perfectly okay to tell a woman she looks fat in something, you seem to have that psycho-babble about grief bullshit down pat."

He ran his hands across her thighs. "It's not babble. Once I understood that the anger was my way of avoiding how her death affected me, I was then able to let the rage go."

"Let's say I believe all this shit. What do I need to do then to make my new narrative so I don't try to jump your bones again?"

"You need to be honest with yourself, and other than talking it through, I have no idea." He tapped her knee. "I'm a good listener."

She smiled. "For a guy who can't keep a girl, you're shockingly kind and warm."

"Well, what you're going through I understand. But I won't pretend to understand you as a woman."

"We're not some super-secret puzzle. I'm beginning to suspect that you look for women in all the wrong places. Not only that, your eyes are so dark and rich and when I look at them." She leaned in, pressing her hands on his knees. "All I see is a warm and loving man and I think at your core, that's who you are."

"Nice way to change the subject."

"What are you talking about?"

He arched a brow. "This shouldn't be a lesson in how I'm supposed to talk to women. It's about a friend being there for another friend."

He dropped his hand, resisting the urge to kiss her, because friends don't swap spit. Boy was he glad he didn't say that out loud.

She smiled. "Thanks."

He nodded. "Now on to a different subject for now. I need a copy of that illegible note. I've got a couple of forensic guys who said they'd look at it."

"Will that cost a lot?"

"Won't cost you anything," he said.

"Thank you. The note is on the table." She let out a long sigh. "I need to go call a defense attorney that the estate attorney recommended."

"Who?"

"A woman by the name of Jillian White or Sutten or both."

Tristan pushed himself from the bed, holding his hand out. "That's Stacey's step-mom. Let her know we're friends and maybe she'll drop her fee."

"I hate fucking small towns," Brooke muttered. "I don't want or need handouts."

"You asked me to help, that's what I'm doing."

She waggled her finger. "You really want to help? Get six men who can carry my grandfather's casket because all his friends are eighty and older."

"Done."

"Of course it is." She waltzed through the door, her hips rocking in that natural swagger she had. "While you're at it, find me a place to have a small gathering of his close friends and I suppose whoever else attends the ceremony. He'd never forgive me if I didn't."

"Have it here and I'll take care of the catering."

She looked at him, her nose crinkled. She managed to make a scowl sexy.

"Last minute, it's all your gonna get."

"Fine," she said, hand on her hip. "But I have a budget, so you've got to stick with that, okay?"

"Got it." No point in arguing with her. "Doug will be by this afternoon to look at the key and take measurements of the house."

"Cool." She glanced over her shoulder and smiled. "Thank you for today."

"You're welcome." He made his way through the house toward the front door contemplating how long he'd have to wait to ask a broken-hearted girl out on a date.

CHAPTER 4

Brooke tapped her cell phone, satisfied that the funeral arrangements were complete and grateful that Tristan managed to snag a few of his buddies to help, but not thrilled with the idea of having the gathering right here at home. But it did make the most sense. She glanced out the window at the female state trooper running around the yard with a toddler, feeling guilty she'd been holed up in the kitchen, ignoring the woman, her kid, and her hunky husband who was still taking measurements.

She was sure the woman was nice enough, and as open as Brooke had been her entire life, talking about being arrested wasn't something she really wanted to do with a female officer of the law.

After her night in jail, she spent a week in a hotel room, working on her resume, calling a head hunter, and doing everything she could to keep from falling apart. Her little tirade in the office had scared her because she could barely remember what she'd done, but the feeling associated with that day will never leave her.

Ever.

Nor would having cold metal restraints slapped on her wrists.

When the doctor from the hospital called to tell her about her grandfather, her mind and body went numb until she walked through the doors of this house. Ever since then, she had no idea who she was anymore.

Or what she wanted.

Damn Tristan for making her see all this shit. Ignorance was bliss.

But she had to admit, she enjoyed having people around. The idea of being alone in this house now gave her the chills and Tristan wouldn't be off work until midnight. While he was a nice guy, she shouldn't be relying on him for anything, not even moral support, but the fact her grandfather seemed to have spent more time with Tristan in the last few months than anyone else, made her feel somewhat closer to the old man.

She set her phone on the table and made her way outside where Stacey's little boy, Brandon, giggled and laughed like no tomorrow as he chased his mother with a squirt gun.

"Hi!" the little boy squealed as he ran by.

"Where's Doug?" Stacey asked. She smiled and laughed, but her eyes had a tired look about them.

"I'm right here," Doug yelled from the side of the house. "Brandon, come help Daddy measure the perimeter."

Stacey rubbed her swollen belly. "Thank god," she said, taking one of the folding chairs and sat down, glancing over her shoulder as her son ran toward the house. "This second pregnancy is killing me." She unraveled her long blonde hair from the bun she'd put on top of her head. The way Stacey carried confidence put Brooke's self-assurance to shame.

"How far along are you?" Brooke made sure the other chair was secure before turning it to face Stacey.

"Five months." Stacey pulled the small table over, kicked off her shoes and rested her feet on the table letting out a long sigh. "Sorry about intruding on you today, but my husband won't be able to sleep tonight if he doesn't get those measurements."

"I don't know if I'll be able to afford this, so I feel bad he's spending the time, but it's greatly appreciated." Brooke barely remembered meeting Stacey and her family the other night. "I'm sorry about my drunken behavior the last time we met."

"We all have had one of those nights." Stacey waved her hand. "I didn't know your grandfather well, but everyone who did, loved him."

"He was a good man." Brooke swallowed. She'd always been friendly. Outgoing. Extroverted. Whatever label you wanted to give someone who never had a problem talking to anyone, which is why sales had been such a great career choice. That said, asking someone about legal advice was something entirely different. "My grandfather's estate attorney recommended your step-mother for a bit of trouble I've gotten myself into."

"She's great at what she does," Stacey said. "I can tell her you're going to give her a call."

"I'd appreciate that." Brooke stared at the petite blonde who she suspected packed a huge punch. "I'm a little surprised you didn't ask why I needed her services."

"I can't say I'm not curious, but it's none of my business."

Brooke respected Stacey's directness. "I hauled off on my boyfriend's slutty side dish and she pressed charges."

Stacey lowered her chin. "First altercation with her? With anyone?"

Brooke nodded. "I speak my mind and can hold my own in an argument. But, I'm not the kind of person that goes off and hits people. It was just the perfect storm of events."

"Why don't you come over for dinner and I'll introduce you to Jillian. It sounds like a simple plea bargain case."

"I don't want to intrude."

"Are you doing anything else this evening?" Stacey asked.

"Well no."

"Then I won't take no for an answer."

"I have a feeling that you'd drag me kicking and screaming." Brooke hadn't meant to accept the invitation, but truthfully, spending the next few hours alone wasn't all that appealing.

Stacey laughed. "I wouldn't go that far, but I'm glad you agreed."

"Have you lived here your entire life?" Brooke asked.

Stacey nodded. "Born and raised. You can see my father's house from Tristan's dock and my house is right next to it."

Brooke's heart skipped a beat. She'd run from her parent's house the moment she graduated high school. She loved her parents and she'd never gone through a rebellious stage. Her decision to go downstate had more to do with wanting new experiences and having ambition. She certainly wasn't running from her parents. But Plattsburg was the most God-awful place on the planet. "Is it weird living next to your folks?"

"I can see how other people might think it's strange, but it works for us."

The familiar hum of a motor caught Brooke's attention. She watched the big metal gate at Ramsworth Manor swing open. A large, dark SUV, exactly like the one her grandfather drove for them, pulled out on to the main road, heading south toward the country store. "Do you know the Ramsworth's?"

Stacey let out a sarcastic laugh. "I've known Wendell since we were kids. My father used to do a lot of construction for them, but he won't do it anymore."

"Why not?"

"They change their minds halfway through jobs, expecting the contractor to absorb the cost. They don't pay on time, but mostly the way they treated Doug."

"They look down on everyone." Brooke glanced over her shoulder, catching a glimpse of Doug helping his son with the measuring tape. "If you're not from their same social whatever, you're beneath them."

"My father could handle their judgements considering all he had to overcome being a single dad at the age of seventeen." Stacey folded her arms, resting them on her belly bump. "But he couldn't handle the way they treated an innocent young man."

"What do you mean?" Brooke's eyes grew wide.

Stacey waved her hand in the air. "To make a very long story short, when my dad first met Doug, he was a fifteen-year-old homeless boy. My dad gave him a job and moved him in with us."

"How old were you?" Brooke tried to hide her shock by keeping the muscles in her face tight, only she forgot to close her mouth.

"Six." Stacey lowered her chin. "But that has nothing to do with what the Ramsworth's did to Doug."

"I'm listening." Brook snapped her lips together.

"When they found out Doug had been homeless most of his life, they told my father that Doug wasn't allowed into their home. They were concerned for their safety." Stacey held up both hands, making the quote sign with her fingers. "My father told them that where he went, Doug went, and if they didn't like it, then they could find someone else to do the job."

"I bet that really pissed off Grandma Ramsworth more than anyone else."

"To this day, if she sees my beautiful gentle giant of a husband, she walks on the other side of the street, clutching her purse."

"What a bitch."

"You can say that again," Stacey said, shifting her shoulders.

"Mommy!" Brandon yelled as he raced toward his mother, arms flapping about. "Daddy's all done and I got the messsureints right!" The boy jumped into Stacey's lap. "I'm going to build things just like daddy."

"That's awesome." Stacey rubbed her nose against the little boy. "You can be just like dad and papa."

Doug sat on the grass and stretched his legs out, setting a notebook on the ground. He had soft caring eyes and by the way he looked at his wife and son, they were his world. "My measurements aren't adding up. Do you know if there was any work done on the house over the last ten years?"

"The interior was painted, but I think that's it," Brooke said.

"I believe there is some dead space in the walls between the master bedroom and the guest room, behind the kitchen, but I'd need to look at original plans and any modified plans after that." Doug ran a hand through his thick, long hair. He looked like the kind of man who should be gracing a hot body calendar and while his facial features showed him to be kind and sweet, he wasn't Tristan.

She blinked. Where the hell did that come from? She meant Larry. Didn't she?

"Do you mind if I request the blueprints from the town and any permits for construction?" Doug asked, snapping her out of the insanity finding Tristan more attractive than her ex-boyfriend and her new friend's yummy husband.

"I don't mind, but what does it cost?" Brooke had spent her entire career perfecting the killer close. For the last three years, she had either been the top sales person in her division, or led the team that had the most sales. But sitting here with this family, she realized that all she'd tried to do with Larry was close the marriage deal.

"At most, a couple hundred, but don't worry about it for now. If you decide to hire me, we can talk about it," Doug said. "But I suggest you talk to a couple of other contractors, just to get a feel for different things."

Brandon climbed down off his mother's lap and tugged at Doug's tool belt. Watching how natural and comfortable the couple was with their son made Brooke realize how uncomfortable she'd been the entire time she'd been living with Larry. The constant walking on eggshells, wondering if he was cheating. Who he was cheating with.

"I appreciate the candor," Brooke said.

"I'd like to take the key over to an antique dealer I know." Doug said as he held one end of the tape measure so his son could measure his own foot. "He might be able to give us some insight."

"I don't know how to thank you."

"Tristan's family, so we've always got each other's back." Stacey shifted again in her chair, still rubbing her belly. "I invited Brooke over for dinner and she's accepted."

"Awesome," Doug said as he stood, holding his hand out to his wife, his son perched on his hip. "We'll see you tonight. Around six?"

"I'll be there." Brooke watched as Doug buckled his son in the car seat in the back of the truck before helping his wife into the passenger seat. They all waved as the dark truck made its way down the street.

She fingered the pendant dangling between her breasts, tears burned in her eyes. Her parents had been the greatest people on earth and she missed them desperately right now.

I'm a good listener. Tristan's words rattled around in her mind. She liked him. He made her laugh and had a way of breaking down barriers she didn't know she'd constructed. The rapport she had with him would have taken years to build with anyone else. She wondered if her feelings for Tristan came from his vast knowledge of her grandfather or something else.

She pulled out her phone and tapped his contact information.

How are things at work?

She stared at her phone for a good three minutes. Nothing. Well, he was at work. Her phone buzzed.

Long day so far. How'd things go with Doug?

Her heart fluttered like a girl waiting in line for cotton candy at the state fair.

Good, I think. He took measurements. Stacey invited me to dinner so I can meet her step-mom and maybe talk about my case. Why a long day?

The bubble blinked.

That's good. I'm hoping to have something regarding the note by tomorrow.

Her heart thumped. He hadn't answered her question.

Why a long day?

She shivered, sensing frustration and concern.

Dealing with a murder case. Nothing you need to worry about.

She swallowed, looking around the front yard.

Be safe out there.

She stared at her phone.

I still don't think you should be alone in the house, so I'll be there by 12:20 ish. Have to respond to a call, but I'm here if you need me.

Tucking her phone into her back pocket, she folded the chairs and stared at the house. It might have only been twelve hundred square feet, but it was filled with family and love.

What more could anyone ask for?

Happiness.

Her grandparents and her parents had it in spades. Now she had to find it.

Tristan rubbed his eyes as he reached for the morning paper. The sun wasn't even up yet, but the moment he'd cracked open the door to Brooke's house, the humidity smacked his skin like a water balloon, only it wasn't refreshing, coating his skin with a splash of warm Florida pool water that made you do a double take, making sure you hadn't been splashed with hot oil. The only thing worse than that had to be the chills that crept across his body from the air-conditioning as he carefully pushed the door shut.

When he rounded the corner into the kitchen, he hadn't expected to see Brooke at the kitchen table. But there she sat, face in a bunch of papers, twirling her hair, wearing a tank top and a pair of shorts. He stood at the entryway for a long moment, soaking up her beauty. They'd stayed up 'til two in the morning discussing her legal issues and watching an episode of *Bloodline*. He'd never heard of it before and she insisted he watch at least one episode. It took a lot of control on his part not to watch another one. Crazy good.

But the company was better.

"You're up early." He tossed the paper on the table as he padded his way across the kitchen to pour a large cup of coffee, ignoring his need to draw her into his arms. Getting involved with woman fresh off the cheating ride was a sure-fire way to have a short-lived relationship.

"If my grandmother were here, she'd be yelling at you for being half naked in the kitchen."

"I'll go put on a shirt." He scratched the center of his chest, feeling the massive poke his mother would have given him.

"Not until you explain this." She shoved the questionnaire he hadn't finished in front of his face.

"I started it, but then had to go to work."

She tapped on one particular question. "You promised you'd be honest."

He held the paper between is thumb and forefinger, staring his answer, contemplating his response. "I was honest."

She shook her head, snatching the paper from his hands. "You can't compare what you want in a woman with someone else, especially someone you barely know."

Maybe I don't want someone else and would rather get to know you? "I don't see how filling that thing out is going to help me with diarrhea of the mouth."

"Really? At the breakfast table?" A quiet laugh followed her sarcastic words. "All I'm trying to do is help you find out what kind of person you want to be with and then go back and look at your last few girlfriends to see if you're even close and what may have caused the relationships to go sour."

"I didn't love them," he said as he poured her a second cup of coffee. "Which could be part of the problem."

"Not one of them?"

He joined her at the table, leaning back in his chair, staring into her warm eyes, amused by her pursed lips and crinkled forehead. As much as he liked her, he'd have to be patient, something he knew he had in him. "I wanted to fall in love with them. I tried."

"Love doesn't happen like that." The way her fingers twisted and glided her hair into a side braid mesmerized him. "Have you ever been in love?" she asked.

He nodded. It had been a long time since he let his mind wander to the girl that broke his heart.

"With who?" She tucked her foot up under her butt. The skin on her thigh glistened in the morning sun peeking through the window. "When?"

"I'll tell you the story on one condition."

She cocked her head.

He mimicked her look, only he added a grin.

"What's the condition?"

"You tell me what made you fall in love with Larry and what went wrong."

She nodded. "You first."

He leaned into the table, fingers fiddling with the handle on his coffee mug, staring into the dark liquid. His mind easily conjured up her image. "I was a junior in college, studying pre-law with the idea

I'd finish Law school and go on to Quantico to become an FBI agent."

"You became neither."

"She was part of that decision." Carefully, he raised the mug and blew before taking a large gulp, letting the coffee burn the inside of his mouth. Anger had left him a long time ago, but sadness could still cut his breath short. "Brenda and I met in our intro to criminal law course. Swear to God, for me it was love at first sight."

"That's infatuation."

"Maybe, but the moment she asked if the seat next to me was taken, I was lost in her. Everything about her. The way she laughed. Her voice. I could sit and listen to her for hours and be the happiest man alive."

"So, it wasn't just her looks that attracted you to her."

He closed his eyes, feeling the same ripple of heat burn his skin, only this time Brooke caused the sensation. "She was drop dead gorgeous, so her looks certainly helped, but she's the smartest woman I've ever known." He blinked a few times, avoiding Brooke's stare. He might be talking about Brenda, but what stirred inside him now had nothing to do with his past girlfriend and everything to do with the woman sitting across from him. "I'd been dating someone else when I first met her, so I didn't act on anything, but Brenda was all I could think about. She consumed me."

"Did you cheat on your girlfriend?" Brooke's tone remained even, but her words had some bite.

"No. I broke up with her because of my feelings for Brenda, though Brenda didn't return mine, at least not at first. Took three months to convince her to go out on a date with me."

"Impressed by your determination. But what about those things that pop out of your mouth at the wrong times."

He shrugged. "They happened left and right, but she honestly didn't seem to care." He laughed. "The first date was actually horrible for both of us. My car broke down. We missed the dinner reservations and then I got the movie times all screwed up and our only choice was to see a teenaged comedy sex flick." He glanced up to see Brooke covering her mouth, trying to stifle a laugh.

"It didn't end there." He smiled. "We stopped for ice cream and I managed to spill my chocolate cone all over her white blouse then tried to clean it up, essentially groping her."

"What did she do?"

"Pushed my hands away, called me an asshole, and proceeded to shove her cone in my face. It quickly turned into us having an ice cream fight at the picnic table before we ended up in a lip lock." He remembered her strawberry lips as he touched his own. "Someone yelled at us to get a room and we sat there, staring at each other until we burst out laughing. I took her back to her dorm and said goodnight. Thought that would be the end of it, but the next day in class, she kept finding ways to put her hand on my arm, or lean into me. After class, we went back to her dorm and I guess the rest is history."

"Why'd you break up?"

"She never loved me." His heart skipped a beat. "I'd tell her I loved her and she would respond with 'awe, you're so cute'. I asked her about it one day and she told me 'sorry, I don't feel the same way, just having fun'."

"Ouch."

"Tell me about it."

"How long were you together?"

"A little over a year. After she admitted she didn't love me, I tried to stay with her, thinking I could somehow make her love me back, but I was miserable. A few months later, she started dating my college advisor. They got married right before she want to law school and now they have a kid with another one on the way. I opted not to go on with my education and went into the State Police Academy." He let out a long sigh. He'd always wanted Brenda to be happy and didn't have any ill-will toward her or her husband. However, that didn't change the fact she'd broken his heart.

"How long before you started dating again?"

"I don't know, maybe six months or so. A couple of girls I've dated I've really liked, but either I'd say something so stupid and that was it, or my 'lukewarm-ness' put an end to it."

"I have a hard time believing anyone would call you lukewarm." She twirled her dark hair around her finger. "You're very attentive."

"Some of the women I dated said I was distant and hid behind humor."

"I might buy the latter," Brook said. "Are you sure you loved Brenda?"

"Are you sure you loved Larry?" He arched a brow.

"Touché," she said, tipping her head. "Did you ever think that you say and do dumb things around women because it got you the one you loved?"

He opened his mouth, then slammed it shut. She had a point.

"You could also be sabotaging yourself because you're afraid you're not loveable."

"I'm loveable. My mother even says so." He winked. "The family dog adores me."

She shook her head. "And there is the humor you hid behind."

"I don't think I'm hiding. I've always been a bit sarcastic. It's part of my charm."

"You are charming, but you're afraid of getting hurt, so you've built up some powerful mechanisms to protect yourself."

"Now who is full of psycho-babble shit." He drew his hand down his face, bringing his forefinger and thumb together at his chin. "You could be right."

"What about girlfriends before Brenda? How'd those relationships go?"

"I didn't date much before I meet Brenda. After Tamara died, I was a mess and girls really didn't want to go out with me. I had maybe four relationships before Brenda, but that was it. Now that I'm about to turn thirty and my best friend is getting married soon, I'm thinking I want to settle down and have a family." He smiled. "Thanks. That was insightful."

"Wow. You took being told you have deep seated fears quite well."

He shrugged. "If it's preventing me from finding someone to share my life with, then I'm willing to look at it."

"Well color me something. You are a sweet man." She raised her mug.

"You're turn." He smiled as he clanked her mug.

"I didn't like Larry when I first met him. I thought he was an arrogant, pompous ass."

"So, why'd you go out with him?"

She tossed her head back and laughed. "I worked with him, well, more like for him and God, what a horrible boss. I kept bitching to my girlfriend about him and she decided a blind date would be the best way to make me feel better and her fiancé's best friend just happened to be available."

"Larry was your blind date?"

She nodded. "I took one look at him and nearly turned around and left, but he stood, and pulled out my chair. Greeted me with kindness. It was like he was an entirely different man."

"You had a good time on the date?"

"He was charismatic and charming. I was stunned. We had lunch the next day and found out we had so much in common."

"What happened when you went back to work?" Tristan had seen his share of Jekyll and Hide men, and it was never pretty for the women involved with them.

"He remained an asshole. He'd text me an apology, saying he couldn't afford to treat me differently at work and we kept our relationship a secret for a year."

"From everyone? Or just work?"

"Just work. We're both ambitious. I wanted his job, and he wanted to be V.P. of Product Development. Even when we made our relationship public knowledge, we kept a safe distance from each other at the office."

"Sounds awkward and uncomfortable."

"I thought it worked for us. When we were at work, we were focused on our own careers and advancement. At home, we had romantic dinners, watched television, and went on long walks. I had no idea he'd been unhappy." She picked at her fingernail. "That's not entirely true. Once we moved in together, he became distant. At first, I thought it was because I pushed marriage, so I backed off.

But he started working late at the office during the week. Later than usual. I knew he was pushing for another promotion, so I thought he was just dedicated. I had no idea he'd been doing the nasty with my assistant for six months."

"Why did he stay with you?"

She ran her fingers across the top of her head, gathering her wavy hair and shaking it out. "I never asked him. Haven't talked with him since I moved out." She pushed her phone across the table. "He's been texting me for the past few days, offering his condolences and wanting to know if there is anything he can do to help. He also says he misses me."

"You haven't responded?" He glanced at the phone, but decided he didn't want to look at the texts. He'd heard enough.

"Hell no." She pulled one knee up to her chest, resting her foot on the chair next to her butt. "I don't want to hear his excuses, rationalizations, or anything else. Cheating is a deal breaker for me, so I have no problem saying good-bye."

"Good for you. But it's still got to be hard. You obviously loved him."

"I loved the idea of him." She tilted her chin and her gold eyes locked with his. "If I'm being honest, my outburst in the office had more to do with being angry at myself for ignoring the signs that he'd been cheating. After I was arrested, I didn't really focus on the loss of him as much as the loss of my job and not having a place to live. When I got the call about my grandpa, I will admit that the grief for both losses overwhelmed me, but I'm starting to see that maybe I didn't love Larry like I thought I did."

"Do you mean that? Or are you pushing things down again?"

She smiled, which sent a warmth across his entire a body.

"I mean it. I'm more upset about losing my job than him. I'm not saying I didn't love him, because I did, but I knew it was over before it was over and I just didn't want to let it go."

"Had you dumped him when you realized that, you wouldn't have gotten arrested, lost your job—"

"Thanks for the reminder." She smiled, picking up the paper

and tossed it at his face. Luckily, he had good reflexes and snagged it from the air before it had a chance to take his eye out.

"You're welcome." He pulled the newspaper out of its plastic bag and went searching for anything printed regarding Richie Rayburn, a man wanted for questioning in an open murder investigation. The all-points-bulletin had gone out a few days ago and was of the highest priority since the man was considered armed and dangerous. As he flipped the pages open, he peered over the top, checking out Brooke's ass as she rose and moved about the kitchen.

She glanced over her shoulder, and he quickly diverted his gaze to top article. He coughed, staring at her mug shot. The headline read: *Long standing resident's family name shamed.*

"Fuck," he muttered.

"What?"

He sucked in a deep breath as she made her way around the table until she stood behind him, hands resting on his shoulder for a brief moment until she yanked the paper from him.

"What the…this happened a little over three weeks ago? Why are they doing this now?"

"I wouldn't be surprised—"

Ding Dong!

Saved by the bell? "I'll get it." Tristan squeezed her shoulder, but she waved him off, eyes scanning the paper. He hiked up his jeans, zipping the fly just as he opened the front door.

"Oh, well…" Mrs. Ramsworth and her grandson, Wendell stood at the front door. "Um, excuse me. Is Miss Fowler here?"

Had it just been the old lady, Tristan wouldn't think to mess with her. But Wendell? Life was too short not to make that man squirm in his shoes.

"Hey babe?" he called over his shoulder. "Bring me my shirt." He smiled at the woman who looked like she might have a heart attack. Perhaps she'd never seen a bare-chested man.

Be nice, Tristan Jordan Reid. His mother's voice boomed between his ears.

"The Ramsworth's are here to see you, hon."

"May we come in?" Mrs. Ramsworth asked.

"Not my house, so I'll let Brooke make that call."

"Tell them to go away," Brooke yelled from the other room. "It's too early for company."

Tristan fisted his hands as Wendell moved closer to the front door, the newspaper pinched under his arm.

"We need to talk to her about something important." Wendell lifted the paper, showing Brooke's not so attractive mug shot.

"That has nothing to do with you." Tristan rested his hands on his hips.

Wendell tapped the newspaper so hard he poked a hole in it. "She's wearing my great-mother's necklace, which was stolen years ago. We'd like it back."

Tristan leaned in, looking at the necklace in the picture. "My mother has a necklace that is similar. I'm sure it's not—"

"It's a one of a kind handmade heirloom." Mrs. Ramsworth fanned her eyes. "I don't like to speak ill of the dead, but it went missing when Ashley Fowler was our employee."

The floor boards rattled.

"What?" Brooke let out a huge puff of air right in Tristan's ear.

It didn't calm him down, but it certainly had a different effect on his body and he no longer wanted to throttle Wendell. Just slam the door in his face and do a few unspeakable things to Brooke.

"Are you accusing my grandmother of stealing?" She tried to shove past Tristan, but he looped his arm around her, keeping her from lurching toward Wendell.

"That…." Mrs. Ramsworth pointed to the pendant dangling around Brooke's neck… "is my mother's. We reported it missing years ago. Please, give it back."

"She will do no such thing." Tristan moved his arm in front of Brooke, pressing his hand against the door frame, ignoring her glare.

"Look at this picture." Mrs. Ramsworth shoved an old black and white picture in front of Brooke's face. "That necklace is identical to my mother's."

Tristan took the picture and glanced between it and the locket that Brooke gripped between her fingers. "Looks similar, but until you have some kind of proof—"

"You're an officer of the law. I demand you do something." Mrs. Ramsworth yanked the picture.

"There's nothing to do. If you want to persue this, I suggest you hire a lawyer, dig out the last appraisal on the item, find the original police report, and go from there."

Mrs. Ramsworth drew her lips into a tight line, eyes narrowed. "That's my family's property. I'm going to get it back."

"Go to the car, grandmama," Wendell said, resting his hands on the woman's shoulder and turning her toward the street.

Tristan looped his arm over Brooke's shoulder, getting her attention. Her eyes turned a fiery orange. Not a good sign. He leaned in, kissing her temple. "Relax. Let me do the talking," he whispered. He squeezed her shoulder when Wendell turned his attention back toward them.

"We'd thought that necklace was gone forever." Wendell planted his hands on his hips. "It was meant to travel through the family from wives and daughters. It now belongs to my wife and soon my daughter. I'm going to do whatever it takes to get it back." He waggled his finger in front of Brooke. "Anything."

"I wouldn't threaten her if I were you." Tristan would like nothing better than to egg Wendell on, giving him any excuse to arrest the asshole again. "If there is nothing else, please leave."

"You haven't heard the last of this." Wendell stuffed his hands in his trouser pockets. "You'll be hearing from our attorney." He turned on his heels, but then paused, glancing over his shoulder. "Good luck getting a job."

"Asshole," Brooke muttered, shaking out her hands. "I bet he handed that article to the local paper."

"I wouldn't put it past him." Tristan cupped her face, searching her whiskey-colored eyes. "He's still looking at us."

"So?" Her hands slid up his hips to the bare skin of his lower back.

"Just thought a little public display of affection might be in order."

"I'm beginning to think you're an exhibitionist."

He smiled. "It bothers me the way he looks at you and not just because he's married."

She leaned into him, her chest heaving with labored breath. "Are you jealous?"

"God no," he said, his fingers gliding down the side of her neck, tracing a path to the locket dangling between her breasts. "And this has nothing to do with them. I've been thinking about kissing you since I walked into the kitchen this morning." Not wanting her to react, he licked his lips, then brushed them against her like the soft stroke of an artist's paint brush on a canvas, creating a masterpiece.

Her lips parted, giving him full access to her hot mouth. Her tongue swirled around his in a tender dance as her hands pressed harder against the small of his back.

The roar of an engine echoed in the background. Part of him enjoyed the idea that Wendell and his family believed that he and Brooke were an item. The other part wanted Brooke to be in his life in a girlfriend kind of way.

He continued to thumb the locket with one hand, the other cupped the back of her neck, desperately trying to keep the kiss controlled. He could easily lift her into his arms and carry her to bed. Sex had always been the easy part.

Maybe too easy.

Pulling back, he glanced down at the necklace in his fingertips. "What's inside?"

Her fingers split open the sliver trinket and exposed two wedding pictures. Both black and white. The same ones that hung in the family room above the sofa.

"They've never seen you wear this?"

"I really don't know. I almost never take it off, so one would think so, it's possible they haven't seen it on me. Not like I spend a lot of time with them." Her eyelids fluttered as she lifted her gaze. "You don't believe them, do you?"

He swallowed. There was no mistaking the hurt in her eyes. "No. But considering the break-ins, we need to get this appraised and take it to a specialty jeweler and see if we can find anything out about it. My mom has a really good one. I can ask her for the name."

"I appreciate that, but it sounds like you think I should be worried."

"Not worried, but you need to protect yourself." He dropped the pendant, letting it bounce off her skin between her luscious breasts. "Go on a date with me."

"What!?"

"You heard me" He shook his head. "Go on a date with me. Dinner and a movie."

"I don't do teen sex flicks." She laughed, stepping back.

"Now you're the one hiding behind humor."

"You can't be serious?" She titled her head.

"I think the way I kiss you should be hint enough of how serious I am."

She waved her hand. "Come on. You do that to fuck with Wendell."

"I will admit that's fun." He inched closer, lifting her chin with his fingers. "But they aren't looking now."

Her lips parted and he took that as an invitation. Pressing his mouth against hers, he slipped his tongue inside her mouth in a slow, controlled kiss.

She pulled away. "This isn't a good idea."

"It's the best idea I've had in a long while." He kissed her cheek. "You are going to go on a date with me."

She cocked her head. "Let me get through my grandfather's funeral and then I'll think about it."

"Deal."

CHAPTER 5

Brooke pulled into the packed parking lot of the Boardwalk restaurant in the village of Lake George. Saturday nights were always happening at this place in the summer, and tonight was no exception. At first, she'd turned Tristan down for dinner, not wanting him to think it was a date, because she'd decided that was never going to happen, no matter how much she liked him. She had too much to deal with and getting involved with him would just complicate her life.

But after spending the day on the phone, she decided it would be good to get out of the house. Besides, she had one last thing to take care of for her grandfather's funeral in the morning, and after careful consideration, Tristan was the only logical choice.

After closing the top on her convertible, she glanced around, looking for Tristan's car, but no luck. She glanced at her watch. He'd said seven and it was seven fifteen.

"Over here," Tristan's voice echoed over the noise of the blended sounds of people deep in conversation. He leaned against the fence, holding open the patio door. A man of medium height and slender build stood next to him.

She clicked her car locked and dumped the keys in her purse, trying not to admire the man she wished she'd seen more of over the course of the last two days. Sure, he stopped by when he wasn't working, but now that her security system was completely on-line, he'd stopped spending the night on her sofa.

"Where's your car?"

He drew her in for a quick hug and a peck on the cheek, before escorting her across the crowded patio. "I rode in with my boss this morning because we both had a court appearance. I was hoping you could drive me home."

"I don't know. It's such an inconvenience to turn that corner."

His laugh filled her ears, sending warmth throughout her body.

She resented the way he made her feel because she knew it wasn't real. A woman would have to be dead not to find him attractive, but he would be a rebound experience. No. Worse. He'd be revenge to toss in everyone's face. That's the one thing she decided he was right about. She'd never gotten over the betrayals in her life and she was a walking time bomb, which meant dealing with it so she didn't do something crazy.

Which meant no rebound, no matter how awkwardly adorable he was.

"This is my buddy, Cade Nash."

"Are you a police officer too?" she asked.

"I'm a fireman."

"That's cool," she said.

"I met your grandfather a few times. Stand up guy. Was very sorry to hear about his death" Cade took her hand and kissed it.

"Thank you," she said.

"Cade and some of his fellow firefighters will be pall bearers."

"I really appreciate it," she said, swallowing. All of a sudden, she'd felt shy. Something she wasn't use to.

"My pleasure. Tristan gave us the details, so we'll be ready tomorrow morning."

Tristan pointed to a table in the back already occupied by two men and a female. "I hope you don't mind dining with Cade and a couple other friends of mine."

What was she going to do? Say no? Her heart beat faster. She didn't want to ask a favor in front of his friends, which is why she'd been disappointed they weren't' alone. "Not a problem. It would be nice to meet more people around here. Maybe one of them can help me find a job."

"Well, we're being joined by a fellow trooper and his fiancé who is an author/advertising copy editor or something or other. Maybe she can help you."

A woman standing at the hostess station, waiting to be seated, gave either Tristan or Cade the once over. Both were handsome men, but Tristan had that something extra, so she figured the woman was interested in him over Cade.

Maybe pushing Tristan toward this woman would help divert her own attraction to the man.

"Brooke, this is Josh and his fiancé, Delaney," Tristan said.

Brooke shook hands with a very sweet looking man and a knockout blonde with a matching sweet smile.

"Good to meet you," the couple said in unison.

Brooke took her seat next to Cade, across from Delaney, while Tristan took the chair at the end of the table. "Cade, how did you know my grandpa?"

Cade took a swig of his beer. "There was a fire at the house down the street about a year ago. He called it in. But it was a week later when I saw him and Tristan having a beer at the Mason Jug and I joined them."

"Did he talk about me like he did with Tristan?" She glanced at Tristan, who smiled, sending her stomach on a roll.

Cade shook his head. "I'm sorry, but not really. He mentioned you, but that's about it. We mostly talked hockey."

"He loved hockey." Brooke ignored the tickling in her brain about why her grandfather chose to keep his conversations about her limited to Tristan. It was both sweet and annoying.

"Tristan tells us you're planning on flipping your grandfather's house," Josh said. His hand looped over the back of Delaney's chair. She leaned into him, hand resting on his leg. New love. Hopefully a lasting love.

"That's the plan. I think I even have a contractor picked out," Brooke said, trying not to stare at Tristan.

"You've decided to use Doug?" Tristan arched a brow, smiling.

"He seems to think he can do it within my budget, but it's not a done deal yet," Brooke said, smiling back. The man was irresistible.

"That's good news." Tristan squeezed her hand before reaching for his drink. "I won't have anything on the note you gave me until Monday or Tuesday. The forensics' guy, however, thinks the note was written in the last couple of years because of the paper that was used."

"That's amazing they can find that shit out." Brooke smiled, staring into his captivating gaze, trying to blink, wishing she could turn away. "What about the key?"

"Doug has an antique key expert looking at it who thinks he can trace it since there were numbers on it, meaning it may have come with something specific like an antique lock box. But he also said it could be a replica, so he will be testing the metal."

"The process of all this is fascinating." Brooke tore her eyes off the sexy man leaning across the table, intently staring at her. She looked about the room, catching the same woman with short dark hair eyeing the table. Brooke still couldn't tell if the cute woman at the bar gawked at Tristan or Cade, but she decided to use the situation to deflect her own crazy attraction. "Someone's checking you out." She nudged Tristan.

"What?" His face scrunched as if she'd just punched him in the stomach.

"A woman at the bar." She nodded in the girl's direction. "She couldn't keep her eyes off you as we walked in."

The waitress appeared at the table. "Are you ready to order."

"Yes," Tristan barked. "Ladies first." He tapped her hand.

She gave him a sideways glance. But she knew what she wanted and went ahead and ordered. By the time everyone had told the waitress what they wanted, the girl at the bar had been seated at a table on the other side of the restaurant with two other girls.

"You missed a chance to go talk to her," Brooke said.

"Didn't want to." Tristan turned his attention to the other side of the table. "Is everything all set for the wedding?"

The happy couple looked at each other and smiled.

Stupid young love.

"Nothing left to do but show up," Delaney said. " Did you find a date yet?" She winked at Brooke, which Brooke thought was weird.

"I'm not bringing a date." Tristan tossed a napkin on the table.

"If you'd talk to that girl, you might have one by next week." Brooke tried to give him her best smile, but by his narrowed glare, she figured she'd come off sarcastically.

"I think we should leave the poor man alone," Cade interjected with a wave of his hand. "Besides, he's my date."

"Oh no," Delaney leaned forward. "What happened to the girl you've been seeing?"

"Crashed and burned worse than Tristan ever could." Cade laughed.

"That's impossible." Josh continued to find ways to touch his fiancé and it was starting to annoy Brooke. Larry had never been like that, not even when they first started dating.

"I didn't say it was me who crashed. She made fun of my dog and her name. Not once, but twice and thought it was funny."

"Everyone makes fun of Baby's name." Tristan shook his head. "Who the hell names a 100-pound German Shepard Baby?"

"I don't understand why she'd make fun of that name?" Brooke stared at Tristan.

"It gets better." He nudged her knee with hers. "The dog is named after Baby from the movie Dirty Dancing."

Brooke covered her smile, but it didn't stop her laugh from traveling across the room. "Seriously?"

Cade rolled his eyes. "It's my mother's favorite movie."

"Awe, that's so sweet." Brooke patted his shoulder. "Did you tell the girl that?"

"Yep." Cade tipped his beer. "She called me a mama's boy, so that was the end of that."

"You are a momma's boy," Delaney said. "Which is adorable, so screw her."

"Exactly." Cade pushed his empty beer glass to the side as the wait staff brought over their food.

"So, where's your wedding going to be?" Brooke loaded up her cheeseburger with all the toppings, smothering it with ketchup and mustard. The smell of caramelized onions filled her nostrils. She couldn't remember the last time she had a good old fashioned American Cheeseburger. She held the thick sandwich in her hands, studying and squeezing it so she could manage to take a bite.

"At a friend's house, just down the road. They have a beautiful front yard overlooking the lake." Delaney had a voice of a school teacher, soft with a gentle firmness to it.

But all Brooke wanted at this moment was to taste the hunk of meat in her hands. She took a big bite and part of her tomato fell out the other side, but she really didn't care. Closing her eyes, she chewed slowly, letting the tastes of bacon, cheese, lettuce, and all sorts of treats melded together in a symphony of perfection. "Oh… my…God. Best cheeseburger ever." She opened her eyes to half the table staring at her.

"You got a little…" Tristan dabbed his napkin in some water then reached out toward her shoulder, his hand hovering as he stared at her chest.

She looked down at a glob of ketchup and mustard on her left boob. "Shit," she muttered, taking the napkin Tristan offered, knowing she'd never get this stain out right now.

"I'll be right back." Tristan squeezed her shoulder. "Key." He held his hand out in front of Josh, who smiled, forking over a set.

Before she had a chance to ask where he was going, he disappeared into the crowd of people gathering to hear the band. She gave up cleaning her shirt, and went back to eating her burger, being a tad more careful this time.

"Where are you going on your honeymoon?" Brooke asked.

"He won't tell me." Delaney said.

"That's romantic." Brooke scanned the room and choked on a tiny piece of pickle when she saw Tristan with a backpack flung over his shoulder, talking with the hot chick that had been eyeing the table earlier. Well, she did tell him he should go talk to her.

Tristan took a piece of paper the woman gave him and strutted back to the table, smiling. He dumped his bag on the chair and pulled out a T-Shirt, handing it to her. "So you don't have to walk around with a target on your chest."

"Thank you," she stammered out, impressed he'd thought to get it, annoyed he'd smiled so wide after talking to some random hot chick. "I saw you talking to that girl?"

"Oh yeah." He reached across her and handed Cade a piece of paper. "She said text her when we're done if you want to have a drink."

Cade took the paper and looked across the room. He smiled, giving the girl a little wave and holding the paper up before taking his phone out.

"Whoa, wait." Brooke blinked. "You screwed up that quickly?"

"No." Tristan laughed. "She's not my type and I knew she was checking out Cade."

"How do you know she's not your type? You barely talked to her?" Brooke asked, stunned by the butterflies flapping around in her gut.

"I'm not interested in her," he said, shaking his head. "Why don't you go change and I'll pay the bill. We can stay and watch the band for a bit if you want."

"That would be fun." She snagged the shirt, quickly covering her breast. "Let me know what the damage is so I can pay my part."

He held out his hand out, helping her out of her chair. "Do you want another drink?"

"If we're staying a bit, yeah, I'll have another beer." She let her hand linger in his a little longer than she should have, causing a long awkward stare.

"I'll come with you," Delaney said and she stood. "Get me another glass of wine, please."

Brooke had never understood why women went to the bathroom in pairs. A few times, when out with friends or business associates, women would leave the table, staring at her, giving her the evil eye when she didn't join them.

She followed the friendly blonde across the restaurant and into the bathroom, where thankfully, there was no line. "Where do you and Josh live?" Brooke tore off her shirt, rinsing it in the sink.

"For now, right above this restaurant until we find a little house we like on the water in our price range."

"Lake front is so expensive." Brooke held up her shirt, satisfied she'd gotten most of the stain out before pulling Tristan's shirt over her head. She adjusted the oversized shirt, staring at the words across the front. "Not sure if having NY State Trooper across my tits is any better than a ketchup stain."

Delaney laughed. "At least he thought to get you a shirt."

"This is true." Brooke fluffed her hair. Tristan had been a life saver in so many ways. He'd been correct in his assessment of her current state of mind, but this dependence she had on him had to stop.

After the funeral, she'd put an end to it. They could be friends, but not friends glued at the hips.

"Tristan talked about your grandfather a lot. He was real fond of him."

"It's weird. My grandpa didn't talk about him. Well he did, but not by name. Considering he wanted to fix me up with Tristan, I'm a little shocked my grandfather never said his name." Brooke folded her semi-wet shirt, tucking it in her large purse. "Though I did have a live-in boyfriend and wouldn't have allowed my grandpa to even discuss the possibility of meeting someone else."

Delaney leaned against the wall near the hand dryer. "Now that you've met Tristan, what do you think?"

"I think he's a nice guy who took pity on a girl when she was down. He's been very helpful." Brooke leaned into the mirror and puckered her lips. "Have you met many of his past girlfriends?" *Shut the fuck up, Brooke!*

"Not really. The last year he's been gun-shy."

"Why is that?" Brooke leaned against the sink. Based on everything Tristan had told her about his past relationships she could see why he'd been a little afraid of jumping in with two feet, but she could tell having a long-term girlfriend meant a lot to him.

"Josh thinks part of it has to do with the loss of his twin."

Delaney lowered her gaze to her hands. "I shouldn't have told you that."

"He told me about his sister, just not how it happened."

"Josh said something died in Tristan when she passed. Add in the fact he's not the most romantic guy, says what he thinks when he thinks it, and he's been told most of his adult life he's not marriage material, I think he believes it."

"Self-fulfilling prophecy," Brooke said, understanding more about the man who had her stomach tied in knots. "I told him he needs to find a woman who appreciates his flaws."

"She's out there, somewhere."

Brooke's phone buzzed. She dug through her purse, finding it at the bottom. She laughed looking at Tristan's text. "Seems Tristan is wondering if we are having a lesbian love affair."

Delaney's eyes went wide. "He didn't say that, did he?"

Brooke held up her phone. "Men and their obsession with girl on girl action."

"I can't believe he texted you that." Delaney shook her head.

Brooke waved her hand. "It's hysterical, if you ask me." She swallowed, keeping her smile light. No denying she and Tristan had a physical connection. The way his lips molded to hers like peanut butter and chocolate left her wanting more.

It's only rebound feelings. It's not real.

She pushed from the sink and took two steps before Delaney curled her fingers around her biceps.

"You see the way he looks at you, right?" Delaney asked.

Brooke took in a deep breath, letting it out slowly. "I don't know what he's told you about me, but I'm just out of a long-term relationship and I have so many problems that I couldn't even consider dating anyone. Besides, I'm not the girl for him."

"Are you kidding? You're perfect him." Delaney looped her arm over Brooke's shoulder, hip checking the bathroom door, pulling them both into the crowded room. "But I understand needing time after a break-up, but you'll see how perfect you are soon enough. Hey. You should come to my wedding. Consider yourself invited."

Before Brooke should respond to the insanity spewing from the bouncy blonde's mouth, she was standing face to face with Tristan on the deck of the restaurant. The band had started, playing a popular country song. She leaned against the railing next to Tristan, watching Delaney drag her fiancé onto the dance floor.

"Where's Cade?" she asked, trying to ignore the pull to lean into Tristan's strong body. She'd have to be blind not to find him the sexist man in the room with his chiseled facial features and deep eyes. She glanced in his direction and swallowed her breath when he smiled.

"Over there." He pointed across the deck to a couple dancing in the corner.

"Wow. He can really bust-a-move."

"His mother was a dance teacher and rumor has it, he took lessons for years. He says he named his dog for his mother, but secretly we all think he watches *Dirty Dancing* all the time."

"He'll have to do the final dance at his wedding."

Tristan laughed as he slid his hand across her lower back, hooking his fingers into her belt loop.

She swallowed. "What do I owe you for my dinner?"

He frowned, narrowing his eyes. "Don't insult me."

"You don't have to buy me—"

He covered her mouth. "No. I don't. But I wanted to, okay?"

She nodded as he dropped his hand. "Thank you," she said as she rubbed her hands across her jeans.

"You're welcome." He took one of the beers on the railing and handed it to her. "This band plays here at least once a month. Probably the best one in years."

"Do you want to dance?" She blinked a few times, pressing the long neck to her lips, wishing she could take the words back.

"I'm not much of a...Fuck it," Tristan said as he put the beers back on the railing and took her by the hand, leading her toward the band. As the song winded down, he leaned in and said something to the guitarist, who nodded then turned his attention to the rest of the band.

"What did you do?"

"Requested a slow song. I can dance to a slow song." He pulled her closer, his hands on her hips, thumbs rubbing slow circles on her waist. A country balled came on that she vaguely recognized.

Her heart beat erratically as she pressed her hands on his shoulders, eyes locked as they swayed back and forth. If she continued to stare at him like this, she'd kiss him. Leaning closer, she broke the mesmerizing trance by resting her chin on his shoulder.

His arms circled her waist, hands resting just above her ass. His hot breath tickled her ear. Staring at him might have been less exotic than this sensual embrace. Her body shivered from desire. He guided her in a slow circle, rocking their bodies to the beat of the music. She glanced around the dance floor at the sea of lovers kissing, touching, and smiling.

She closed her eyes.

You know I'll always support you, her grandfather's voice echoed. *But I don't trust Larry with your heart and I don't think you love him. Really love him.*

Tears stung in her eyes. Her grandfather had been right. She wanted to love Larry and maybe they could have if they hadn't been so ambitious, putting their careers before each other. He'd even talked about how his career was more important than family. No wonder he ran for the hills the moment she brought up marriage.

You're so much like your father and you need a partner that will support you no matter what. I know the kind of man you need.

She dropped her head, nuzzling her face into Tristan's neck.

"You okay?" Tristan whispered in her ear.

"I was just thinking about my grandfather." She clasped her fingers around his neck. "I was supposed to come see him the weekend before he died, but I cancelled. I didn't want him to know what I'd done or that Larry cheated on me. I should have come to see grandpa."

"He understood."

"How do you know?"

"I had dinner with him that weekend. He didn't know what was going on. Suspected you weren't totally up front with why you cancelled but he understood. Only thing that bothered him was I actually had that entire weekend off and he planned on introducing us at dinner Saturday night."

She jerked her head back. "You didn't tell me that?"

He traced his thumb over her cheek bone. "I wasn't sure how you'd take it that I was desperate enough to let the old man fix me up with his granddaughter who was already living with some dude."

The corners of her lips turned upward. "That's pathetic, you know that, right?"

He nodded, cupping the back of her head. "I would've done just about anything your grandfather asked. I really am going to miss him."

"That reminds me." She swallowed. "I have huge favor to ask."

"Anything."

"I know this is last minute, but I can't do his eulogy and the few friends he had left aren't the right people to do it. So, I was hoping you would."

His eyes went wide and his lips parted.

"I know it's a lot to ask."

"Not to mention I've got no time to prepare anything."

"I would understand if you say no."

"I'd be honored to give the eulogy." He smiled. "But I can't guarantee it will be any good."

"All he'd want is your honesty, and I have the feeling he'd be pleased that I asked you."

Tristan's hands slid up her spine, forcing her to arch into him. Quickly, she stepped back. "I really appreciate it." She patted his chest before turning and making a beeline for the railing where her beer waited.

"Either I'm doing this really all wrong, or you're just not interested in me." He stood so close she could see his pulse beat in the side of his neck. "I've never had a problem sending the vibe that I like a woman until you."

"Liking someone and being attracted to them are two different things and people often mistake one for the other."

"I like you AND I'm attracted to you."

"You're timing sucks," she said softly. "You're sexy as hell and a damn nice guy, but I can't go there. Even you said I need to deal with all this emotional baggage I've been carrying around."

"You do." He had the nerve to smile. "And I can be patient when I want something and right now I want you."

CHAPTER 6

Brooke took the hand Tristan offered as she slid from the back of the limo. She adjusted her sun glasses, keeping her tear-filled eyes hidden. She scanned the cemetery. Cars lined the windy road and a sea of people dressed in black made their way toward a small tent. Cade and his buddies stood next to the hearse, hands clasped in front of them, standing stoic, waiting to carry her grandfather's casket to the grave site.

"Are you ready?" Tristan rested his hand on the small of her back. His thumb tracing a tiny circular pattern, making her feel less alone.

Unable to speak, she nodded. Her entire family had been laid to rest in this spot and she was the last living relative. She swallowed a sob. Her parents raised her to be a confident and strong woman, telling her to always keep her chin high. When they died, her grandmother told her strength was both a blessing and a curse.

Brooke finally understood what her grandmother meant by that.

The walk to the gravesite seemed to take forever. The majority of the people who came were friends of her grandfathers, most of whom she'd met over the course of her life. But the only friend she had?

Tristan.

Her strength had kept her a safe distance from the world.

She'd thought about inviting some of her friends from the office, but then it dawned on her, not a single one of them had texted or called to check in with her. To see if she were okay after the incident at the office, or the announcement of her grandfather's death.

Not a single one.

A tear rolled down her cheek as she took her place in the front of the tent, watching Cade and his friends lift the casket in their firemen uniforms.

A strong hand squeezed her shoulder. She glanced over at Tristan, who took a few steps back and turned.

"Please don't go," she whispered. "I don't want to be up here by myself."

"Okay."

The muscles in her legs trembled. The casket now in front of her and the men who'd placed it there stepped back, standing to the side, heads down, hands clasped in front of them.

The preacher greeted the crowd, giving her a nod and a weak smile.

Tristan tugged at her arm, helping her ease back into the chair. The sun shone through the trees, its rays breaking apart, casting streaks of sparkles against the backdrop of a shadow. She heard a crow in the background. It was the kind of beautiful day that would make her grandfather take a stroll down the road, stopping to say hello to his neighbors, waving to children he didn't know, smiling at everyone.

"I first met Russell Fowler, better known as Rusty, when I was barely twenty-five. His son and beautiful wife had just passed." The preacher held his bible open, a red ribbon dangled down between the pages. "He and *his* Ashley, as he always called his lovely bride, were not religious, and they let me know that straight away. They wanted a simple ceremony that celebrated life, not death. They didn't want a lot of scripture or ceremonial traditions. They wanted only a proper way to say, and I quote, 'see you on the flip side.'"

Brooke squeezed her eyes closed, pushing out the moisture that had welled. The past and the present collided in her mind. Being a young woman at this very grave site, her grandmother the pillar of strength as they lowered her parent's caskets into the cold, hard ground.

"I remember vividly the joyous words Rusty and *his* Ashley had to say about the wonderful life their son and daughter-in-law had carved out for themselves. How much they enjoyed life, even when things didn't go their way."

The sound of the preacher's steady voice gave Brooke the power to open her eyes.

"A few years later, Rusty knocked on my door, sadness etched in his tear stained eyes. While I could see the pain, I also saw something in Rusty that both astonished and humbled me. I saw life in the wake of death. He buried *his* beloved Ashley." The preacher pointed to the tombstone where Ashley Tindle Fowler had been laid to rest. "When he left that day, he made me promise that when his time came, that I'd make sure his service was about love and life. He wanted to give his family and friends what they needed for grief, so this," the preacher raised his bible up, "simple setting under the watchful eye of the Lord above, is Rusty's way of saying, 'I'll see you on the flip side'". The preacher closed his bible and raised his hands. "I will not say a prayer out loud as I know that is what Rusty would have wanted. But please, take a moment to say a silent prayer, or simply remember Rusty in the fondest of ways."

Tristan's warm hand covers hers with a powerful grip, easing the pain set deep in her bones. Her breath shook as she filled her lungs with air, letting it out slowly, trying desperately not to sob.

He gave a good squeeze before he stood and made his way around to the other side of the casket. He cleared his throat as he pulled a piece of paper from his pants pocket. For a long moment, he stared at it. His fingers fondling the edges of the paper. Finally, he folded it and shoved it back in his pocket.

"Rusty and I had dinner at least once a week for the last year."

Brooke sniffled.

"The thing he was most proud of was his family. I gladly sat through many dinners listening to stories of his wife, son, and granddaughter. Rusty reminded me of the importance of family and how short life could be. At the end of every dinner, he'd slap my back and say, 'kid, there are two things in life you never want to say no to, and one rule to live by. The first: never say no to the love of a good woman. Second: the thrill of giving her everything she wants, even when you know it's going to break the bank.'" Tristan wiped his eyes. "He'd end with his golden rule, which was a quote from a song: 'love like there's no such thing as a broken heart.'"

Searing tears flowed down Brooke's cheeks, remembering her grandfather saying the exact thing, only he'd change it to the love of a good man who was willing to do anything to make your life better, even if it broke the bank.

"Rusty taught me to go after what I want in this life so that when I'm old and look back, I won't have any regrets. I honestly believe he didn't have a single one. He truly was the happiest man I have ever met and that is nothing short of a miracle when you consider all the death he had to endure during his life." Tristan loosened his tie. "Rusty was a firm believer in truisms. He always told me clichés were some of life's best realities. That struck me as odd, but I'm beginning to see how Rusty was right in his sentiment. He told me nothing happens in a vacuum, everything happens for reason, even if we don't know why. He was a great man who lived a humble life. I will miss him and always remember how he made my life richer. Rest in peace, my friend."

Brooke allowed herself to smile as Tristan sat down next to her, taking her hand. She continued to cry, but her heart warmed for the man who'd taken time from his own life to befriend her grandfather and now help her. "Thank you," she whispered. "My grandfather would have loved that."

Tristan wiped his face before covering his eyes with dark sunglasses. "I hope so."

For the next fifteen minutes, she stood next to Tristan as people walked by, giving their condolences in a hushed tone before dropping a rose on the casket. She managed a polite smile when Mr. and Mrs. Ramsworth, the grandparents, made their way through the line.

The old woman barely looked at her, but the old man took her hand into his frail cold grasp and looked her in the eye. "It takes a special man to do the things your grandfather has done. Always remember that."

She had no time to contemplate the meaning of those words when Wendell's parents stepped in front of her. His mother nodding respectfully, his father managed a weak smile before placing their roses on the casket.

Bile gurgled from her stomach to her throat when she laid eyes on Wendell and his pregnant bride.

Michelle leaned in and kissed her cheek. "I'm so sorry. I know how much you loved him."

Be kind because it's good for the soul and makes the people who want to push you down, crazy, her grandmother's voice whispered in her mind.

"Thank you," Brooke said behind gritted teeth.

Wendell nodded as he walked by, unwilling to say a word, much less shake Tristan's hand.

She waited for the last person to walk away before approaching the wooden box. Reaching out with a shaky hand, she placed her rose on top of the others, resting her hand on the hard casket. A warmth rushed over her body, as if her grandparents and parents had reached5` down from wherever they were and hugged her. "You were right Grandpa. You were always right." She kissed her fingers, then tapped the casket four times. "See you on the flip side."

She laced her fingers around the inside of Tristan's elbow. A vivid memory of her parents helping her move into her dorm room at college. Her father laughing, tossing a pillow at her mother. Similar images of her grandparents floated across her mind. Both couples had the kind of love people searched for their entire lives, some never finding it.

The sun beat down on her face, drying her tears. A few people lingered, chatting by their cars. Others drove off down the windy, narrow road. Of all the people who attended the graveside ceremony, she suspected only half would come to the house.

She could only hope the Ramsworth's had something better to do.

"Who's that?" Tristan pointed to a man leaning against the limo.

"You've got to be fucking kidding me." Brooke squeezed Tristan's arm as tight as she could. "That's Larry."

"Normally, I'd offer to give you some privacy, but in this case, I'm afraid you might cause bodily harm and I'd have to slap on the handcuffs, which is not how I want to tie you up."

"That's beyond inappropriate." She laughed. "But I think you have a point with regard to me causing damage to that man. I'll ignore the rest of the statement."

Larry pushed himself from the vehicle. As always, he dressed to the nines with a dark designer suit, red tie, and those damned imported Italian shoes. His brown hair parted neatly on the side with a poof of hair pushed up in the front, sides cut much shorter, almost buzzed.

"What are you doing here?" she asked.

"Mind if we have a moment?" Larry addressed Tristan.

"He stays." She dug her heel into the ground. "If you came to pay your respects, go ahead. But don't give me any condolences."

"Your grandfather wouldn't want me anywhere near his resting place."

"Then why are you here?"

"I've been worried. You haven't responded to a single text or phone call."

"You're an asshole," she muttered. "Unless you want something else tossed at your head, and this time I won't miss, I'd leave if I were you."

"I never wanted to be on the other end of your temper," Larry said, shifting his weight. "You've never learned to forgive, much less let go of anything, and that's your problem."

"What do you want?" she asked with her fist clenched at her side.

Larry looked between her and Tristan. "I'm not comfortable talking in front of a stranger about this."

"I'm not a stranger to Brooke and if she wants me to stay, I'm staying." Tristan clasped his hands and widened his stance.

"We need to talk." Larry had the nerve to reach out and rest his hand on her shoulder.

She brushed it off. "I have nothing left to say to you."

"You've never let me explain."

"I think cheating is explanation enough," Tristan said in a dark tone. "This is not the time or place."

"I have no idea who you are or what you know about me." Larry took a step forward with his chest puffed out. "But I'd appreciate it if you'd kindly back away and let me speak to my girlfriend alone."

"I'm not your girlfriend." Brooke maneuvered herself between Tristan and Larry. "I don't care what you say about what happened or didn't happened."

"I still love you," Larry said.

"Should have thought about that before you stuck your dipstick in someone else's oil."

"Come on, sweetie. You at least owe me the time to tell my side of what happened."

"She doesn't owe you anything." Tristan inched forward, putting his hands on his hips, spreading his jacket, showing off his weapon.

Larry's Adam apple bobbed.

"Your presence here is disrespectful to both Brooke and her grandfather's memory. The idea you want to have any kind of discussion about your cheating and subsequent break-up on the day of Rusty's funeral is not only ill-mannered, but it's repulsive. So, I suggest you leave."

"Are you threatening me?" Larry's eyes went wide.

Brooke hated herself a little for enjoying watching Larry squirm.

"What makes you think that?" Tristan asked.

Larry pointed to the gun on Tristan's hip.

"I'm a State Trooper." Tristan flashed a smile at the same time he pulled out his badge. "My weapon is with me at all times and by no means is that a threat. Just fact. That said, I believe Brooke has asked you to leave and not contact her again."

"She said no such thing," Larry said with a snarl.

"Then let me say it now." Brooke stood tall, feeling empowered,

JEN TALTY

without rage. A nice change of pace considering her behavior for the last few weeks, months. "You're not welcome here and I never want to see you again."

"You heard the lady." Tristan stepped around Larry and opened the limo door.

She eased into the seat. Larry stood there, scratching his head, looking like an idiot.

"In the end, you did me a favor. Like my grandfather always said: everything happens for a reason."

As soon as Tristan slipped into the limo with her, before he could close the door, she wrapped her arms around him, kissing him passionately.

He gently pried their lips apart before slamming the door shut.

"Sorry." She adjusted her skirt, crossing her legs, fingers trembling. "It was a childish thing to do."

"I quite enjoyed the kiss." He winked. "And it's better than hauling off and hitting the asshole." He leaned back, stretching both arms out across the back of the seat. "Total dick move for him to show his face here, wanting to explain his affair. But," Tristan lowered his chin, lifting his brow, "at some point, you're going to need to hear him out so you can have closure."

"I don't want to agree with you," she said, reflecting back on her outrageous behavior and insane thoughts since she'd found out about Larry's affair. "But if I don't, I'm going to go through life angry and unable to find true happiness."

If she were being completely honest with herself, she was going to have to hear Michelle out as well.

Change is good for the soul.

⬥

Tristan sat on the fireplace hearth watching Brooke as she closed the front door.

"I'm glad that this is over with." Brooke pressed her back against the wall, and slid down until her ass hit the floor. "But I dread cleaning up this mess."

"I hired a cleaning service, which is already paid for. They will be here in twenty minutes." Tristan braced for impact. He'd stuck within her budget for everything, even letting her pay for it all when he would have preferred to foot the bill. "You're exhausted and I wanted to do this for you."

"You've done so much already. I don't think I'll ever be able to repay you."

"I'm sure I'll think of something." He stood, snagging his sport coat and tossing it over his shoulder. "Let's get out of here." He held out is free hand.

"Don't we have to wait for the cleaners?" Her face paled and dark circles had formed under her sad eyes.

"My boss's wife is still in the kitchen. She knows they are coming, so let her deal with it." He knew it would take time for Brooke to get past the utter sadness over the loss of her grandfather, among other losses. But he could feel the core of her personality would pull through in the end.

Brooke nodded, letting him pull her to a standing position.

"Where are we going?"

"For now, just a walk. You need some fresh air."

The fact that she didn't argue about the cleaners or leaving the house, told him her level of mental exhaustion had gotten the better of her.

She leaned into him as they strolled down the street. The afternoon sun warmed his face. The sounds of boats zooming up and down the shoreline filled the air. It was the kind of evening Rusty would often show up, asking Tristan to have a beer.

He held her close, hand running up and down her arm. "Let me drop my coat off so I don't have to carry it. Maybe change my shoes."

She looked down at her feet. "I forgot I put on sandals."

"It's been a long day." He guided her down the driveway toward his modular home. "Want to sit down on the dock?"

"I'd like to come in, actually." She tucked a strand of hair behind her ear. "See how you live."

The screen door shuddered as he pulled it open. "It's your

typical bachelor pad." He followed her into the kitchen area and tossed his coat over a chair, suddenly aware he still had a tie around his neck. He enjoyed living in a world outside of what he grew up in. Even though he knew he had money in the bank, and he certainly didn't have to worry about paying his bills, he got to see the world from a different perspective.

Especially when the people around him had no idea who his father was or how much money his family was worth.

But he knew he'd somehow pay a price with that secret when it came to Brooke. It sucked because he hadn't planned on ever making the fact he was the son of Albert Lawrence Reid, the founder and CEO of Highlands Pharmaceutical, known to the world. He didn't feel the need to share it with people because that was only one aspect of who he'd become as a man, and a very small one at that. His co-workers and friends all knew, or at least he suspected they did, but no one said a word, and they didn't treat him any differently, which had been the point.

"Are you going to give me the five-dollar tour?" For the first time in hours, she smiled.

"More like the ten-cent tour." He tossed his hands. "This is my kitchen." He pointed to the far end of the double-wide. "That is the one and only bathroom, but the shower is big and it has great water pressure. It also doubles as my laundry room."

"That's always a plus."

He tugged her hand, pulling her into the main living space. "Welcome to my family/gaming room."

She glided her hand across the leather recliner. "Nice furniture."

"My parents let me take it." He blinked a few times, shaking his head. "I think that is the lamest thing I've ever said."

"You sound like a twenty-year-old getting his first apartment." Her laugh filled his ears and warmed his skin like he'd just slid into a hot-tub.

"You have a flare for decorating."

He looked around the room. Cream colored valances lined the top of the windows. Honeycomb blinds, pulled halfway up, graced the glass panes. A few tasteful decorative lamps and wall hangings he'd picked up at a well-known upscale store accented the light furniture.

Perhaps his simple lifestyle wasn't as simple as he thought.

"How many bedrooms?"

"Three, but I use one as my office." He led the way to the front of the modular home.

She peeked her head into his office and guest bedrooms, which were tiny and not very exciting.

"Wow," she whispered stepping into the front bedroom, overlooking the lake. "What a view."

He shoved his hands in his pockets and leaned against the door jamb. She stood at the foot of his bed, looking out the double window. The sunrays kissed her dark hair. Her skin shimmered against her black dress. Beautiful didn't do her justice. "I never lived on a lake before until I moved here."

When she turned, her face silhouetted in the bright light, cutting his breath short.

"Where did you grow up, anyway?" she asked.

"Saratoga. My parents and brothers still live there."

"You never did tell me where you went to college when you told me about your one long-lasting relationship."

He swallowed, wondering how best to toss his education out there. "Harvard."

"Holy shit." Her golden eyes grew wide. "Impressive."

"I wanted to be a lawyer, remember?" He undid his tie, tossing it on the bed. He wanted to draw her into his arms and hold her, kissing her forehead. Her body fit against his so perfectly. It seemed like a waist not to keep doing it, but he thought better of it. Today wasn't the day.

Follow their lead. Her words hung in his mind like bee over a flower.

"I can't imagine what the loans are like on a school like that." She turned her back, once again staring at the water.

"My parents helped out a little." Ha. They footed the entire bill.

His heart hammered liked a drum. Sitting on the edge of his bed, all he could do was stare at the most perfect woman he'd ever met. Confident. Strong. Passionate about life on so many levels.

She lowered her head. "Is this you and your sister?" Lifting a picture frame from the small table under the window, she faced him.

He nodded. "Two weeks before she died."

"You were both go-cart racers?" She tapped the picture. "Is there really such a thing?"

He let out a small laugh. "She was so much better than I was." He leaned forward, reaching out for the picture. It felt heavy as Brooke placed it in his hands. "It's how she died."

"Racing?"

He traced a finger across the frame, down the glass, and over Tamara's flawless face. "It was a hobby for me, but she wanted to be a race car driver. She'd been practicing, buying time in cars at different races." He tapped the picture. "This was to be her last season of go-carting before moving up to a car."

"Wow. That's cool." The bed shifted as Brooke eased herself on the end of the bed.

"Tamara was cool." Tristan continued to look at his sister. Her long hair, which matched the color of his. Eyes also identical. They looked so much alike, yet she was so feminine and he her masculine counterpart. He tried to remember her alive every day, but today, the moment she had taken her last breath filled his mind constantly. He didn't want to say anything because today wasn't about him or his sister. It was about Rusty and his beautiful granddaughter who'd been given a shit hand, but managed to play the cards she'd been dealt with style and grace.

"You were very close to her," Brooke said as a statement of fact. Her eyes shifted colors yet again, into a soft yellow-brown that reminded him of the changing colors of the leaves in the fall. "You said she died in your arms."

Tristan sucked in a harsh breath.

"I'm sorry. You don't have to talk about it if you don't want to."

"It's not that." He patted the mattress. "Sit here, it's a better view." He fluffed up a couple pillows, while she crawled across his bed. "Today is about you and Rusty. Not me."

"But I want to know. Seems we're sort of drawn together in a morbid way."

The corners of his mouths drew upward, but it didn't last as he let the images flood his brain from that fateful day. "I didn't love racing the way she did, so I spent more time on her pit crew than actually racing. She wanted to go out with a big win and I think since she'd been racing cars, she pushed the go-cart too hard and too fast. She was in the lead. I told her she could take the corners easy. She didn't listen to me, knowing she could easily break a world record." He paused to control his escalating pulse. "I could see her coming around the corner, wheels on edge and I knew she was going to crash, so did she because she said, 'oh shit'. I ripped off my head gear the moment I saw the go-cart roll the first time." He grabbed the center of his gut. "I felt the cold metal bar rip through my stomach, even though it was happening to her. I could hear her scream out in pain inside my head."

Tristan wiped his face. He'd never once been able to tell the story without shedding a tear or two. A constant purge of pain and sorrow. A necessary evil to keep from going crazy.

"When I got to the wreckage, the frame of the go-cart was ripped apart. I reached in to pull her out, but stopped when I saw part of the roll bar had sliced through her stomach. I climbed in as best I could. Held her steady, waiting for the ambulance and fire trucks. Her breath was so ragged she couldn't speak, but I could feel her thoughts, and I didn't like them one bit."

A guttural sob came from Brooke. He glanced over at her to see her hand covering her mouth, eyes wide and filled with tears.

"Don't cry, babe." He wrapped his arms around Brooke. The heavy burden he'd bared had gotten lighter over the years. He could never pin-point the event that triggered this sense of calmness, or maybe acceptance until right now. This moment. It was as if Brooke sucked up some of his pain.

"You're going to think I'm crazy, but I think you just put those thoughts in my head."

He kissed her temple. "Tamara knew she was dying. She held my hand, staring into my eyes, telling me it would be okay with her thoughts. That I'd be okay without her. She closed her eyes and took her last breath. Something inside me snapped in half. I held her for another ten minutes before they made me get out so they could remove her body."

"I can't imagine," Brooke whispered, resting her hand over his.

He entangled their fingers. His own tears dried up as a warmth spread from his belly to his mind.

I'm still with you.

His body tensed for a moment. The shrink had suggested that he let the connection snap with his twin out of anger and grief.

Abandonment.

The same emotion he accused Brooke of not dealing with.

"My turn to say something crazy," he said.

"What's that?" She titled her head, gazing up at him.

"We were destined to meet." He took her chin between his thumb and forefinger. "I hadn't realized that I still haven't completely allowed myself to forgive my sister for leaving me."

"She never left you." Brooke tapped his chest. "She's always been right here, and also in your mind. I sense her. I know it sounds weird, but it's impossible not to see and feel the closeness you had… still have. It's so special and strong." She kissed his cheek. "You're special."

"No. You're extraordinary and I wish I had met you sooner." He searched her eyes and face for a reason to keep his lips from entangling with hers, but the same questioning stare fired back at him. "You know I want you."

"I do," she said in a soft purr. "It's wrong for me to want to be with you when I know it's about rebound, revenge, fear."

"I think you're wrong about all that except for fear, but not in the way you think."

She cocked her. "What does that mean?"

"I saw the way you were with Larry today. It's been a long time since you really loved him." He cupped the back of her neck, pulling her closer, feeling her hot breath on his face. "This thing with us? It's not revenge or rebound. It's real and that frightens you." He paused, waiting for her to speak, but all she did was open and close her mouth. "It scares me too," he admitted.

"The only thing that is real here is we both hurt for different reasons."

"No." He pressed his mouth against hers, smiling when a soft moan escaped her parted lips. "Tell me you don't want me."

"I'd be lying if I said that, but this is purely physical"

His body craved the woman in his arms, but his conscious wouldn't allow it if she truly believed what they felt for each other wasn't real or some manifestation of collective pain. "Are you positive about that? Because I know without a shadow of a doubt that I like you. Really like you. The kind of like that goes beyond hanging out, shooting the shit, and I'm not talking about being fuck buddies either."

"Oh, my, God." She rolled her eyes. "That's so romantic, how could a woman resist that?" The words could mean she was about to get out of his bed, but she leaned into him and her eyes sparkled with mischief that told him she wasn't going anywhere.

"Aren't you the one who said I needed to find a woman who thought my idiosyncrasies were adorable?"

"I'm not that woman."

He arched a brow, his hand resting on her hip as he shifted her sideways.

She didn't try to wiggle away and she smiled.

He took that as a good sign as he gently brushed his lips against hers, keeping his eyes open and focused on her dark pupils as they dilated. "You think I'm funny."

"I think you're weird."

He kissed her cheek, moving toward her ear, and down her neck. "You like weird."

"I do," she said softly. Her chest rose up and down with deep breaths as he circled his arms around her body, kissing his way down to the pendant dangling dangerously close to her cleavage. Tangling the locket between his fingers, he glanced up. She stared down at him, lips parted, eyelids fluttering. Purposefully, he glided his hand from her hip across her middle, resting his palm under the swell of her breast. She rewarded him by sucking in her lower lip.

"Tell me you don't want this and I'll stop." He needed her to say the words. Maybe this would be one night, maybe it would be more, but if she didn't want to find out, then he'd have to walk away.

His heart wouldn't survive if he didn't.

"What do you want, Brooke? Are you willing to take a leap of faith? Give this...us...a good old-fashioned college try?"

"Oh, my, God. Just stop talking." She smiled. "I want you."

His insides shook with the power of an earthquake registering a ten on the rhicter scale. Her hands glided up his back as he pressed his knee between her legs, kissing his way to her lips, which greeted him with insatiable hunger. Her tongue darted in his mouth, taking control.

Her passion flooded his mind and body like gale-force winds smashing against the beach, out of control. Rolling to the side, he found the zipper on the back of her dress and eased it down, his fingertips skimming across her smooth, silky skin.

She thrust him onto his back, straddling him as she tore her mouth from him to lower her dress, exposing her black, lacy bra.

"You seem to like this position."

She smiled. "I'm a control freak."

He arched a brow. "That makes two of us." He cupped her ass as he sat up, the small space between her breasts called to him as he pressed his lips on the top of her mounds. "This could be interesting," he whispered as he flipped her over.

"Whoa!"

He stood at the end of the bed, tugging her dress over her hips, exposing black, lacy boy shorts, matching her bra. At least he thought they were called boy shorts. Whatever they were, they looked damn sexy on her. "Do I need to worry about this dress, or can I just toss it to the floor."

She'd raised up on her elbows, tossing her head back, laughing. "I can't believe you asked that?"

"I don't want to get into trouble later for ruining your dress." He decided, based on the feel of the fabric in his hands, the dress needed to be hung up in his closet. When he was done, he stood at the side of the bed.

"You're turn." Her dainty fingers easily undid the buttons on his shirt. Kneeling in front of him, her dark hair flowed over her shoulders, covering her breasts.

He tossed his shirt to the floor, and quickly pulled his t-shirt over his head. His stomach muscles tightened and twitched when her plump lips kissed the center of his bare chest. The palm of her hands brushed against his nipples.

"Come here." He fisted a large clump of her hair, tugging at it, exposing her beautiful long neck.

Her seductive smile sent his blood boiling. The color of her eyes shifted to a deep copper tone. For a long moment, he stared at her, soaking up her beauty, imprinting this moment on his brain forever. When his lips met with hers this time, the urgency had dissipated into a romantic slow dance, savoring every swirl of her tongue against his. He captured every sweet moan her throat eased out and swallowed them as if they were the finest full-bodied Cabernet one could buy.

The faint humming of boat engines on the lake echoed in the background as the late afternoon sun cut through the window, heating their already hot bodies.

Her fingers pressed against his stomach, undoing his belt. She yanked it so hard it made a snapping noise as she released it, sending it across the room.

"That could have hurt," he whispered. He desired a woman who could match his thirst in the bedroom, but more importantly, he longed for a strong, intelligent woman.

He wanted the undeniable connection that bound two people together.

He wanted Brooke.

"Hurt so good," she responded, her tongue tracing a path form the corner of his mouth to his earlobe, sucking it into her mouth.

He hissed. His body went taut with desire so powerful it consumed every cell. Reaching around her body, he unclasped her bra, drawing it down over her shoulders, her nipples hard and ready to be touched. He teased them with his thumbs, barely applying pressure, feeling them harden even more.

"You're beautiful," she whispered, kissing his chest as she eased his pants over his hips.

"Oh…Christ." He gritted his teeth.

Her hands gently glided over him like warm oil. Her fingers torched his skin in a fiery blaze of hunger.

He kicked out of his pants and pushed her back on the bed. "I think this is going to end up as a battle of wills to see who is dominant."

"Is that a challenge?" She smiled, still holding him in her hot hands, squeezing the base, fanning her thumb across the tip.

He groaned, pressing his hand against her belly, tucking his fingers under the top of her panties.

She grabbed his wrist. "Before we go any further," she panted out. "Do you have protection?"

He nodded.

"Proceed then."

He growled, shoving his hand inside, cupping her heat, wetness trickling over his palm. She arched as he floated two fingers inside her, her hips moved against his hand. He'd considered himself a decent lover. At least the women he'd been with never complained about the actual art of sex, only the things he said after. Or before. Sometimes during. He'd become so self-conscious of his thoughts, that he tried to say the exact opposite, which ended up being worse.

With Brooke, he no longer worried about saying the wrong thing. Or trying to find the right words to express himself. He knew deep down, she understood him.

But did she know that?

He bent over and kissed her belly button, her hands clutched his head while her hips still moved in a circular motion, her throaty, high-pitched moans filled the room.

"Oh, God,' she whispered. Her head thrashing back and forth.

"I'm winning."

"I'm letting you," she said, gasping for air. "For purely selfish reasons."

He laughed, pulling his hand out so he could roll her panties down to her ankles and admire every inch of her body. Her freshly shaved womanhood called out to him to be touched. Licked. Devoured. Wetness pooled at her thighs, her skin glistened in the sun's rays.

"You better not be stopping." She lifted her head, her chest heaving up and down.

"What will happen if I do?"

"Nothing that will feel good." She bit down on her lower lip, eyes narrowed.

He let his gaze roam from her angelic face, to her round breasts. He cupped them both, fanning his thumbs across her hard nipples, enjoying how her eyelids fluttered.

"Better?"

"Hands good there." Her raspy voice made him shiver. "But mouth needs to stop talking and do something else."

"Are you trying to talk dirty to me?" Gliding his hands down her firm stomach, he admired her sensual body. His fingers traced the folds between her thighs and the beginning of her sex. She squirmed.

"Do you need me to spell it out?"

He laughed as her hands gripped his hair, pushing his head between her legs. "I get the picture," he whispered as he kissed her intimately, pushing himself deeper inside her. She tasted like honeysuckle and felt like sunshine.

Her body shifted as he continued to tease her, keeping things slow and tender, knowing it drove her mad. Understanding her body, without having to explore it, humbled him.

And frightened him.

He spread her legs as wide as he could, wrapping his arms around her so his hands pressed against her stomach. He worshipped her hot nub with his tongue, drawing it into his mouth and sucking until she moaned so loudly he thought the neighbors could hear.

"Oh, my…Oh…God." She threaded her fingers in his hair, pushing and pulling while her hips rocked up and down. Her thighs clasped to the sides of his head as more sweet juices flowed from her body.

He pressed open her legs, lifting his head, catching her laden filled gaze. Eyes wide as she licked her lips.

"Do NOT stop!" Her words sounded more like one long moan.

"Who said I was stopping?" He used his finger, rubbing in a gentle circular motion, occasionally dipping two fingers inside her.

"You are such a tease," she ground out, dropping her head back and fisting the sheets. "Be careful, pay back is a bitch."

"God, I hope so." He watched his fingers disappear deep inside as he sucked her hard nub into his mouth, running his tongue over it.

"Oh good, Lord," she cried. "Make me cum...oh, Tristan..." Her hips lifted as her stomach began to quiver and shake.

He pressed his hand on her stomach, feeling every tremor as her insides clenched around his fingers, wetness pouring out of her body.

She kept trying to close her legs, but he wouldn't have it, still lapping at her sweetness as mild shudders rippled across her skin.

He kissed his way to her lips. "Taste you on me." He shoved his tongue deep inside her mouth, twisting it around hers. His erection pressing against her. Her legs wrapped tightly around his waist. He reached toward the end table.

"What are you doing?"

"Getting a condom."

She looked over her shoulder. "It's in that drawer?"

He arched a brow.

"I'll get it when *I'm* ready." She pushed him to his back, her hand gripping his hard cock.

He sucked in a deep breath.

"My turn to play."

"What exactly are you going to do to me?"

Her hot, pink tongue darted out of her mouth, lapping over the tip of his throbbing cock like an ice cream cone.

He groaned, staring down at her.

She sat up, stroking him with her hand as she looked around the room. "Where'd that belt go?"

"What!?"

She obviously ignored him as she jumped off the bed, bending over, showing off her ass along with her sexy, wet folds.

"Stay just like that," he said reaching for a condom in his nightstand.

But she didn't listen. Instead she held his belt in his hands, toying with the buckle, smiling like the devil as she crawled her way onto the bed. "Scoot down, hands over your head."

"Fuck," he whispered, understanding her thirst for total control. "Do you know what would happen if I suggested anything like this the first time with anyone?" He knew it wasn't the brightest question, but since he was flat on his back, while she secured his hands over his head, successfully tying him to the bed post.

"I'm not anyone."

"That's for damn sure." He hissed as her teeth brushed against his nipples.

Taking his cock in her hands, she smiled. "Can't say I've ever tied anyone up."

"You've got to be joking." All of the muscles in his body tightened as she nibbled her way down his stomach, her hands cupping him. He wanted to tangle his fingers through her hair, hold her down while he pumped himself into her, but the belt successfully kept his hands above his head.

She licked her lips, her mouth hovering over him, teasing him with her hot breath.

"I've always wanted to tie a man up."

He felt his eyes go wide.

She slid her mouth over him, nestled between his legs, keeping her eyes open as her hand followed her lips from the base of his cock to the tip. Her tongue swirled over him just as she sucked him back into her mouth.

His lungs burned as he took in heaving breaths. The belt tight against his wrists as he clenched his fists, trying desperately to break free, only he didn't really want to. The loss of control so intoxicating he thought he might pass out. He blinked his eyes a few times, watching her devour him. Every time she lifted her mouth off him, her smile ignited a fire across his nerve endings.

"Brooke…" he panted out, dropping his head to the bed, flexing all his muscles. "You've got to stop."

"Why?" her sultry voice echoed in his ears.

His chest tightened, making it hard to take a deep breath. "Let's move to that other position you like."

"What's that?"

Her finger glided over his tip.

"Get the condom and fucking straddle me before I go mad." He closed his eyes tight, hoping the room would stop spinning, praying his outburst didn't offend her, but sensing it didn't, somehow. The bed shifted and he heard the sound of the drawer opening. Blinking, he turned his head, watching her tear open the foil. "Where the fuck have you been all my life?"

Goosebumps spread across his body as she wrapped him in protection and guided him inside her.

He dug his heels into the bed, lifting his hips, watching her toss her hair over her shoulders, cupping her own breasts. Her hips rolled over him, causing intense friction as her insides gripped him tightly. She flicked her thumbs over her nipples, moaning.

The bed shook as he yanked his arms, but the belt didn't give way at all. She just smiled and continued to ride him, touching herself, one hand on her breast, the other moving over her midsection until she rubbed herself slowly with two fingers.

"Fucking untie me, now," he barked.

She stopped moving, but he keep his hips rocking, easing in and out of her.

"Untie me," he ground out.

She leaned over, bringing her breasts close to his mouth. He sucked in her nipple, swirling his tongue over the hard nub. She rewarded him with a high-pitched groan.

As soon as his hands were free, he grabbed her ass and flipped her onto her back, ramming himself deep inside her, stopping for a moment to gaze at her beautiful eyes. "You are a wicked woman." He kissed her nose. "You're the perfect mixture of strength, confidence, intelligence, wits, and by far the hottest woman I have ever met. I want to make you cum so hard you scream again." He shoved his tongue in her mouth as he pumped uncontrollably inside her, losing all restraint. His movements were wild and messy.

Raising up on his elbows, he broke off the kiss. Their eyes locked and he nearly exploded. "Cum for me, Brooke," he whispered.

Her eyelids fluttered as she lifted her hips, grinding against him, wetness seeping out all around him.

"Oh, my…my…God!" She arched her back, tossing her head to the side. "Tristan, oh…." Her body quivered underneath him. "Yes, oh…Tristan," she screamed.

He thrust into her over and over again. His toes curled as he let out a guttural groan, his own climax spilled out inside her. She clenched herself around the length of him. The way she stared at him, chomping down on her lower lip, her stomach rippling from delight, sent a warm shiver across his skin.

"You're amazing," he said, still stroking her slowly, staring into her big golden eyes, his breathing slowly returning to normal.

"You're not so bad yourself," she said with a smile.

He lowered himself, easing his full weight on her, nuzzling his face in her neck. "I'm probably going to get kicked out of this bed in thirty seconds, but fuck, that had to be the best sexual experience of my life."

"I aim to please."

He burst out laughing, and so did she, her hands still roaming up and down his back.

A few minutes ticked by as their laughter eased. He rolled to his side, taking the small blanket from the foot of the bed, and covering their bodies.

"I've never met anyone like you before," he admitted. "You're so open and…" he held her chin between his thumb and forefinger. "I've never been with a woman like you and I think you ruined me for forever."

"How so?" She pulled the blanked up around her breasts, fluffing a pillow, leaning against the headboard.

He wanted a better view of her perfect body and face, so he snagged a few pillows, shifting his body, so his head was at the end of the bed.

"Now you can't see the lake," she said.

"I'd much rather look at you," he said, kissing her big toe. "You even have sexy feet. I mean, feet are usually a bit of a turn off, but not yours."

Her smile filled the room with a warmth stronger than sunshine. "Still want to know how I ruined you."

Time to get real.

"I honestly told myself I would not sleep with you until we'd gotten to know each other better and had a few dates."

"We haven't had any dates."

"I have a confession to make," he said.

She scrunched her forehead. "Okay…"

"When I asked you to help me with women, I was serious, but I spent so much time listening to Rusty talk about you, then meeting you, well it didn't take long for me to want to learn how to talk to you. I like you. A lot. More than any other woman I've dated in a long time. I wanted to try to romance you, but then we end up, in this bed, fucking like there is no tomorrow. Hell, I even let you tie me up and I hate not being in control."

"I got news for you." She pressed her hands against his feet, massaging firmly. "You were never in control, not even when you asked to be untied. I didn't have to do that."

He growled, dropping is head to her ankle. "You make me crazy," he muttered. "I don't want this to be some random sex act. I want to date you and fuck you."

"Oh, my, god." She wiggled her big toe on the side of his head. "You're lucky I don't mind that word as a descriptor for sex, only, it would be nice if you said it differently when asking me to date you."

"So, we're dating?"

"I haven't said yes.

"You haven't said no." He took his finger and traced the small heart shaped tattoo she had on her ankle.

"On one condition."

"You and your conditions." But he'd give her whatever she wanted.

"You don't try to be something you're not and get all wrapped up in the crap I've been telling you."

He arched a brow. "That was crap?"

She shook her head. "No, but I want you to be yourself."

"All right, but you have to do the same in return."

"Deal," she said. "Now, I saw a nice bottle of wine in your kitchen. Do you have any cheese to go with it?"

"I do." He leapt from the bed. "Let's take it down to the dock and watch the sunset." He tossed her one of his T-Shirts and found a pair of boxers that could pass for shorts on a woman. As he hiked up his jean shorts, he realized he'd gotten himself a girlfriend.

Don't fuck this up.

CHAPTER 7

Exotic, wild sex, no matter how good or empowering, doesn't mean Brooke should have said yes to dating Tristan. They fucked. Kinky, dirty, fucking. Letting off some steam, dealing with the incredible sexual tension between them, topped off with a good dose of grief, brought them to bed. It wasn't supposed to mean anything, much less end up with her dating the sexy Trooper, who'd essentially been a stranger to her a week ago when she'd asked for his help.

She snagged her dress from his bedroom closet and made her way to the kitchen, wearing a pair of his boxers and T-Shirt.

"I hope you're hungry." Tristan stood in front of the stove. The crisp smell of bacon and…she sniffed again, catching a whiff of cinnamon and coffee.

"French Toast and bacon," he said.

"I could eat that." She plopped her dress on the recliner before maneuvering around Tristan, who smacked her ass while she poured herself a cup of coffee. Leaning against the counter, she blew into her mug and admired the fine specimen of a man flipping some bread. She'd always enjoyed sex, when she had it. Though the last year of her relationship with Larry, she could count on one hand their sexual encounters, and they hadn't been good ones. More like hurried, let's get the obligatory screw out of the way.

Her and Tristan had sex, made love, screwed, whatever you want to call it, three times. She squeezed her legs together, the soreness of having him inside her so many times, for so long, and occasionally being rough felt so good she blushed. She liked to express herself during sex and generally that came in the form of colorful language, only Larry didn't think a lady should be saying things like, 'oh yes, there, fuck me there'. Not that she said that often, but sometimes, when the sex was raw, it was necessary.

"You're deep in thought." Tristan kissed her temple before putting two plates on the kitchen table.

He did say some things that some women could take the wrong way, but nothing so horrible it warranted breaking up with him over, especially considering how attentive he'd been with her all night. Holding her in his arms. Gently caressing her. Giving her something to wear before she had to ask for it. She really wanted to meet some of these idiotic women he'd been dating because the man was a sweetheart who knew every erogenous zone on a woman's body and how to make her scream in delight. Who wouldn't want a man like that?

And by the smell of things, he could cook too.

She sat down next to him, slicing into a thick piece of French toast drizzled in syrup, cinnamon, and a bit of powdered sugar. "Any ex-girlfriends you can introduce me to?"

"Why the hell would I do that?" he stuffed an entire piece of bacon in his mouth.

"I want to see the kind of women who would turn down someone as good in bed as you and who can cook too." She held her fork up before shoving a large piece of toast in her mouth. "Oh, my, God. That is soooooo good."

"I'm hurt. I'm more than a sex slave who can prepare a decent meal."

She laughed, tossing a napkin at him. "I didn't mean it like that."

He arched a brow.

She rolled her eyes. "Seriously. Now that we are sort of dating."

He kicked her under the table. "We're dating. Not sort of."

"Fine." She took a couple more bites of her food, contemplating how she landed in Oz, because there is no way in hell she should be doing anything with Tristan, other than saying thank you. "I want to meet just one. You make it sound like all of them but Brenda ran for the hills the moment you opened your mouth."

"Come with me to Delaney and Josh's wedding. My last girlfriend will be there."

"Delaney already invited me."

He laughed. "So, that means I'm still going stag."

"You're a pain in the ass," she muttered.

They ate the rest of their breakfast in silence, passing the newspaper back and forth.

"I've got a busy week coming up." Tristan stood, taking the plates in his hands.

"I'll do the dishes. Least I can do since you cooked."

He kissed the top of her head. "I've got it," he said. "Anyway, I work today at nine, so should be home by six. Then the rest of the week I've got SCUBA recertification. Generally runs eight to seven ish."

"Sounds grueling."

"It is."

She leaned back, watching as he did the dishes. His biceps flexing as he scrubbed a pan. Most men…most people, she could peg quickly, but she had to admit, she'd had him pegged all wrong. She thought his awkwardness with women came from some insecurity or feelings of inadequacy, but that couldn't be further from the truth. If her theory was correct, his problem with women began the day his sister died.

Brooke understood deep seated connections. She had that with her grandmother. Sure, her mother was fantastic. Her father, spectacular. Her grandfather, her biggest cheerleader. But out of everyone in the family, it had been her grandmother she'd felt the deepest connection to and when she died, Brooke felt more lost than she did when her parents had passed.

If she were being totally honest, the day her grandmother died was the day Brooke changed, and not necessarily for the better.

"I can feel you watching me." Tristan turned to face her as he towel dried a pan. "What's going on in that beautiful mind of yours?"

She fingered her necklace. "I'm honestly worried about what will happen when Jillian talks with the DA this morning, looking for a plea bargain, and then what might happen next with the civil case." Not a down right lie, but she didn't want to get into her thoughts too deeply, not yet anyway.

"Didn't you tell me she already spoke to the DA's office and they seemed agreeable to dropping the charges after some community service?"

Brooke nodded. "But she also said she couldn't be sure and to brace myself for the worst."

"Come here." He waggled his finger.

She didn't hesitate. Being in his strong arms gave her courage, even when her confusion was over him and this connection she wanted to fight, but couldn't.

"There's nothing you can do about it right now, so let Jillian take care of things. She's good at her job." He cupped her chin, pressing his lips against hers in a wet entanglement, his tongue probing the inside of her mouth.

Her body soaked up his energy, consuming it for herself, making her stronger. Making her want things she thought she should run from.

And run fast.

He squeezed her ass with one hand, while the other managed to unhook her bra. Even if she wanted to resist him, she couldn't. No, she wouldn't. For the first time in a long while, she felt like a whole woman. One that could be desired and worshiped like a temple at the same time being treated like an equal and with respect.

He spun her around, shoving her stomach against the counter, ripping her shorts and panties to the floor.

She gasped, gripping the counter, kicking the boxers to the side. "What do you think you're doing?" Her body melted at his tender touch. His arm around her body, fingers sliding between her legs, teasing with feather-like circular motion.

"I think I'm getting ready to make you cum again." He shoved a couple of fingers inside her.

"Oh...ah..." She tossed her head back, reaching her hand around his neck. His lips kissing her earlobe, making her body shiver in anticipation. "Maybe we should go back to the bedroom?"

"I want you here. Like this." He fingered her with one hand, while the other plucked and pinched her nipples, bringing them to tight, throbbing nubs.

"Condom," she said with ragged breath, clenching her insides tightly around his fingers as he continued to ease his way in and out.

"I brought one." He pinched her nipple, twisting to the right.

"Yes..." she breathed out. She no longer had control over her body as she moved her hips with his fingers. The need for him to take her body, claim her, choked her common sense. "I want you inside me now."

A deep growl vibrated against her ear as his hot breath tickled her skin. He pressed his erection against her ass, bare skin to bare skin. She spread her legs a little wider, bending at the waist.

"Take me now." She'd never been one to beg for anything. Begging wasn't in her wheelhouse. If she had to beg for something it wasn't worth it.

He was most definitely worth begging for.

With labored breath, he backed away, his hands brushing against her ass as he wrapped himself with protection.

She gripped the counter top with one hand, her other still wrapped around his neck. "Please...oh God," she screamed as he rammed himself inside her so fast and hard she had to brace herself with both hands.

"Hold still." He kept himself deep inside her as he reached around and ran his fingertips across her hard nub.

Her body shivered. Her muscles tightened. She tried to stay still, but she wanted to feel him move inside her as she squeezed him as tight as she could.

"Do I have to beg again?" She squirmed, but he still wouldn't stroke her.

"Beg all you want, babe, it won't change how we're going to do this."

His fingers were like magic, working her into a frenzy. He'd switch between slow and light, too fast and hard, driving her body and mind crazy. The moment she'd be near the edge, he'd change it up, doing something different.

She clutched her insides as tightly as she could around him, then released before doing it again, and again, creating as much friction as she could. With each squeeze, he'd moan, rubbing her just a little harder.

"Please…" her plea came out more as a throaty groan.

He chuckled in her ear. His large hand covering both her breasts, toying with her nipples.

Gripping the counter, she squirmed, determined to make him stroke her, but all he did was pinch her hard nub.

"Oh…God." The orgasm started at her toes, rippling across all her muscles. She slammed her fist into the counter, while he gripped her hips, finally slamming into her, creating multiple mini convulsions on top of the wickedest, most intense, orgasm known to mankind.

He grunted as he pumped faster. His lips on her shoulder, kissing and licking wildly until she felt him explode. She actually worried the condom might break.

With her elbows on the counter, he continued to slowly stroke her. His long fingers glided down her spine and massaged the top of her ass. She wanted to look over her shoulder and tell him to spank her, but no way would she. Hell, she didn't even know if she liked to be spanked.

He smacked her ass with the palm of his hand. Not hard, but with enough vigor it made a loud noise.

"I can't believe you just did that," she said, her breathing still labored.

"Sorry. I won't do it again." His hand smoothed over the spot where she wondered if it were a little pink.

"No, that's not what I meant." She let her forehead drop to the counter. No man she'd ever been with had been as demanding, yet giving, rough, yet tender while having mad, passionate sex for the sake of sex. "I had been wondering what that would have been like, then you did it."

She sighed, feeling her wetness drip down her legs when he pulled out. The sound of the faucet running reminded her she was bent over the kitchen counter, with her bare ass in the air.

"Whoa," she said, feeling a wet cloth between her legs. "Oh… thanks," she whispered.

"You're welcome."

Glancing over her shoulder, Tristan held up her panties and boxers. "You were actually thinking you might like it if I spanked you?" he asked with an arched brow.

Nodding, she hiked up the boxers, balling the panties in her hand. "Do you have a plastic bag I can put these in?"

He smiled. "I'll wash them for you."

She wanted to protest but was too stunned as he took them from her hand. "I think you've been lying to me about your problems with women." Reaching under her shirt, she clasped her bra and stared at him as he closed the bathroom/laundry room door. "Other than some women might not like your tastes in bed, you really are adorable."

He laughed. "Because every guy wants to be called adorable." He poured himself a cup of coffee, raising the pot in her direction and she nodded. "I can't say I'm usually that aggressive and honestly, I don't take all the women I date to bed."

"Are you serious?" Their fingers glided against each other as he passed her the mug, sending a tiny wave of desire across her belly.

"In the last year, I've had sex three times, not including being with you." He took a sip of his coffee. "I've taken maybe fifteen girls out on dates, but I've only slept with one other woman, besides you in this last year."

"Why are you telling me this?"

He set his mug down and folded his arms across the chest. "About this time last year, without getting into all the crazy details, I dated a woman who turned out to be working for a man who wanted to kill Josh and Delaney."

"That's fucked up."

He nodded. "I really liked her. But she played me and that just brought up all that weird shit about Brenda, so I didn't date for a long time." Tristan ran a hand over his head. "I promised to be myself with you, so here goes nothing."

She swallowed, wondering if this was going to be the moment he crashed and burned.

"Just now, I sensed you wanted me to pat your ass. Not hard. Not enough to hurt, but something you wanted."

"I don't know why I wanted it. Kind of silly."

"It's not silly. Smacking someone's ass is generally affectionate." He titled his head. "You don't think it's weird that I sensed that? Or last night, that I knew you'd untie me as soon as I asked? Because otherwise, I would never have let you do it in the first place."

Her heart pounded in steady beats. "Are you saying you sense this stuff with every woman you sleep with?"

"Not really. Not like with you where it's so tight it feels natural. That's only happened with you. It's impossible to explain without sounding like an ass."

"Try me," she said.

"I can sense things with people I'm close to, like family, though it's nothing like what I felt with Tamara. But with you, it's different."

"Can I ask you something?" Minoring in Psychology had been helpful in her sales job, but not so much anywhere else in her life.

"Ask me anything."

"Do you like being in crowds?"

He furrowed his brow. "Hate them. Why?"

"I have noticed you're an introverted kind of guy, in general, but I also think you have great empathy."

"What does this have to do with anything?"

Talk about something that was impossible to explain. "I suspect crowds bother you because you feel every single emotion in the crowd. It's brain overload."

"Now you sound like my mother."

"My job has always required me to be a good read of people. In sales, I do that very well. In my personal life, I've always tried not to be like that, which is why I ignored the signs that Larry was cheating." She breathed in deeply, letting it out slowly. "I want to say something to you, but I don't want you to get mad or upsct."

"Say it," he said it as a command, even though his tone was soft.

"You told me when Tamara died, something snapped, and part of you went with her." Tentatively, she moved across the kitchen and rested her hand on the center of his chest. "I believe the whole twin thing. I also believe there are people we have deep connections with, mine was with my grandmother. It's weird, my entire life, she'd look at mc, and I sense this great burden she carried, but I never knew what it was. I think your twin connection helped to make that stronger with anyone you care about, or want to care about, and that scares you. But the bigger problem is not knowing if they have that same intuition about you."

He laced his fingers around her wrist and kissed the palm of her hand. "Talk about psycho-babble bullshit."

"Your problem with women isn't because you're not what everyone thinks romantic should be, or that you like to talk dirty when you get laid, or whatever. Your problem is, you don't think someone will be connected to you again. Might have started with Tamara's death, but Brenda killed it."

"Maybe."

"Maybe my ass."

He circled his arms around her waist, drawing her against his chest. "I like your ass."

"Now you're changing the subject." She pounded his chest. "And we're not going another round because I can barely walk as it is."

He tossed his hands wide. "If I had made any mention of having that kind of effect on a woman after a night of tantalizing love-making, I'd get slapped."

"Yes, you would." She leaned up and kissed his cheek. "Time for me to take my stroll down the walk of shame avenue."

CHAPTER 8

TRISTAN STOOD at the printer in the Trooper satellite office, hands looped into his belt, tapping his fingers against the leather as the paper slowly appeared in the tray. Twelve pages of forensics on one piece of paper along with six more on a skeletal key. He looked over his shoulder sensing his boss, Jared Blake approaching.

"I need a minute," Jared said as he leaned against the wall. His wide, muscular frame intimated everyone. But it was his serious facial expressions, never letting anyone know what he was thinking, that made him the most frightening man Tristan had ever served under. Only, once you got to know Jared, you quickly found out he was a fair man with a big heart.

"I know I shouldn't have asked our team to take a look at these items from Rusty's granddaughter." Tristan figured best not to beat around the bush.

"What lab rats do on their own time is none of my business." Jared arched a brow. "They didn't use state resources, right?"

"No." The printer shot out another piece of paper, five more to go. "Except the paper it's being printed on."

"Fair enough." Jared had been the Sergeant in charge for about thirteen years now. He ran a tight ship, but he treated every single one of his troopers as family. "I've met Brooke a few times when she was little. My sister babysat for them a few times. The Fowler's were always a nice family, but they never really socialized with the neighbors."

"But he was such a friendly man, at least to me," Tristan said.

The last paper shot out of the printer. Tristan gathered them, tapping the bottom of the pages on the table, making sure they were straight.

"Let's take this in my office," Jared said. "Sutten!"

Stacey stepped from the small reception office. "I've been married for seven years. The last name is Tanner." She tapped her name tag. "How many times do I have to tell you people that?"

"You'll always be little fouled mouth Sutten to me," Jared said taking the stack of papers. "Make two copies of these, then read it. When you're done, come into my office and tell us what you think."

Stacey rolled her eyes. "Doug told me being second meant being your lackey."

"Damn straight." Jared laughed. "But I'm thinking retiring on my fiftieth birthday, then you can get your own lackey."

"Does Ryan know? Because I think your wife would strangle you if you were under her foot all day." Stacey took the papers. "Anything else?"

"That's it." Jared smiled.

Tristan followed Jared into the office. While he appreciated another set of eyes on the reports, he wanted to sit down and look at them before heading home. He took the seat in front of Jared's massive desk.

"Did you known Brooke's grandmother had a catering service?" Jared eased into his office chair, leaning back and clasped his hands behind his head. His standard position when shooting the shit.

"Rusty mentioned it a time or two."

"My mother loved Ashley's cooking. Every event my mother had, Ashley almost always catered, but because of something old lady Ramsworth said, Ashley's business took a big hit and she lost a lot of customers, but she still managed to maintain a few loyal patrons, and my mom said she was busy enough."

"What did Mrs. Ramsworth say?" Tristan asked, knowing it wasn't good.

"A. Bad service. Bad food. Stealing."

"Stealing what?" Tristan rubbed the back of his neck.

"I can dig up the police report, but it said a set of emerald earrings and a thousand in cash went missing during a party Ashley catered."

"During a party? Anyone could have pocketed those items. Along with any of the other staff."

"That's what I told them, but they insisted it was her."

"You investigated this?" Tristan asked.

"I was a rookie and happened to have stopped off at home to get some dinner, so I was two minutes away when the call came in." Jared dropped his elbows to the desk, leaning forward. "That wasn't the first-time old lady Ramsworth accused Ashley or Rusty of doing something."

Tristan didn't like the pattern that had started to develop. "Wendell and his grandmother showed up at Brooke's the other morning accusing her grandmother of stealing some heirloom necklace. They said the one that Brooke wears all the time went missing when Ashley had been working as a cook for them."

"My mother told me that Ashley and…what is the old lady's name?" Jared looked toward the ceiling. "Georgina? Yeah. That's it. Anyway, they went to middle school or something together and at one time were friends."

"Can't picture that woman being friends with anyone who can't afford their own private plane."

Jared laughed. "She didn't come from money, she married it and she's had that chip on her shoulder ever since. My mother told me she'd be at parties with her, and she'd be going on and on about her childhood and living abroad, and all sorts of fabrications. No one called her on it, except my mother, who then became the brunt of a few rumors herself. My favorite being my father had another family in Canada."

"You're serious?" Tristan shook his head. "I feel like I just walked in on a bunch of high school girls gossiping."

"I know." Jared ran a hand down his face, drawing his thumb and forefinger over the shape of chin. "My family has avoided the Ramsworth's and their kind for years, only dealing with them when we had to."

"I really only have a beef with one of them: Wendell." Tristan shook his head. "His wife and Brooke used to be best friends."

"I'd heard that," Jared said. "I need you to watch your back with that one, got it?"

Tristan nodded. "So, why do you think the Ramsworth's had it in for Rusty's wife?"

"That's the million-dollar question. My mom enjoyed Ashley and often asked about the conflict, but Ashley would smile and say that Georgina was the kind of person who needed to put others down to lift herself up and that she just felt sorry for the old woman."

"What about Brooke's parents? Did they know any of this?"

Jared nodded. "Russell's ten years older than me, but I knew who he was. Nice guy. Kept to himself. Graduated from high school and moved away, but he came home to visit a lot. He wanted his parents to move closer to him and his family, but they wouldn't."

"Why?"

"I have no idea. They didn't seem to care what people of thought of them, and no matter what, they always seemed to be happy. But it's always bothered me how the Ramsworths treated them."

"I would guess they treat everyone that way."

Jared nodded. "This is true, but it always seemed like the old lady had a grudge against Ashley so deep, it consumed her."

A knock on the door sounded.

Tristan craned his neck.

"Interesting reading," Stacey said, patting her pregnant belly.

"Come in and have a seat." Jared waved her in, holding his hand out for one of the copies.

She handed Tristan a set before settling down in the chair next to his. "The pen used is a standard brand name blue pen sold at every store."

"That's not helpful." Tristan flipped through the pages, but Stacey grabbed them, setting them on the desk.

"Let me tell you what I know, then you can read them."

"She's way too much like you," Tristan said, pointing to Jared. "Go ahead."

"They were able to capture four finger prints. Thanks to Brooke's arrest, we know one set is hers."

Tristan closed his eyes, trying to push that mug shot out of his head.

"Two of the prints, we can't identify, but the last one is where it gets interesting."

"How so?" Tristan asked.

"They matched the prints we took from Wendell the night you arrested him." Stacey gave Tristan a sideways glance.

"I don't like the sound of that," Jared said.

"Me neither." Tristan pinched the bridge of his nose. "But considering Rusty worked for Wendell, it's possible his prints could be on anything Rusty might have carried with him."

"I'm shocked to hear you give him the benefit of the doubt," Jared said.

"I'm not," Tristan said. "But, I know he's been inside the Fowler residence a time or two."

"You know this for a fact?" Stacey asked.

"I stopped by Rusty's to invite him for a beer once when Wendell was there. When I asked Rusty why, he said Wendell dropped off his paycheck, which I didn't believe, but didn't push."

"Considering what they uncovered from the note, this gets really dicey," Stacey said.

"What does that mean?" Tristan swallowed the heartburn bubbling to his throat.

"The paper has traces of glue at the top, so most likely a tear off pad. There was a name and address in a light pink ink, but they couldn't recreate the letters. Still working on that, though I suspect it belonged to Ashley Fowler based on the contents of the note."

Tristan rubbed his temples, visualizing the kitchen table at

Brooke's house. "I think I saw a pad of paper with pink lettering. I'll check with Brooke on that."

"The techs were able to decipher most of the words based on looking at the slight indentation in the paper. Kind of like writing with a pen with no ink and then running a crayon over it."

"I'm aware of how it works," Tristan said.

Stacey pulled out a piece of paper from her stack. "The note is on page three of the report. Want me to read it out loud?"

"Go for it," Jared said.

"Brace yourself," Stacey said.

Tristan gripped the armrests.

"*My Dearest Rusty,*

I shouldn't have kept this from you. It is the only lie I have ever told you and I have regretted it. This necklace, Wendell gave me a few weeks after Russell was born along with offering me money. He said the pendant belonged to the oldest son's wife. Technically, that meant it belongs to Georgina, but he wanted OUR Russell to have it, give it to his bride, then their daughter or daughter in law. Guess that's how its passed down through the generations. I shouldn't have taken it, but I did. Probably to hurt Georgina. She's been distraught over the damn thing for years and I've secretly had it hidden in that box you gave me, along with a few other things I shouldn't have allowed Wendell to give me. Now that I'm dying, I needed you to know. Do with them what you need to. Thank you for loving me. I'll see you on the flip side.

YOUR Ashley."

"You've got to be fucking kidding me." Tristan stared at Stacey with wide eyes.

"Jesus Christ," Jared muttered. "That's a shocking twist. Do you think Brooke knows?"

Tristan pushed back the chair and began to pace, going over the words from the note and their meaning. "She doesn't know and I suspect neither does Wendell and his wife Michelle."

"Why do you think that?" Jared asked.

"When her grandmother died, Wendell hit on her. By the way he looks at her, he's still got the hots for her. His wife believes all Brooke wants is Wendell and his millions."

"They're cousins," Stacey stated the obvious.

"No shit," Tristan said under his breath, going over in his head how he was going to break this news to Brooke. "What other shocking insights are in that report?"

"That's it," Stacey said. "They were able to trace the key. It's an original and goes to a girl's keepsake box. It also has a matching diary with smaller key."

"I take it the brand name and details on where it was sold is in that report." Tristan stopped pacing, taking in a deep breath.

"The company that made them was local, went out of business thirty years ago. I've seen many of the boxes at garage sales, antique shops," Stacey said. "There are pictures of all the box styles in the report."

Tristan shivered. His mind sensing something about Brooke. Anger? Yeah, she wasn't going to be thrilled when she heard that her beloved grandmother had an affair with Wendell's grandfather.

A sharp jab hit his chest. He looked down, nothing had touched him. The pain all in his head.

Couldn't be, could it?

"Can I clock out a few minutes early?" Tristan asked. His body tensed. He told himself the sensations that something had Brooke upset was because he knew how she'd react to the news, not that he was that deeply connected to her. "My shift ends in twenty anyway."

"Go," Jared said waving his hand. "But stay the fuck away from Wendell and his family."

"I think I can manage that considering the news." Tristan flew out of his boss's office, confusion and fear tugging at his heart. He understood the concept of an empath. Even believed in the ability to sense other people's emotions since he'd experienced it himself with Tamara. He'd always been overwhelmed by crowds and the affect they had on his mind and his own emotions. But those were general sensations, not pinpointing any one person, but a collective rush of feelings?

That was different.

Brooke puckered her lips, putting on fresh lip-gloss. She hadn't felt this light in years. It sucked that she and Tristan wouldn't last, but rebound relationships never did. And he'd see that soon enough. Besides, she wouldn't lead him on. She'd set him straight when he got home tonight, especially about last night being more about her needing someone to be there for her. To hold and comfort her in her time of need.

Crap. That sounded like she used him for her own selfish needs and then was tossing him aside, which wasn't what she wanted.

I want him in my life, as a friend.

So, what had the quickie in the kitchen been about?

And why was she primping for him?

The doorbell rang. She glanced at her phone. Tristan said he'd be back around six. It was a little after five. Maybe he got off early. She valued he didn't take liberties, like walking in her home, just because they were sleeping...slept together. With a wide smile strapped across her face, she opened the door

She quickly frowned, staring at a man dressed in golf attire.

"Ms. Brooke Ashley Fowler?" he asked.

"May I help you?" She looked him up and down, thinking he looked harmless enough. Probably selling something.

But he knew her full name.

"Are you Brooke Ashley Fowler?" the man repeated.

"Yes."

He handed her a legal sized envelope. Without thinking, took it, but the warning bells went off loud and clear.

"You've been served."

"Shit. Again?"

The man turned and walked toward his small economy car parked in the street.

"Served for what?" She sat down on the front steps reliving the day she'd shown up at her old apartment to collect her things and the doorbell rang. She was on her way out, so she opened the door and a man handed her papers, serving her with the lawsuit from her ex-assistant, Debbie.

With shaky hands, she opened the envelope and pulled out a thick document. She read the first page, letting her know the Ramsworth family was suing her for a million dollars.

"What the fuck!" She flipped through the pages, but the words blurred together. She wanted to rip the document into tiny little pieces and toss them into a fire. The heat of pure fury started at her toes and burned like a raging wildfire up her body. She knew in a matter of minutes she'd be in an all-out rage.

That wouldn't be good.

She sucked in a few deep breaths, collecting her thoughts, forcing the increasing tingle across her skin to settle into the back of her mind.

She shivered. *Tristan.*

Blinking a few times, she managed to pull up Jillian White-Sutten's phone number and tapped the speaker button. Jillian had talked the DA in the criminal case to agree to drop all charges after Brooke served a hundred hours of community service and went through anger management classes, which couldn't start soon enough.,

Even with deep breaths, the rage just wouldn't go away and thanks to Tristan sharing his own life experiences, she could actually see how she'd been spiraling out of control.

"Jillian White-Sutten," a woman's voice echoed.

"Hey Jillian, this is Brooke Fowler. Do you have a minute?" Brooke squeezed her fist, digging her nails into the palms of her hands.

"Sure. What's up?"

Might as well lay it all out there. "The Ramsworth's are suing me for a million dollars."

"What the hell for?" Jillian asked. "You have the paperwork?"

"I do."

"My husband won't be home until around ten tonight. Why don't I come over?"

"You don't have to do that. I can make an appointment." Part of Brooke really didn't want Jillian to go out of her way. Everyone in Tristan's life had gone above and beyond to help a perfect stranger. That said, Brooke missed having a woman to talk to.

She missed her grandmother.

"Nah. I'll bring a bottle of wine and I'll look over the suit and we can go from there."

Brooke's phone vibrated, Tristan number's popping up. "Tristan is calling, so I need to take it. You know where I live?"

"Yep. See you in about thirty minutes."

Brooke tapped the phone. "Hey," she said. Her pulse still wild and out of control.

"Are you okay?" Tristan asked.

She blinked. "No. But how'd you know I might not be okay?"

"Something happened?" Tristan's voice was tight and laced with tension, which unsettled her even more.

"The Ramsworth's held good to their promise and are suing me," she said behind gritted teeth. The overwhelming urge to hurt someone still tickled the back of her throat. She swallowed.

"For the necklace?"

"For a million dollars." She stood, staring down the street. The gate to the Ramsworth Manor opened for a large SUV. "I'm going to march down there and tell them what they can do with their law suit."

"Don't you dare," Tristan yelled. "I'm fifteen minutes from home. Stay put. I've got the forensics back on the key…and the note."

"Why do I think I'm not going to like this?" She plopped herself back on the stoop.

"Just stay put, okay?"

"Yeah," she said. "I called Jillian. She's on her way over."

"Good move." The timbre of his voice settled her rising blood pressure. "I'll be there soon, babe."

The humid air clung to her lungs, making it difficult to get enough oxygen. If she did do something, she knew that she'd get herself in trouble before Tristan made the turn onto Cleverdale.

Ryan had left a bunch of leftovers in the fridge, might as well pull some out for dinner. Even if no one ate them, it would fill the next few moments.

Brooke dumped the lawsuit papers on the family room coffee table. They skidded across the top, knocking over the empty candy dish, breaking it into three pieces. She shook out her hands. Her entire career, she'd been decisive and in control. This anger wasn't her and she needed to make it go away.

She pulled together a chicken Caesar salad, knowing Tristan had liked it since that was all she'd seen him eat at the funeral yesterday. She set up a folding table on the side of the house. One of her biggest bone of contentions with her grandfather was that he never built a deck or patio. He'd often say he'd get to it, but never did, not even when she offered to help him pay for it.

The sound of tires squealing across the pavement stole her attention. She peeked around the front of the house to see Tristan swing into her driveway. The smell of burning rubber stung her nostrils.

He jumped from the car and before she had the chance to open her mouth and say hello, he had his arms wrapped around her and his tongue swirling inside her mouth with a combination of fierce protection and loving concern.

She welcomed him with the same desperation. Her body relaxed immediately in his arms. Her anger dissipated into something similar to simple annoyance. She wanted to resent how he made her feel safe with him. She needed to take care of herself. Relying on him would only cause one of them to be hurt in the long run.

As the kiss moved from wild to tender, it dawned on her that Larry had never greeted her like that. Hell, no one had ever seemed that excited to see her.

Her hands massaged his shoulders as she gently pried her lips from his. "Well, hello there," she said. The heat produced by rage quickly changed to a different kind of burn. One that scared her as much as it excited her.

He cocked his head back. "I was worried you were all pissed off and ready to go drive your car through their gate and castrate Wendell."

She tossed her head back and laughed. "The thought did cross my mind, but I opted to make some dinner. Hungry?"

He kissed her nose. "I am, but we need to talk."

The roar of another engine rolling down the street interrupted him as he glanced over his shoulder.

"Jillian's here," he said. "Where are the papers you got served today?"

"Inside."

"All right, I'll go get them," he said with a dark tone.

"You're freaking me out." She'd just gotten rid of the rage and now fear prickled the back of her neck.

"I'm going to get a beer. What do you want?"

"Jillian is bringing wine, so we just need glasses," she said, staring up into his dark eyes. "That bad?"

"I'll fill you in after I get that drink."

She'd never been one to let things like that hang, wanting to know what was going on as soon as possible, but when she held him in her arms, she felt the tension in his strong frame, which caused an electric connectivity to ripple through her body. Her grandfather had always said he'd fallen in love with her grandmother at first sight. He said he couldn't explain how it happened other than it felt like someone took an electrical current and connected it from her to him.

That's couldn't be what she felt with Tristan.

"Thanks for coming," Brooke said as Jillian made her way to the picnic table, holding a bottle of white wine.

To Brooke's surprise, Jillian pulled her in for a brief hug before setting in one of the Adirondack chairs.

"I needed to get out of the house after a day of babysitting my grandson." Jillian laughed. "I love that little boy, but I do love to give him back to his parents."

"He's a cute kid." Brooke eased into a chair. "And very polite."

Jillian nodded. "So, tell me what you can about this suit."

"Tristan is getting the paperwork and some wine glasses, but essentially, they think my grandmother stole this necklace." She held up the pendant.

"And it's worth a million dollars?" Jillian's forehead crinkled.

"Something about pain and suffering."

"Yeah, they tossed some weight and money around to get that lawsuit to go through."

Tristan stepped from the back door wearing a pair of shorts and golf shirt.

"Where'd those clothes come from?" Brooke immediately wished she hadn't asked, remembering he'd left an overnight bag the first few nights he'd slept on the sofa.

He cocked a brow. "I hope it's okay I hung my uniform in your closet, along with my weapon."

"That's fine," Brooke said.

"Hey Jillian. How are you?" Tristan handed over the paperwork.

"I'll be better when I get the chance to put the Ramsworth's in their place."

"What's your beef with them?" Brooke asked, taking the glass of wine Tristan offered.

"Before they knew I had married Stacey's father, they wanted to hire me to defend Wendell after his DUI. My husband never cares what cases I take or don't take, so I was put on retainer. The moment they found out I was related to Doug, they fired me and tried to ruin my reputation, unsuccessfully, I might add." Jillian put on a pair of eye glasses and started to scan the legal documents.

"Well, shit," Jillian said, holding a piece of paper up. "They have documentation that the necklace was made using an old family crest from the late 1800's and is one of a kind. They also submitted Brooke's mug shot with an image of Great Grandmama Ramsworth wearing the necklace."

"That's still a little weak to sign off so quickly on a million-dollar lawsuit, isn't it?"

"The image with the crest is pretty telling. Sure, someone could have knocked it off, making a fake. We'll find out soon enough when an independent jeweler checks it out."

"While that will be necessary, I'm pretty sure the necklace around Brooke's neck belongs to the Ramsworths," Tristan said, standing in front of Brooke.

"What the hell? You think my grandmother stole it?" She squeezed the wine glass so tight she thought she might smash it in her hand.

"Not at all." Tristan pulled a folding chair over. He sat down leaning forward hands on her knees. "Jillian, can you give us a moment?"

"I'm her lawyer, I think I need to hear this."

Brooke's gaze locked with Tristan's. His eyes filled with a combination of concern and a sense of sadness.

"She stays."

Tristan nodded. "It seems Wendell's grandfather gave Ashley the necklace."

"Why the hell would he do that?" Brooke continued to stare at Tristan. His pupils widened and his face contorted as if someone put a knife through his chest. "That makes no sense at all."

"Actually, it does." Tristan took her hand. "Take a deep breath."

"Just fucking tell me, would you, please?" The last thing she needed was her boyfriend…her friend…her whatever, patronizing her.

"The note implies that your dad's biological father is old man Ramsworth and Ashley mentions him giving her the necklace, among other things."

Brooke opened her mouth, but only a horrid nose that sounded like a dying cow came out. She blinked a few times. "Do you know how crazy that sounds?"

"I do."

"That note was illegible. They could have it wrong." Brooke squeezed Tristan's hands so hard her fingers ached.

"This is good news," Jillian said.

"I don't see how." Brooke snapped her head in Jillian's direction.

"It means the necklace belongs to you and the lawsuit is dead in the water. Especially if it turns out you're the daughter of the oldest son." Jillian peered over her cheaters. "Your father was older than Wendell number two, right?"

"I think so."

Tristan wiggled his hands free. "Let me get the forensics from the car."

Brooke sipped her wine as she watched Tristan saunter to his car. How he'd managed to wiggle into her life so deeply frightened her, but also comforted her when she had no one else to lean on. She understood part of that was her own fault, hiding behind her career. Her job had been her life, more important than anything. "This is crazy. No way did my grandmother have an affair with a Ramsworth." If that were a fact, her grandfather wasn't hers biologically…AND that made Wendell the III, her cousin.

Gross.

"I didn't mean to be so flip about this," Jillian said, resting the papers on her lap. "I tend to focus on the legalities. I apologize for my insensitive attitude."

Brooke let the crisp, pear-tasting wine linger in her mouth before swallowing. She wanted to guzzle it, but knew that would lead her nowhere and fast. "The last few weeks of my life have been a roller coaster ride and I'm ready to get off of it."

"I can't image being in your shoes right now, but I will do whatever it takes to make sure this suit goes away."

"Why?" Brooke stared at the older women, who held herself with more class than the entire Ramsworth family.

Jillian took her glasses off, resting them on top of the legal document on her lap. "There are a lot of reasons. One being personal. I'd like to see the Ramsworth's get a taste of their own medicine. The second one, and maybe the more important one is something that took me a while to get used to. Stacey is my husband's world and by extension mine. Her co-workers are her extended family, which means they are ours too. They have her back every day on the job, so we take care of them and their families when asked."

"I'm not family."

"Maybe not, but Tristan is and he loved your grandfather."

"I'm beginning to think their friendship was much deeper than Tristan makes it out to be." Brooke took in a deep breath, letting it out slowly, eyeing Tristan as he walked toward her with an envelope in his hand. Thinking back over all her conversations about her love life with her grandfather, she realized his probing questions were all leading up to him introducing her to Tristan. She looked to the sky, squinting. Life might work in mysterious ways, but love didn't happen like this. Not a love that would last.

Your grandmother and I had a love that could endure the worse, and still survive. When it's real, it lasts forever.

"This is all the forensics on the note and the key." Tristan set the envelope gently on her lap, letting his finger dance across her knee for a lingering moment. "To sum it up simply: the note was written by your grandmother to your grandfather about the necklace. It's inferred your grandfather knew he wasn't the father."

"They did have a shotgun wedding. Everyone knew that." Brooke's fingers curled around the envelope. Her muscles rattled against her skin. "Grandma worked as a cook in the Manor until right after she gave birth to my dad."

"So, this scenario is possible?" Jillian asked.

Brooke nodded, closing her eyes as she dropped her head back. "If it's true this lawsuit goes away and I potentially have a claim to the Ramsworth fortune." She blinked, focusing on the clouds floating in the sky.

"That's true,' Jillian said. Her voice strong and steady. Brooke admired her grace and style. Something about her oozed confidence and kindness at the same time.

"But you'd have to prove it." Tristan sat across from her, his feet pressed against hers. "And that could be a public spectacle, potentially bringing up a lot of crap from your past."

"I doubt the Ramsworth's would want that kind of scandal. It doesn't serve their greater good, only potentially makes them look bad." Jillian put her glasses back on.

"They will find a way to spin it against me. They are brilliant at deflecting." Brooke had spent a life time listening to stories about how the Ramsworth's treated her family, and everyone else. She had tried to warn Michelle, but she wouldn't listen.

And now she was one of them.

"They won't be able to spin this, nor will they want to," Tristan said.

"Why not?" Brooke wasn't sure she wanted to know the answer.

"Your grandmother's note indicates Wendell number one knew he was the father and either tried to bribe her to keep quiet, or gave her things out of guilt." Tristan kicked off his sandals, rubbing his big toe against her ankle.

She should brush him off, but the contact kept her fury at bay.

"So, why the lawsuit?" Jillian asked.

Brooke's mind snapped into focus, but she didn't like where it went. "Deflection and the assumption I don't know." She lowered her head looking at Tristan. "The break-ins. They could have been looking for evidence of some kind."

"Making sure it doesn't see the light of day," Tristan said, shaking his head. "Wendell number three's finger prints were on the note."

"Can I see the forensics?" Jillian asked. "That's a good piece of information if we can link him to the break-ins."

Brooke handed her the envelope. "But if he broke in and saw it, why wouldn't he take it?"

"We don't know when the note was damaged, so it's possible whoever broke-in didn't read it." Tristan rubbed the back of his neck. "The note also mentioned a box that Rusty gave his wife that contained 'other things' but we don't know where that box is or if they have it."

"Which means they might not know exactly what they are looking for." Jillian rose, moving to the picnic table, spreading the papers out. "We also don't know who in the family knows about the affair, if anyone, since they are claiming it was stolen."

"We need to find the box." Brooke shivered, clearing her mind of the idea she might actually be a Ramsworth of some kind and focused on how to make sure she wasn't sued for a million dollars and got to keep a necklace her grandmother or grandfather or both had wanted her to have...for whatever reason.

Tristan leaned forward, taking her hands. His soft, caring eyes melted her heart into a puddle of warm chocolate. "Doug is obsessed with the dead space behind the kitchen and the fact it's not in the plans. Can I have him come over and put a couple of holes in the wall?"

"Go right ahead." She let out a long sigh. "I'm really struggling with all this. It's too much to process."

He nodded. "I don't understand why, if Rusty knew his son biologically was a Ramsworth, why he'd live here his entire life, much less go to work for them."

"The best revenge is success? But that doesn't really work since old lady Ramsworth tried to destroy my grandmother's business more than once." Brooke swirled her wine glass.

"But she didn't and your grandparents lived a happy and good life," Tristan said.

"Do you think he could have known there was question of his paternity?" Jillian asked.

"I have no idea." Brooke had never questioned anything about her family life. Her parents were loving and they adored her grandparents. Family gatherings were always free of conflict or feuds. There were the occasional disagreements, but they were always resolved with humor and love.

Tristan leaned forward, cupping her face. "We're going to figure this all out." He brushed his lips against hers, but quickly pulled back. "Don't push me away."

"I'm not going to have any regrets, but—"

"No buts." He fanned his thumbs under her eyes.

Her heart pounded and warmth spread across her body like a shot of whiskey and a dose of sunshine. His eyes showed more love and compassion in a single gaze then any gesture Larry could have mustered up and that scared her because she realized she'd never given her heart fully to anyone.

Not even herself.

"Tristan."

He hushed her with his finger. "There are no guarantees in life and I've spent my entire life worrying about what might happen a few months down the road." He smiled. "Love like there's no such thing as a broken heart."

"How about we amend to really, really like, like there's no such thing as a broken heart."

"Whatever works for you, babe."

CHAPTER 9

THE FOLLOWING EVENING, Tristan stood in the middle of Brooke's bedroom with a crowbar, waiting for Doug and Jim to finish their assessment of what might be behind the wall.

"I think this entire wall was added and we don't have to worry about any wires," Jim said, running a hand across his buzzed, greying hair. In his late forties, it was hard to believe he had a daughter in her late twenties, a grandson, and another grandchild on the way.

"Let's cut a small hole here." Doug tapped the wall near the corner.

"Hit the music." Jim pointed to Tristan.

"What?" Tristan was handy…with a car, capable of rebuilding an engine, but handy around the house? Could barely paint a wall without screwing it up. "Music?"

Jim gave Doug a dirty look.

Doug tossed his hands wide. "I didn't expect him to be here."

"Then why is he holding a crow bar?" Jim shook his head, pulling out his cell, tapping a few times until *Looking Out My Back Door* by Credence Clearwater Revival boomed out of a portable speaker.

Tristan stood there, watching the two men cut into the wall, pulling some of the drywall off. They worked in unison, like one person. Each man understanding exactly what the other was about to do. They didn't speak a single word to one another as they continued to carefully cut through the wall, trying not to do too much damage, as requested by Brooke.

Occasionally their heads would bob with the music, but otherwise, their attention completely focused on ripping apart the wall.

"Interesting," Doug said, stepping back.

"How so?" Tristan set his tool on the ground next to the toolbox, knowing he wouldn't be doing a damn thing, which was fine by him.

"It's exactly as I thought and there is a box inside." Doug reached his thick biceps into the hole and pulled out an old, metal floral box. "Just like the ones we found that go with that key."

Tristan took the dusty box. He wanted to shake it, but worried something breakable might be contained inside. The cold metal taunted his brain. His sister dying and all the death he'd seen on the job happened hard, fast, and on a permanent server. Brooke's was like an endless mountain of shit that had her putting one foot in front of the other, plowing her way through entanglement after entanglement hoping to find an end to it all, only another shoe would drop.

"I'm going to take this to Brooke," Tristan said, still staring at the dulled pink and yellow lilacs that graced the box.

"We're going to clean up in here and put some cardboard over the hole so Brooke doesn't have to look at it. I'd recommend knocking down this wall during demo anyway," Doug said.

"All right." Tristan barely heard the words as he walked into the kitchen. The smell of burning wood struck his nostrils when he opened the back door.

Brooke sat at the far end of the bonfire, her face slightly blocked from the flames that rose from the wood pile.

The sound of kids laughing and screaming tugged his attention. He hadn't planned on this being some sort of neighborhood party, but Jared, his wife, and four kids had been walking by just as Stacey and her family pulled in. One thing led to another and the next thing he knew, they were sitting around having drinks and making s'mores.

"Are you okay?"

Tristan's body jerked at the sound of Jared's deep voice.

"Hey Tristan," Bella, Jared's six-year-old little girl said from her perch on her father's back.

"Princess Bella." Tristan reached out, taking the girls hand and kissing it.

Bella giggled as her father put her down.

"Go find your older sister and tell her I said to make you one more marshmallow."

"K, daddy!" Bella took off running.

Jared rubbed the back of his neck. "I thought the twins were exhausting."

"We found the box," Tristan blurted out.

"I see that."

"I don't have a good feeling about this." Tristan pushed open the back door, setting the box on the small table, deciding it would be best to deal with the contents at a later time. "She's had a rough time as it is, and to find out she's probably related to those assholes could send her over a cliff.

"You really think she's a ticking time bomb?"

For as long as Tristan had worked under Jared, he'd been more like the big brother Tristan never had. The way he wanted to be with his little brothers, though somehow fell short.

"She's dealing with it and having the criminal case essentially settled, it's taken some of the stress off, but this is a different kind of emotional upheaval. It can change the way a person sees and value's themselves."

"From what I can tell, she's her grandmother through and through, and that lady was one tough bird." Jared squeezed Tristan's shoulder. "You've fallen hard for her, haven't you?"

Tristan shifted his gaze to the bonfire. Brooke sat on the ground, Bella in her lap, holding a long stick over the flames. Bella kept tilting her head up and Brooke smiled down at her. "I've fallen and I can't get up."

Jared laughed. "Good way to put it."

"Dad!" Caitlyn, Jared's oldest child screamed from across the yard, dragging one of her twin brothers by the arm as he dug his heels into the ground. "You're namesake took my phone and texted my friends and now everyone thinks I like some boy that I don't even know and ewe, I don't like boys. Not after having two bratty brothers!"

Jared put his hands on his hips. "Hopefully, she continues to hate boys well into her twenties." Jared turned and strode toward his children, Caitlyn now yanking the boy by his shirt.

The sparks from the fire rose toward the sky, burning out a few feet in the air. Quickly, Tristan made his way toward the fire, sitting down next to Brooke as Bella took off to find someone else to make her 'just one more'.

He reached out, pressing his thumb against the corner of Brooke's mouth, wiping some marshmallow off. He sucked his finger into his mouth. "That was good." He leaned in, eyes locked on hers, his tongue parting her lips, gently entangling hers in a quick dance. "That was better."

"I shouldn't let you do that," she whispered.

"I'm the only one you should let do that." He pressed his mouth harder on her lips, deepening the kiss to the point where all he could hear in the background was the crackle of the fire and the beating of his heart. Cupping the back of her neck, he massaged gently before running his hand down her spine, feeling her body shiver as he found a small section of skin between her shorts and her top. "Only me." With his other hand, he palmed her cheek, his tongue enjoying the sweet taste of Brooke mixed with chocolate and a dash of marshmallow.

She pulled back. "You're trying to distract me because you found something in the wall."

"A little bit, but I really wanted to kiss you." He blinked, no reason to lie since she'd seen it on his face, and felt it in her heart. "A metal, floral box like the one we believe go to that key. I figured you'd want to wait until everyone left before opening it." He adjusted her body between his legs, drawing her back against his chest, arms circling around her warm body. Jim and Doug had joined their wives in front of the fire while Ryan and Jared gathered all the children to be sent back to their house with a local babysitter.

"Beautiful night," Stacey said, sitting in a chair, her arms folded over her swollen belly. Doug sat next to her, hand over hers.

"Thanks for letting us crash the party," Ryan said as she plopped down on the ground. "I'm so glad there was a babysitter available."

Looking around the bonfire, it was difficult for Tristan to not remember Tamara and wonder if she were still alive, how'd she fit in with this crowd.

"Caitlyn is almost old enough," Jared said standing behind his wife. "But she'll end up in an all-out brawl with her brothers while ignoring her baby sister, who would probably burn down the house trying to bake cookies."

"I'm so glad I only had one." Jim sat on the other side of Stacey, in a chair. Jillian between his legs with her arms draped over his knees.

"You're daughter was a holy terror and makes my kids look like saints." Jared laughed.

"My little girl a trouble maker?" Jim asked. "That's putting it mildly."

"You two better shut your traps because my grandparents have told me some pretty wicked stories about you two that I won't hesitate to share." Stacey tossed a twig at her father.

Tristan's sister would have loved being here with this group of people.

Brooke squeezed his thighs, looking up at him, giving him a nod as if she could read his mind.

His breath hitched.

"I've got so many great stories," Ryan said. "Do you know where Jared and my brother got caught—"

Jared bent over cupping his wife's mouth. "Shall I bring another round?"

"Please," Brooke said.

Tristan kissed her cheek. "Are you sure you don't want everyone to leave? Just because they got a babysitter doesn't mean they have to stay. They can go to the Mason Jug for a beer."

"I'm having a good time. I'll deal with the box later."

Jared returned with a cooler full of beer and wine. The fire had settled down to a red-orange glow, which reminded Tristan of Brooke's eyes.

"I know how all those guys met." Brooke waved in the direction of Stacy and her family. "But I don't know how you two met." She pointed to Jared and his wife.

"I've known this clown my entire life," Ryan said, patting Jared's leg. "He was my brother's best friend all through middle and high school."

"The kid sister that always tagged along?" Brooke asked, her body completely relaxed against Tristan.

He ran his fingers through her soft hair, occasionally grazing the skin on her neck.

"Not even close, at least at first." Jared laughed. "She was two and I was twelve the first time we met."

"So, when did you get together?" Brooke asked. "Obviously it wasn't right away."

Laughter erupted around the campfire.

"I had just turned twenty-five and Jared decided he needed a change and took a job across the state. I figured if I could have him forever, I'd have him for one night, so I went about seducing him."

"Two weeks later, she had me brainwashed and I've been wondering what the hell happened ever since." Jared smiled like a big kid.

"I'll tell you what happened." Ryan tugged at Jared's ear. "You finally came to your senses."

Jared laughed. "Yes, dear."

Tristan swallowed. Five years ago, he would have laughed off the idea of getting married and starting a family. Back then, his short-lived relationships had been fine and just the way he liked it, never letting anyone get too close. He knew Brooke had been right when she told him part of his problem with women had to do with his sister's death, as weird as it sounded.

Not only could he see the connection these couples shared, but he felt the bond. It wasn't the same kind of bond a twin has, which has a deeper tether, but nowhere near as intense as each of these couples had for one another.

He had never allowed anyone to get so deep inside his heart and mind. Not even Brenda, and he had loved her as much as one can love a person who doesn't love them back.

He nuzzled his face in Brooke's neck. Her skin smelled of coconut and honeysuckle.

"Do you hear that?" Jared asked. "That's a fire truck."

"Yeah it is." Tristan kissed her neck, before pushing himself to a standing position. "Sounds close."

"Check on the kids, babe," Jared said as he stood and started walking toward the street. "It's definitely coming this way."

Tristan followed his boss to the front yard, noticing a few silhouettes standing in front of the Ramsworth Manor gate. He pointed. "Either they were sitting outside and are hearing the same thing we are. Or—"

"They decided to fuck with Brooke and call in our little legal bonfire in a pit that was built with a permit to be the assholes they are."

The fire truck's siren bleeped as it turned down Brooke's street, a sheriff's car right behind it.

"What a waste of resources," Jared muttered. "You take the fire truck, I've got the local."

Tristan looked over his shoulder. "Shocker. Stacey didn't follow us out here."

"Only because her father is here. I don't think he'll ever truly get past being held at gunpoint with his daughter."

"That will fuck with a man." Tristan strolled to the front of the fire truck, glad to see Cade jump from the passenger side. "What's up?"

"You tell me." Cade stood two feet away, hands on his hips and looked around. "We got a call there was a brush fire of some kind."

"Try a bonfire." Tristan pointed to the back yard. "You should join us for a beer."

Cade laughed. "I wish. But you know the drill. I've got to check it out."

"Be my guest."

Tristan followed Cade to the back yard.

"Any idea who called it in?" Tristan asked.

"No idea, but I'll check the log when I get back to the station." Cade did a quick scan of the area. "Just curious, how big did that fire get?"

"No more than a foot tall and the pit is three feet in diameter. You could barely see it from Ramsworth Manor."

"Those people are whack-a-doodles." Cade laughed, waving his hand in the air like a whirly bird. "Carry on."

Tristan stood on the side of the house, eyes focused down the street. Brooke's possible blood ties to the Ramsworth family could no longer sit on the back burner.

Brooke sat in the middle of her bed, the metal box between her crisscrossed legs. The old-fashioned key placed carefully next to her, sinking into the comforter.

Tristan stepped from the bathroom. He'd offered to leave her alone to go through the box. She almost told him to go home, but the idea of finding out her grandmother, the woman she'd bonded with more than her own mother, had an affair with a Ramsworth, or equally bad, stole from them, made her stomach churn in knots.

The bed shifted her weight as Tristan climbed in, sitting directly across from her. "Are you ready?"

"As ready as I'll ever be." Her fingers trembled. Her hand hovered over the key, but she couldn't bring herself to touch it. "Sit next to me, please?"

"Sure thing."

The bed shook, but for some reason it calmed her. Feeling his body's heat so close to hers, gave her the courage to snag the key.

"What if this isn't the right key?" she asked.

"Do you want me to do it?"

"No," she said quickly.

The key fit perfectly in the hole and the box clicked open on the first twist. Her heart raced. With the lid raised an inch, she tried to peek in, but all she saw was darkness. Sucking in a breath, she pushed the lid so hard the box tumbled over, spilling a few of the contents.

"That's one way to see what's inside," Tristan said.

She let out a dry laugh. "I used to think that relying on someone for strength like this meant you were weak. I mean, at least that's the message I got from my grandparents and parents."

"You misinterpreted what they were telling you."

"How so?" She picked up a small maroon-velvet bag, fingering the contents.

"Your grandparents relied on each other for strength and support. I'm sure your parents did too. People who love…care deeply for one another, that's what they do. Look at Doug and Stacey and what they went through when Doug had been accused of murder. They got through it because they had each other."

She set the pouch on her leg, staring at it. "I've always prided myself on my independence."

"So have I, maybe too much. Another reason why I've ended up single for so long." He pressed his shoulder against hers. "You are one of the strongest, fiercest, women I have ever met. Wanting a friend during the shit storm that's happening around you doesn't make you weak. It makes you human." He tilted her chin with his forefinger.

"Is that what we are? Friends?" Part of her wanted to prolong dealing with the box as long as possible, but the other part wanted— no needed— to define their relationship.

His lips sizzled against hers and his tongue probed inside her mouth with a tenderness that brought a tear to her eye. "Friendship is the basis of all great love affairs," he whispered.

She bit down on her lower lip, stifling a laugh.

"Yeah, I know. I borrowed that one from your grandfather, but it's true."

"You somehow make me feel like no matter what, it's all going to work out." She cupped his face, puckering his lips before giving him a quick kiss. "First order of business." She held up the pouch, tugging at the strings. Holding her breath, she shook the bag upside down.

A coin, the size of a silver dollar fell to the bed, along with a silver bracelet with a large circular pendant. "Wow." Brooke lifted the coin, which seemed heavier than it should. Her fingers, tracing the lettering that had been etched over the same design the necklace she wore around her neck.

"My father's name and date of birth."

"Your name and I assume date of birth on this." Tristan held the silver bracelet between his fingers. "Looks like someone wanted to acknowledge you as a Ramsworth."

"Don't ever say that again." She glared at Tristan, squeezing the coin with all her might, hoping she'd magically snap it in half. "Even if this nightmare is true, I'll always be a Fowler."

"Point taken." He gathered up a small notebook. "May I look inside?"

"I'll do it." The pages had yellowed and only a few of them had any written words on them.

She read the first page to herself.

I can't believe I left Russell in the bassinet to talk to Wendell. But I didn't want him to see the boy. Crazy. He'd see him eventually considering we are right down the street. But only in the summers. I know Rusty knows the truth, but I still can't ask him to sell the house he'd worked so hard to buy. Also, I think for my Rusty, it's a form of revenge.

Wendell stopped by to drop off two things. A necklace for me. Like I'd ever wear it. But he said it should be passed down to whoever MY son married. At least he didn't try to call the boy his own.

The second item was a collector's coin. I think the only reason I accepted them was if I needed to get his bitch of a wife off me, or maybe hock them someday.

"It would appear my grandmother and the original Wendell did indeed have an affair and my father was the result. Worse, my grandfather knew."

Tristan's arm looped around her shoulder. "Biology doesn't make you one of them."

"That statement I will agree with." She turned her attention back to the book.

Next page:

It's been YEARS since Wendell has shown his face anywhere near me and my family, though his bitch of a wife keeps trying to take me down. Never going to happen because I have something she doesn't.

I have true love.

Today, Wendell gave me money for Russell's graduation to help with college. Ten grand. Barely enough to do anything with and really, I didn't want to take it, but somedays I can be a bitch. Will I spend it? Not unless someone is dying.

"Look for a wad of money." Brooke really didn't think there'd be a stash of large bills, but it would be nice if there were.

Tristan dumped the rest of the contents on the bed. "Well, I'll be damned. Two large stacks of cash." He tossed two white envelops in her lap.

"Holy fuck."

"How'd you know there'd be money?"

She tapped the notebook, showing him the words before flipping the page. "Two more entries."

. . .

The nerve of that man to show up after the birth of MY granddaughter. This time I told him to take whatever he was offering and leave, but he said he had a bracelet for Brooke and a request. He wants me to, when she was old enough, to give her the pendant and this bracelet. He's nuts. No way in hell would I do that. I have half a mind to send Georgina the stupid necklace. She hasn't shut up about it missing for years.

Final entry:

I did the one thing I swore I'd never do, and that's contact Wendell. But I can't have him or anyone in his family showing up at MY son and his beautiful wife's funeral. I begged him not to send flowers or even a donation of any kind, anywhere in their name. Wendell, the bastard offered to pay for the funeral. He tried to fake cry. He doesn't even love the son he adopted. Thankfully, Wendell adhered to my wishes. Now I just have to keep him the hell away from Brooke.

"What the heck?" Brooke re-read the entire paragraph. "Did you know the middle Wendell was adopted?"

"Someone might have mentioned it."

"I had no idea," Brooke said. "Anything else in the box?"

"One more envelope, addressed to you."

She glanced at the paper in Tristan's hands. "That's my grandfather's handwriting." All the notes and lies had gotten under her skin. She hugged herself. "Read it for me, please?"

"Are you sure?"

She nodded, leaning back against the headboard and closed her eyes.

"*Dear Brooke. If you are reading this, then I'm waiting for you on the flip side and you found our family's skeleton in the closet. I told you every family had one.*"

Tristan rested his hand on her thigh.

"*After your grandmother died and I found this box, with all the things I knew she'd been given, I took out the note she wrote me and the necklace. I honestly hadn't meant to give it to you, but you saw me holding it, so I lied and said it was meant for you, which wasn't a lie, but telling you it was your grandmother's favorite and she wanted you to have well, that was one big lie."*

Brooke swallowed a sob. "I remember him sitting on the sofa, the pendant in his hands. He'd been deep in thought and hadn't even heard me come in." The memory so vivid, she could smell her grandfather's pine cologne.

Brooke fingered the locket. "Help me take this thing off." She leaned forward, bile rising to her throat. The day her grandfather gave it to her, she'd pushed, desperate to have one thing of her grandmother's she could have with her at all times. Something to keep that bond strong and alive.

"Are you sure you want to do that?"

Taking the damn necklace off was about the only thing she was sure about. Tristan's fingers tingled the skin on her neck. He easily undid the clasp before resting it in her hand.

"Keep reading, okay?"

"Not much left." Tristan cleared his throat.

"I'm hiding the box with all its contents in the wall. Well, except the original note about the necklace. I needed you to know the truth. I worry that someday someone in that family will see it and go after you. The note at least explains it. I'm still contemplating about telling you where this box is, only because I know you, and I know you don't want any of this, so for now, it's all hidden away. The important thing is that you're our granddaughter and we love you with every fiber of our being. Stay strong. I'm hoping that I've either had the chance to introduce you to your perfect match, or that you've managed to meet him on your own. Once you figure out he's for you, you'll understand why it was so easy for me to be the best and only father to your dad. I was very proud of the man he became and am enjoying the woman you are growing into. Call my friend. His card is tacked on grandma's board. I'm torturing her with how I tacked it. Love, Grandpa."

"Wow," she whispered, blinking, trying not to look at Tristan, but found it impossible. "He was talking about you."

"I don't blush often, but I am now." Tristan rested the note in his lap, staring at her. "I know he wanted us to meet and always told me he knew we'd hit it off, but wow. Just wow. To leave that in a note like this. I'm stunned."

"Me too," she whispered. "But can we talk about that later?" More memories of her grandfather talking about the perfect man flooded her brain. She'd thought he'd been talking figuratively, but all the while, he'd meant Tristan.

"Of course. There is a lot to take in and that is something we can deal with later." He pressed his lips against her temple.

She shuddered. "My father always told me that lies, even the ones we tell to protect our loved ones, are usually not worth it in the long run."

"Do wish your grandmother had been upfront about your father's paternity from the very beginning?"

For a long moment, she stared at the pendant holding both her parents and grandparents wedding picture. "Hell no." The necklace felt heavy in her hands. "If it weren't for this stupid thing, I might have been able to go on with my life, oblivious of this truth. Imagine what my father's life, my life, would have been like if we had to deal with them as family our entire lives. They would have treated me like the red-headed ugly step-child."

"Do you really think your father didn't know?"

She pondered that question as she put the necklace in the pouch. Her father had left Lake George right after he'd graduated from high school. First spending a summer working at a camp as a counselor. He'd met her mother their first week at SUNY Plattsburg, and much like her grandparents, fell in love quickly. "I think he believed in the life my grandparents created. He always loved coming back here, said they looked to live here, but there just wasn't a job for him or my mom."

"They both taught at the college there, right?"

She nodded. "My dad never paid any attention to the Ramsworths. Never said a bad thing about them, but certainly didn't say anything good either."

"We need to hide this box again, and I don't want to leave it here. Something tells me, those break-ins have something to do with the contents of this box."

"What am I going to do?" She turned and looked at Tristan. His dark eyes staring deep in her soul as if he were trying to reach inside and kiss her heart. Her breath hitched. "I've got to do the community service and anger classes. I've got this pending lawsuit. I need to get a job, which I suspect is going to be impossible until the arrest is off my record for good."

"I might have a job prospect for you. It would be in Saratoga."

She narrowed her eyes, balling her fists. "I don't want anyone pulling strings for me."

"I'd only be able to get you in the door, and that's only if there's a job opening. You'd have to sell them on why they should hire you and then you're the one who has to keep the job, not me."

"I'll take the opportunity, if that's the truth."

"It is." He tossed two envelopes of money in her lap. "Pay cash for groceries, gas, anything you can."

"I'm not using this money." She glared at him. "My grandparents didn't."

"Your grandparents weren't being sued for a million dollars and until we figure out how exactly we're going to make that go away, you need to save your money so you can flip this place and move past this shit."

Other than the last few months, Brooke had spent her entire life living off logic, never making a rash decision. Even moving in with Larry had been carefully planned out. It had made Larry nuts, considering he'd tossed the idea out there one night over dinner. He'd said it wasn't planned and by the way the words spewed from his mouth, she believed it and that freaked her out. She spent the next three weeks contemplating and planning the best way to go about taking the next step in their relationship, which meant marriage needed to be on the table.

Talk about not being romantic.

"You're right. I'll take the money."

"I want you to let me take the jewelry to the place my mom uses. I think we need to have these items valued."

"Couldn't it then become public that I have the items and cause people to wonder why I have them? I really don't want attention brought to me or my father's paternity."

"Neither do I." He took the box and set it on the nightstand. "Jillian said she was going to come up with a plan after looking into some laws or whatever. We sit tight and do nothing until we've talked to her. Then we make the shit go away."

"Thank you." She slid down the bed, rolling to her side, tucking her hands under her cheek.

"For what?" His fingers tangled in her hair, putting pressure on her scalp.

She sighed. "For picking up the phone when a stranger called."

He laughed, tugging her head into his lap, fingers dancing up and down her arm, across her neck. Hard to believe any woman wouldn't want to be curled up in his arms.

"I almost never answer calls from numbers I don't recognize."

"Then why'd you answer?"

"Pulling you over had put me in a bit of a sour mood. I figured Rusty was waggling his finger at me for not saying anything to you considering all of our conversations. I assumed it would be a telemarketer and since I had no plans, I thought I'd entertain myself by harassing the person on the other end."

"That's mean." Draping her arm over his thighs, she let her mind wonder back to their first encounter. The way he looked at her had been with compassion, not judgment. Not something you'd expect from a police officer who had pulled you over for reckless driving.

"I was bored, but also wondering what would have happened if Rusty had been able to introduce us."

"That's an interesting thought." Even early on in her relationship with Larry, there'd been a distance between them. She'd told herself she didn't want to let anyone in too fast because that's how people get hurt.

"I feel connected to you," he whispered. "I have from the moment I laid eyes on you and I've only felt that way once before, but it wasn't even remotely as strong as this."

Admitting she felt the same way would make her vulnerable in a way she'd never been before. Being vulnerable meant being weak, or at least it used to. She took risks all the time when it came to work. Closing a deal often meant playing your boss and the customer, trying to do right by both of them. Being with Larry, she'd treated it much the same way. A business deal.

She closed her eyes. This thing with Tristan started out the exact same way.

A deal.

She took a deep breath, blinking a few times, her focus landing on the box. "I asked you to help me with the key, and you've done that. You don't need to do anymore. I'm not really sure I helped you with women, but I think we've kept our promises to each other."

"What the hell are you talking about?" His hand dropped to the bed. "I tell you I care about you and start babbling on about an agreement we made, that quite frankly, I only suggested because I wanted to be with you." He lifted her head, resting it on a pillow as he stepped from the bed. "You're really going to push me away now?"

Was that what she was doing? "I don't mean to." She wanted to get out of the bed, put her arms around him, and kiss him like there was no tomorrow, but she couldn't bring herself to do it.

"Really? Because I just told you I'm falling head over heels for you, putting my heart out there, and you're just going to toss it aside. Jesus, Brooke. That's really cold."

The bed shook as he stomped out the room. Moments later, she heard the fridge slam shut.

What the hell was she doing? Tristan had been nothing but kind to her and she genuinely liked him. Fuck. It was a hell of lot more than like, but the connection scared her.

Not having the connection, though, would be worse.

She took in a deep breath and made her way to the kitchen. He leaned against the doorjamb into the family room, swigging a beer.

"I'm sorry," she said. "But I just broke up with a man I thought I wanted to spend the rest of my life with. I don't think I'm over it yet. It wouldn't be fair to you to keep this going."

Tristan laughed, only it wasn't a ha ha funny laugh. "You've been over that asshole for some time now. The only thing that's got you tied up in knots with regard to him is the fact that you lost control. But more importantly, you're mad because you saw it coming and you didn't do anything about it. Just like when my sister got into that go-cart, I reminded her of her times, and how close she was to a world record, putting that thought in her head."

Brooke covered her mouth, squelching a gasp. "Your sister's death isn't your fault."

"No, it's not, but it's a statement I carry around with me. I knew before I said it, she was planning on going for it. Even when I told her to take the corners easy, I could sense her adrenalin and I knew she'd push hard." He turned, taking another long draw from the glass bottle. "You were right when you said my problem with women started when Tamara died and then got worse when Brenda didn't return my feelings. If you don't feel what I do, fine, just say it. But don't insult me and use Larry, the loser, as an excuse."

"It's not Larry that is the issue." Brooke ducked her head into the fridge and pulled out a beer for herself. "Larry and I were set up, but the beginning of our relationship was much like a business arrangement. Kind of like, I scratch your back, you scratch mine. You and me?" She waved her finger between them. "Feels like a business deal, so no matter the connection, I don't trust it." She started to pace behind the small kitchen table. Her pulse raging. "Being with you feels comfortable and I don't know what to make of that. I've known you for what? A couple of weeks? And just a few minutes ago, when you stepped from the bed, I felt you retreat. Fuck, Tristan. I felt whatever you did and that I just don't know what to do with."

"You accept it," he said sternly. "Or you build a wall to prevent it. From the time Brenda broke up with me until this moment. I've been building walls. I didn't know that's what I was doing, but I suppose it was some defense thing, protecting myself, but I'm tired of it and I care about you and want to be with you. What do you want?"

She stopped pacing, sipping her beer, staring at him. His dark eyes lacking their usual spark and she'd done all that because she didn't want to be vulnerable and was too scared of knowing what he felt all the time.

"I want to understand."

"Understand what?"

"My grandmother and I were connected on so many levels. It used to bother me that I didn't have it with my parents, and I loved them deeply." She wiped the tears that she had no control over. Not being able to be in charge of how her body reacted to emotions scared her so much she wanted to lock them up in a deep, dark corner of her brain. "I used to think there was something wrong with me that I couldn't connect with my mother the same way and let me tell you, she was the best mother ever."

"Tamara was the only one where the connection was so deep it would totally freak anyone out. I once woke at two in the morning, startled. Her plane had just landed and I think it was the jolt."

"Seriously?"

He nodded. "No-one but twins can have that kind of deep-seated connection, I think. But we have deep emotional ties to certain people. Outside of Tamara, my grandfather on my dad's side and I have that kind of bond. Growing up, he always tried to treat us grandkids the same, but I think my siblings and cousins sensed it. It's not that he loved me more, or I was extra special or something, just a simple understanding."

"Well, I don't understand it with you," she said, slamming her beer on the counter. "I did push you away because this connection or deep bond or whatever this is, it's freaking me the fuck out."

Tristan laughed.

"It's not funny."

"If you saw your face, you'd think it was funny."

She pursed her lips. "Doubtful." But she couldn't help cracking a slight smile. "You make me crazy."

"Hopefully, that's a good thing."

"No idea," she said. "I do care about you, but I need to know you're here because you like me, not because of some duty or responsibility you feel because of my grandfather, or because I asked you for help.

He quietly set his beer down and closed the gap. Taking her hand, he placed it on the center of his chest. "I'd do almost anything you asked. I want you, and only you. I'm sure I'll manage to say something stupid every now and then, but at least you laugh when I do. As far as what will happen a few months down the road? No idea, but I'm willing to put my heart on the line."

"You are the weirdest, strangest, kindest, most adorable man I've ever met."

He circled his arms around her waist, staring deep into her eyes. "Don't push me away again."

"I can't promise I won't do that."

"At least that's honest," he whispered, before pressing his full lips against hers in a slow, tender kiss. Every cell in her body erupted in a sizzle, similar to those sparklers used on the fourth of July, going off at different times. Her muscles melted into his strong frame. Every time he'd taken her to bed…or took her in general, he'd been attentive to her needs, which seemed like an oxymoron. They'd been wild with sex, but this felt different. Not tame. It certainly got her wet with anticipation, but the way his tongue teased hers, gently stroking the inside of her mouth, told her this would be an experience of a lifetime.

She shuddered.

"Something wrong?" He kissed her neck and she shivered again. "Or do you just like that." He sucked her earlobe into his mouth and she moaned.

"Come on." He took her by the hand and led her toward the bedroom, stopping just as they crossed the threshold. He leaned against the wall, tickling his finger from her chin to her cleavage. "I like everything about you."

She looked down at her heaving chest, two of his fingers running across the top of her breasts. Sucking in a deep breath, she tried to guide his hands into her bra and over her nipples. Instead he cupped the underswell, gliding his hand down to her hips. The way he looked at her set her skin on fire. Normally, this would be the point where her patience would run thin, and she'd push him back, slamming him on the bed, straddling him. Sex had always been a game in gaining power. It was like she needed to be in control in order to keep it…just sex.

Being admired like she was the only person for a man wasn't something she'd been used to, but she never really allowed it.

Too intimate.

Too real.

Yet right now, she wanted to hang her heart out there, even if someday he broke it.

Gently, he tugged her shirt over her head.

She caught his gaze, expecting to see lust, but instead she saw something close to love. Impossible, but that's exactly what her mind and body screamed. Not the desire to be with him physically and have their bodies ravished in the primal need for sex, but the desire to create something magical, even if it did end with the same physical result, but the way you got there was different.

He smiled, as if he knew exactly what she'd been thinking. Feeling.

A quiet laugh escaped her lips.

"It's not going to be easy for me not to bend you over that bed and—"

She cupped his mouth. "Don't go and ruin the moment by putting that vision in my head."

He arched a brow.

"I want you to make love to me." The words tumbled out of her mouth. She'd never been one to separate the act of sex with making love other than most people saw some sexual acts as kinky, or not normal, where she saw all of it as an expression of caring for someone.

Only, this felt very different.

"I haven't been doing that?" he asked with an inquisitive stare.

"Maybe you have, but I've been making it only about sexual release, not feelings. Does that make sense?"

His Adam's apple bobbed up and down. "Yeah, It does."

"Does that scare you?" she asked.

He shook his head. "But your ability to go from pushing me

away, to sucking me in, does." He pressed his hands against the wall behind her.

Resting her hands on his hips, she leaned in and kissed the center of his chest. "What scares me the most is never feeling like I do right now, here, with you, again."

A deep groan vibrated from his throat as he separated her lips with his tongue. His fingers curled around her neck as his thumb gently rubbed her high cheekbone.

With her hand planted directly on the center of his chest, she felt his heartbeat, pounding in unison with hers. Wanting to feel his skin, she slowly lifted his shirt. When their lips parted, she sighed, the words they'd exchanged hanging between them, circling them, binding them, stripping her bare. Thankfully, as soon as his shirt had been tossed to the side, his hot tongue swirled around hers, sending warmth to all the right places.

Her hand shook with uncertainty as she eased her fingers into his belt, releasing the hook. His hands held her breasts with tender care. His lips touched the side of her neck like the magic of a brush against the canvas. Her body shivered and her vision blurred.

The room smelled like Tristan, a combination of sunshine and whiskey. A scent that could easily make her drunk.

His hands made their way to the clasp of her bra, releasing her aching breasts. She leaned against the wall, breathless, not knowing what to do next, as if this were the very first time she'd ever been with a man. Closing her eyes, she tried to regain her control.

"Open your eyes," he whispered.

Her eyes snapped to his, locking gazes as his finger traced a line from her chin, to the space between her breasts, over her stomach, stopping at the top of her shorts, before undoing them.

She gasped when he rolled her shorts over her hips, letting them drop to the floor. Her legs felt like puddles of melting ice cream as he guided her to the bed, laying her down with loving care.

As they removed the last few articles of clothing between them, she continued to be locked in a trance with him, unable to tear her gaze away, until he lifted her foot and kissed her ankle. His touch so affectionate. Sweet. Loving. She swallowed her breath, fighting the urge to throw up all her defenses and turn this into a session of her exerting her dominance to keep from feeling anything.

He worked his way across every inch of her exposed body, worshiping her like a temple. A flash of haze washed over her as his hand hovered over her sex. He touched her so gently she thought she'd cry out, begging him to take her, but instead, she enjoyed the exquisite torture. Her climb up the corporate ladder required her to be somewhat ruthless. Calculating. But always in control. In the bedroom, she wanted to let her hair down and be wild, having nothing to do with love.

She thought of love in terms of simple acts of kindness. Remember a birthday. A romantic dinner. A rose on Valentine's Day. Things that made you feel warm and fuzzy on the inside.

She never expected that sex could be so emotionally earth-shattering.

He stroked her insides slowly, kissing her stomach as if it were her mouth, moving his way up, sucking her nipples into his mouth, swirling his tongue over the hard nubs. His touch needy, but not urgent.

She found herself reaching for him, thinking she wanted to devour him, make him beg for release, but when her fingers curled around him, all she wanted to do was hold him. Gently caress him. Feel his soft skin against the palm of her hands. She wanted to know him. To understand him.

The room spun as he positioned himself between her legs, slowly entering her as if she were the only thing in his life that mattered. For a brief moment, she had no idea what to do.

He cupped her face, pulling back. "What's wrong?"

She blinked her eyes, feeling the sting of a tear.

"Brooke?"

She focused on his warm eyes. Her breath coming in short pants. Her need for him so strong it stunned her, excited her, but also made her feel loved. A slow smile drew across her lips. "Nothing's wrong. Everything is perfect."

He smiled, then kissed her, her tongue greeted his as heat poured out of her body. Tension building in every muscle. All her nerve endings sizzled with an electric current that seemed to be passed back and forth between their bodies until they both rocked with an uncontrollable release, shocking her. She held him tight as she convulsed underneath his weight, feeling his body tremble. Their mouths remained in a wet, passionate kiss while the aftershocks of their climaxes subsided.

He rolled off her, but kept his arms around her. "I'd say that was mind-blowing."

"Oh, my, God. You couldn't have come up with something more romantic than that?"

He laughed. "I could have said what I was really thinking."

"That I'm the best lay you've ever had."

He laughed harder. "Close enough."

"Well, you're the best I've ever had."

"Correction. I'm the best you'll ever have." He kissed her temple.

Her heart skipped a beat at the truth she felt deep in her heart.

The one she'd just given Tristan and she didn't think she'd ever get it back.

CHAPTER 10

Tristan sat outside his home, eyeing Brooke, sitting at the kitchen table with Doug, not looking very happy at all when an older model SUV rolled to a stop at the end of the driveway. A man with greying hair and a slight limp made his way down the pavement with a large envelope.

"May I help you?"

"Are you Tristan Jordan Reid?"

"I am." Tristan balled his fists knowing exactly what the man's next words were going to be.

"You've been served."

"Thanks," Tristan muttered as he took the envelope. No point in taking out his frustration on the poor guy just doing his job.

Tristan tore open the envelope and glanced at the top page, indicating that he was being sued by the Ramsworth's for two million dollars for defamation of character. He shook his head, wondering how on earth they got this lawsuit up and running. Talk about a waste of the court system.

He glanced into the kitchen where Doug held a bunch of papers bound together by a blue, thick piece of paper. The architecture plans had been pushed to the side.

She glanced over the papers, curling her lip into a snarl as she glared at him.

Well, the proposal hadn't been his idea, but he did think it was worth her listening too.

Quietly, he made his way to his bedroom, where he dumped the envelope on his nightstand.

His stomach growled, reminding him he hadn't eaten dinner yet and he really did want to hear what Doug was offering, so he made his way back to the kitchen. But the second he saw the not so happy look Brooke had shot him, a beer seemed appropriate. He stepped into the kitchen, avoiding Brooke's glare. He could only hope her temper wouldn't go off like a skyrocket.

"I think that about covers it," Doug said, gathering up the paperwork. "Not to put any pressure on, but if you could get an answer to us by early next week, we'd greatly appreciate it."

"I won't leave you hanging too long either way." Brooke stood, extending her hand. "Thanks for coming out."

"Later man," Tristan said. "Tell Stacey that I kicked Prichard's ass today."

"Will do," Doug said as he left.

Tristan took a good swing before turning his attention to Brooke.

"You could have given me a heads up," she said as she stood, shoving the contract at his chest.

"I was in the water all day and by the time I found out, he was already on his way here."

"But you knew they were putting together an offer."

He shrugged. "It wasn't my business to fill you in and besides, I didn't know what kind of offer they were making. All Stacey told me was that they had a proposition for you."

"They sure did."

"And?"

"They offered to be the bank during the renovations until my issue with the Ramsworth's is cleared up."

"That's cool."

She shook her head. "I'm not a charity case."

"I never said you were and I doubt Doug treated you that way." He kept his tone level and continued to watch the color of her eyes. He sensed frustration more than anger, but it probably wouldn't take much to set her off.

"When I told him I didn't think I could take the risk on any kind of loan, he offered, that if things went south for me, they'd give me fair market value and they'd flip it, keeping the profits since they would have taken a hit for all the materials and I'd be able to walk away."

"Did he give you a price?"

"He did." She poked her finger at the center of his chest. "You went too far."

"I didn't do anything. That deal was all Doug and Jim." The tension in the room grew and he had to find a way to keep his own temper from flaring up. Her independence was sexy as hell, but her inability to let people just do something for her drove him nuts. "What he offered is a good deal, for both parties."

"Mostly, but he's pretty set on the plans he drew up, so unless I planned on keeping the place, there's room for changes." She folded her arms, leaning against the counter, taking his beer and sipped it.

"He knows what will sell. Trust him."

"Trust him? Either way he's making money. If I take the loan, they are getting two percent, which is way lower than a bank, but still, a profit, and that feels like I'm some pet project of you and your friends."

"You're not. Doug and Jim do this kind of stuff all the time." Tristan reached in the fridge and got out another beer. "It's a fair offer and like you said, they will turn a profit either way, so I don't see how that makes you any kind of project."

"So why me? Why my grandfather's house? What makes me so damn special they decided they had to do the work, willing to take this kind of risk with their business?" She raised her arm, flapping it about in a wild gesture.

"I honestly don't know. When Doug gets it in his head he wants to renovate a property, he pretty much does whatever he can to land the project."

"Doug must be loaded."

Tristan let out a dry laugh, shaking his head. "I would have no idea and I certainly don't care either way, and neither should you. He's a good man."

"Rich people always have an agenda," she muttered. "I don't buy he's just a nice guy who wants to do me a solid."

"Not all wealthy people go around acting like Wendell and his family." If Tristan told her the truth now, she'd go bat shit on him. But if he didn't, and she found out another way, it would be worse. "If you decide to go after the Ramsworth's and paternity is proved, you'll most likely become instantly rich. Will that make you a bitch?"

"That's dumbass logic."

He arched a brow.

"If that happens, I wasn't born in to it, so it would be different."

"Do you hear yourself?"

She nodded. "Still, some rich people are assholes. Is that better?"

He raised the long neck bottle to his lips. The crisp bubbles floated across his tongue. This might be the right moment.

A car rolled down the driveway and she glanced out the window.

He frowned.

"Who drives a Rolls convertible these days?" she asked as looked between the car in the driveway and him.

"My parents do." He'd forgotten he'd made dinner plans with his parent's weeks ago.

"Shut the front door." She stared at him, mouth gapping open.

"I think we should open it, actually."

She narrowed her gaze, then jumped when his father tapped on the door.

Tristan quickly maneuvered around her. "Hey Dad, come on in." His father had gone totally grey, but he wore it well. "You can set that down on the kitchen table."

"Thanks, son," his father said, glancing toward Brooke.

"Mom, let me take that for you." Tristan kissed his mother on the cheek, taking the salad bowl from her perfectly manicured hands. His mother had always had a flare for fashion and style, having gotten her degree in fashion design.

"Brooke, this is my dad, Albert and my mom, Helen."

"Nice to meet you Brooke," his father said. "I hope you're joining us for dinner tonight."

"I hadn't asked her yet." He smiled in her direction, where she gave him a seething stare. "Join us? Please?"

"I don't think so, but thanks for the offer."

"Oh, no, dear," his mother said, taking Brooke's hand. "I insist you stay. We've heard quite a lot about you."

"You have?" Brooke asked with wide eyes, before turning them into tiny slits.

Tristan swallowed. "Your grandfather had dinner with us a couple of times."

"We're very sorry for your loss," his father said. "If you don't have any place to be just now, we'd love to have you join us."

"Thank you." Brooke stepped back. "But I don't want to intrude on family time."

"No intrusion at all." His mother stepped into the kitchen, doing a three-sixty with her arms in the air. "Where are the steaks?"

"In the freezer." Tristan cringed. "I had recertification all day and I forgot to take them out this morning."

His mother laughed. "Pay up." She held her hand out in front of his father. "Then go get the steaks out of the car."

"Son." His father pulled out his wallet and handed his mother a crisp ten-dollar bill. "You owe me ten bucks."

"I'm not the idiot who bet I'd remember during SCUBA week." Tristan ducked his head into the fridge. "I have beer, a bottle of white wine that we opened yesterday, and red if anyone wants that."

"I should go," Brooke said, turning to follow his father out the door.

"Where? You have an appointment somewhere or something." his mother asked.

"No, she doesn't. She's just mad at me." Tristan held up the bottle of white and his mother nodded, holding up two fingers.

He ignored Brooke, since she looked like she might shoot him.

"I'm going to apologize for whatever my son did or said, but he didn't have the best role model in his father. That man doesn't have a romantic bone in his body."

"Neither do you," his father said as he re-entered the kitchen. "This woman's idea of a romantic dinner is a burger and fries at the local greasy spoon."

"Oh, and your idea of a romantic date is any better?" His mother waggled her finger. "He's lucky I married him."

"Please, do tell. I have to know," Brooke said, the lightness in her voice coming back.

"Dad took my mother to see some war movie on their first Valentine's Day as a couple that was so gory, even I wouldn't stomach it." Tristan handed his mother a glass, holding the other one out to Brooke, who graciously took it, but didn't smile at him.

"If you want to neck at the movies, you always take a girl to one where she'll need to close her eyes. She'll cuddle right up against you." His father smiled wide.

"Men. You can't live with them and you can't shoot them," his mother said.

"I'll second that." Brooke clinked her glass with his mother's.

Tristan guzzled his beer, almost wishing he hadn't just introduced Brooke to his parents.

Almost.

At least they'd show her that rich people could be decent, normal human beings, though there was nothing normal about his family, that was for damn sure.

"Shall I go on about women, because I could, you know," his father said.

"Don't even try to go there." His mother lovingly shoved his father's arm. "No need to show what a bunch of adolescents you men are to Tristan's friend."

Brooke laughed. "My grandmother used to tell me she did the happy dance when I was born because she didn't think she could handle having another male who would never grow up."

"I like the way your grandmother thinks." Helen raised her glass again.

"Let's sit outside while we wait for the grill to heat up." Tristan shuffled everyone outside, taking the open bottle of wine and putting it a small bucket of ice with a couple more beers.

They sat on the front patio, facing the lake. His mother and father sat in the two rocking chairs, while he and Brooke shared the love seat, though she sat all the way on the other end, leaning away from him.

The sun still shined over the mountains. It would be another hour and a half before it set. His neighbor's children laughed as they splashed each other in the water.

"So, what do you do for a living Brooke?" his father asked. He'd always been the inquisitive type, asking questions, but he generally didn't pry. That was left up to his mother, but she never stuck her nose in too deep.

"I'm between jobs right now, but my last position was as a regional sales manager." She shifted, but still remained as far away as she possibly could. He really wanted to toss his arm around her and pull her close, just to see her reaction.

She glared at him, probably sensing what he wanted to do. This connection thing kind of sucked sometimes.

"This is the young woman you mentioned that might be looking for a new career opportunity?" his father asked.

Tristan sucked in a breath, letting out slowly, feeling the rage seep from Brooke's skin. "Yes, sir."

His father scrunched his nose. "I'm sorry if I said something I shouldn't have."

"I just hadn't had the chance to tell her the person I'd talked to was my father." Tristan sipped his beer, ignoring the stares coming from both his girlfriend and his mother.

"Feel free to send me your resume and cover letter with references and I'll put it in front of my department heads."

"I appreciate that, but I don't want to take advantage." Brooke set her glass down, shifting again.

"You're not. I can't promise anything other than putting your resume in the right piles. I don't influence my people on who to hire. They won't know who you are or that you're my son's girlfriend."

Tristan tensed, glancing toward Brooke, who pursed her lips.

"Thank you. But before I send my resume, what company is this and where is it located?"

"Highland Pharmaceutical."

Brooke had raised her wine glass, but stopped short as she coughed.

Both his parents exchanged glances.

Tristan looked out toward the water as Brooke put it all together.

"We have offices all over the state. If you'd like, I can get my HR people to send you a list of employment opportunities in sales management and you can apply directly for those."

"I think that's the best way to go about it." Brooke forced a smile, but the tension in the air tripled. "I do have a head hunter looking at various prospects."

"Why don't you boys go start the steaks," his mother said with a sweet, but stern tone.

"Yes, ma'am." Tristan knew better than to argue with his mother, but he wasn't too keen on leaving her alone with Brooke. She never meddled too much, but she did have an intuitive side, and she could be blunt.

Too blunt.

"I think that's our cue to leave." His father rose and headed toward the side of the house, Tristan following behind.

"None of my business son, but what the hell did you do?" his father asked once out of earshot of the ladies.

"It's more like what I didn't do." Tristan opened the grill, hot steam floated out in a big puff.

"And what's that?" Up until Tamara had died, his father had always been a good sounding board. They had a good relationship and most things he'd always been comfortable talking about with his father, including the mandatory sex talk, which had been the most hilarious conversation he'd ever had with his father as a young boy. His father had begun by sitting him down in his office and asked him what he knew about having intercourse with a woman. Tristan, being the smart ass that he'd always been, decided to have a little fun with his father and his knowledge of sex. Besides his father being stunned, Tristan learned he had a few things wrong.

"I didn't tell her the lifestyle to which I was born."

"Why does it matter?"

"It shouldn't, but she literally didn't know until you pulled up and once you mentioned Highland, well, I'm sure she put it all together and it pissed her off. Honesty is a hot button for her."

His father lowered his chin, giving him that obnoxious stare he used whenever Tristan did something or said something stupid. "Lying is a hot button with all women." His father planted his hands on his hip in a father stance.

Tristan unwrapped the steaks and tossed them on the grill, then turned,

For two years after the death of his sister, Tristan couldn't talk to his father about anything and that wasn't just on Tristan. His father had shut down too. The entire family had, but Tamara had been daddy's little girl. She might have been a tomboy, but she'd been daddy's princess. His mother had always told him that there was something special about father's and their daughters.

But during those two years, Tristan not only had to deal with the death of his twin, but his father had checked out for a while as well.

Things were different now, and Tristan worked through a lot of life's issues with his dad, but some of this story wasn't his to tell.

"I can't get into all the details, because that would be breaking her trust, something I can't afford to do at this point."

"You don't have to tell me anything, if you're not comfortable doing so."

Tristan poked at the steaks, sticking a thermometer inside each one before closing the grill. "She's had some problems with the Ramsworth's."

"Who are they?" his father asked, leaning against the side of the house. He'd put on some weight over the years, but he still had a muscular build. Also had a good two inches on Tristan and years of wisdom.

"They live in the big house at the end of Mason Road."

"Oh yeah. Your mother once had words with one of them at a charity event and I believe we turned down some joint venture with the youngest one, who if you ask me is an arrogant ass." One thing his father never tolerated in his children, or the people who worked for him, was arrogance. He'd pull out of any deal if the person he had to work with acted as though they were better than the rest of the world.

Tristan nodded. "They're all assholes and for generations they have been treating her family badly."

"How so?" His father never made a judgment call without having all the facts, so he often didn't give advice if he hadn't been provided all the details. Tristan wasn't looking for advice, but support, and he wasn't sure how to get to the heart of the matter.

"A lot of different reasons. Accusations against her grandmother. Conflict between Brooke and the jackass you turned down."

"I see. But what does that have to do with you not telling her right off the bat about your financial status, which quite frankly, you shouldn't be doing any way." His father pointed a finger at him. "Again, young, rich, attractive man." His father arched a brow.

"Really, dad? We're going to have THAT conversation. I live a modest life for many reasons, one of which is being tired of people treating me differently just because I have money."

"Your youngest brother thinks you're ashamed of it."

Tristan shook his head. "He's not even out of high school yet, what the hell does he know?"

"Everything, if you ask him." His father laughed. "My point is, money, having it or not having it, is the source of many conflicts, but she if she cares about you, and did before she found out, why the hell does it matter now?

"Because money rubs her the wrong way."

"It rubs you the wrong way." His father slapped his back. "Except for that damn car of yours. How'd you explain that one?"

"That I did lie about, saying the bank owned it. But considering where I live, I suppose she believed me." This conversation wasn't going quite as Tristan had planned. It shouldn't be this difficult to have a deep conversation with his father. They did it all the time, but not about love and never about strong connections.

"Don't tell your mother you lied."

"Not planning on it, but she could get it out of Brooke."

"That's true." His father sipped his beer. "You haven't known Brooke that long, and no offense, but you have always had shitty taste in women."

"What the hell is that supposed to mean? I've gone out with some really nice women, Brooke being the nicest one of all."

"I'm not talking about Brooke." His father set the beer down on the side of the grill, looping his arm over Tristan's shoulder. "She's not like any woman you've ever dated that we've met. The others all needed constant reassurance and attention. Brooke seems confident and smart. A woman who knows what she wants and how to get it."

"She's one of a kind."

"I can tell you really like her." His father squeezed his shoulder, before stepping away. "Give her a little time to absorb this new information."

Boy, was his father in for the shock of his life. "You know how mom is always saying I'm some sort of empath or whatever?"

"Her way of saying you've got a big heart, always thinking about other people. I remember when you were little and we were skiing. Someone dropped their glove from the chairlift and you had to hike up the hill to give it to them."

Tristan smiled at the memory. "I'm glad I never went to law school. I love being a Trooper, and helping people is what I'm good at."

His father nodded, his face turning serous. "What are you getting at, son?"

"Brooke, she's in my head."

"What do you mean?" His father reached out, steadying himself against the house, staring at him with wide eyes.

"She's also in here." Tristan tapped his chest. "So much so that it feels like that part of me that died with Tamara never really died, just needed to be awakened."

His father stared at him for a long moment, a single tear rolling down his cheek. "That's some heavy shit, son."

"Dad, I don't know what I'd do if I lost Brooke."

"Jesus, you're in love with her."

The last thing Brooke wanted to do was sit on the front porch with Tristan's mother, but since she chose not to leave when she had the chance, no point in being rude.

"Your grandfather was a class act," Helen said as she glided across the concrete patio to sit on the love seat.

"He was the best." Brooke smiled as sweetly as she could.

"Tristan was quite fond of him. He once told us that Rusty wanted to fix him up with his granddaughter."

Brooke let out a soft chuckle. "I think my grandfather had a man crush on Tristan, more so than he wanted us to meet."

"But now you've met." Helen turned sideways, tucking one foot under her butt. Her pink toes matched the color on her fingertips. Her short bob perfectly styled. She wore little make-up and her skin appeared to be flawless. It was difficult to guess her age, but Brooke figured it was a few years older than she looked. "I will apologize for being so forward, but what did my son do to upset you so much?"

How the hell did she answer that when being truthful about it would make her look like one big ass bitch.

"It's nothing, really."

Helen arched her brow, exactly like Tristan did.

Brooke cracked a smile. "He does that all the time."

"We all do." Helen sipped her wine, before setting the glass on the ground. "My son doesn't often think before he speaks. I'm afraid that's partially my fault because I was one of those parents who couldn't control my laughter at some of the more inappropriate things that came out of my children's mouths."

"He's quite funny, in a weird way," Brooke admitted, wondering why she felt a kindred spirit in Helen. "His blunders make me laugh, though he doesn't do it as often as he thinks he does."

Helen arched both brows. "When he was about three, I had him and his twin sister in a grocery cart, trying to get in a little shopping. He saw an overweight woman with an open bag of cookies and she was munching on them. He stood up and said, 'Mom, that's why she can't lose weight' I damn near died of embarrassment right there."

"Out of the mouths of babes."

"His twin did manage to get him to shut his trap most of the time, but anyone who dared to fish for a complement from Tristan, better be prepared for the truth and not what you want to hear."

That statement hit the nail on the head.

"You're smiling," Helen said.

"Does Tristan date a lot of insecure women?"

"I don't get to meet many of the girls he's dated, but yes. Drives his father nuts." Helen leaned in. "Did he tell you about Tamara?" There was an unmistakable tremor to her voice.

"He did. I'm sorry. There are no words."

Helen closed her eyes and nodded. When she opened them, they were moist. "Those two were inseparable. Neither Albert or I understood their bond. We appreciated it, but twins are unique. They were each other's world and they did almost everything together. It worried me because I thought it unhealthy for them not to have many friends outside of each other. She never had a best girlfriend, and he didn't have many guy friends. As they became teenagers, I wonder what would happen if they didn't go to the same college. When she died, Tristan seemed gone to us too. There was no reaching him. People always say that losing a child is the worst pain in the world, and it is, but losing a twin has to be equally as devastating, and it took Tristan a long time to get to a point where he could live his life without her."

"I've had a lot of loss in my life with my parents and grandparents, but I still can't imagine how you and Tristan feel."

Helen placed her soft hand on Brooke's shoulder. "That's just it, I think you can. I think you feel it."

Boy, was his family into this whole sensing thing.

But she couldn't deny it either. "I can empathize."

"You care about my son. I can tell."

Another thing she couldn't deny. She nodded. "But it's complicated."

"It's only as complicated as you make it." Helen smiled. "You still haven't told me what he said or did that had you so angry."

"I wasn't that angry."

Helen arched a brow and Brook laughed.

"I like persistence." Brooke felt herself melting into this woman's kind heart. There wasn't a single thing she didn't like about her, even though she tried to dislike her outwardly perfection. "He didn't tell me he was the son of *the* Albert Reid, Founder and CEO of Highland Pharmaceuticals." She shook her head. "I did a paper on Highland for one of my master business classes. I can't believe I didn't put two and two together."

Helen waved her hand in the air. "I tried to teach my children not to flaunt what we had. That's just rude, but I didn't want them to be embarrassed by it. Sometimes I think Tristan resents it."

"I don't think it's that at all." Talk about rude. Brooke had known Tristan for a week and here she was telling his mother about the man's inner psyche about his childhood. "I believe it's more about blending in and a way to keep himself cut off enough, that he doesn't have to really let anyone in too deep, even though he says he wants to."

"Wow," Helen said, tucking her hair behind her ears. "That's quite insightful."

"I don't know if I'm right, but from what I know about him, I suspect being a twin made him feel special somehow, having her gone, he's trying to be normal, living without that bond, not forming any new ones."

"Where have you been all his life?" Helen smiled. "That makes perfect sense. Are you sure you're not a psychiatrist?"

"I did minor in psychology. It often comes in handy working in sales and management."

"I bet." Helen picked up her glass, refilling it and Brooke's. "But there is one problem with being that knowledgeable about the inner workings of other people."

"And what's that?" Brooke asked, knowing the answer. Her mind worked on the rebuttal, because she didn't want to believe it.

"You don't truly understand yourself because you're too busy immersing yourself into other people. For Tristan, it's taking on the emotional parts of people, especially in a large crowd and he pulls away because it can be overwhelming. I'm much the same way. For you though, it's different."

"What do you mean?" Brooke found herself sitting on the edge of her seat, as if she were listening to the most enthralling tale, waiting for the punch line that would either send her off in a fit of laughter, or touch her so deeply she could shed a tear.

"Everyone wants to believe they're empathic, and most people are. However, not everyone can sense other people's emotions. I accepted that early on about myself and embraced it. Tristan had his twin, which is an even stronger connection. I suspect you've had a deep connection with someone, but you seem to think being able to feel others versus understanding them, as a weakness. You've spent a lifetime denying your true self. I suspect that has been catching up to."

Brooke blinked. She'd spent so much time with Tristan over the last week, that she can't imagine when he would have had the time to speak with his mother in great detail about her and her situation. Nor did she think he would ever give up that much about her, or anyone. He just wasn't that kind of man.

Helen took Brooke's hand between her palms, holding them firmly. "I'm going to way over step my bounds."

Brooke wanted to tell her she already had, only she enjoyed Helen being in her space. It was like being around her grandmother again.

"I was shocked when Tristan told us, in front of you, that you were mad. Normally, he'd let you leave, shrug his shoulders, and that would be the end of that. But he wanted you to stay, he would have even swallowed his pride and begged."

Brooke opened her mouth, but Helen shook her head.

"And then there is the fact you stayed. You knew he wasn't manipulating you because I believe he knows that no matter how much you care for him, you'll always stand on your own two feet. Independence is intoxicating when you mix it with a desire to share everything with someone."

"That sounds crazy," Brooke said softly.

"Love always is, honey."

CHAPTER 11

When Tristan returned to the porch to inform his mother and Brooke that dinner was ready, he'd been truly terrified about what might have been said. It wouldn't be the first time his mother tried to meddle in his life.

Actually, meddle wasn't the right word, because she'd never told him what to do or how to do it, but she did have a way of saying things that were probably better off left unsaid, often making others uncomfortable.

Brook looked anything but uneasy. She looked down right engaged with his mother.

He stood next to Brooke in the kitchen, taking the dishes she'd washed, drying them before putting them away, while his parents enjoyed the sunset on the dock.

"Sorry I put you in a tough spot when my parents showed up. I appreciate you staying."

She handed him the last dish to be dried. "With everything that has gone on between us, I don't understand why you didn't tell me you were loaded. I mean, can you blame me for being upset?"

"It's not something I go around letting people know the moment I meet them and by the time I deemed it appropriate, you were going to be pissed no matter how you found out." He dried the dish vigorously, before tossing it haphazardly in the pot drawer. "You can be mad at me all you want, but I don't like being treated differently because I come from a privileged background and I sure as hell don't like to toss it around like it puts me above anyone else. My parents are good people and could care less what anyone else has or doesn't have, so please don't go judging them until after you get to know them better." He swallowed. "And if I'd told you my family was rich, you'd judge me to be just like Wendell Ramsworth, and trust me, I'm nothing like that asshole."

"Want to tell me how you really feel?" She brushed her arm against his, taking his hand.

He laced his fingers through hers, a sense of relief eased off his shoulders. "I've wanted to get that off my chest all evening."

"I do know you're not like them, but not telling me feels like you've kept something from me and makes me wonder about last night and—"

He pressed his finger against her lips. "I'm not keeping anything from you and if you asked me who my father was, I wouldn't have lied. As far as last night goes? It was by far the most powerful, amazing sexual experience I've ever had."

She laughed. "Mind-blowing worked better."

He growled. "You make me nuts."

"Good. Someone has to keep you on your toes."

He circled his arms around her, feeling her heart pressed against his, beating in unison. "I should tell you that my father was serious about not giving you a recommendation for hire. Being my girlfriend is kind of a strike against you.:

"Who says I'm your girlfriend?"

"I do," he said. "Anyway, my father never hires anyone as a favor to anyone else. Hell, he even made my brother go through blind interviews. He didn't get the first three positions he applied for and he's making less than I am as a Trooper right now."

"I was a little pissed about that too, but after talking with your dad more, I know I'll be hired only if I'm a good fit."

"I haven't told him that you were fired or the criminal charges."

"I did."

He arched a brow and she laughed.

"That must be the Reid go to expression."

He nodded, annoyed she redirected the conversation. "And?"

"He suggested I wait until the criminal charges have officially been dropped before applying and to make sure I've got top notch referrals to make up for not being able to use my past employer. Only thing is, I'm not sure I can wait that long to get a job."

"You might have to."

She leaned against him, kissing his cheek. "Would you ever go to work for your father?"

"Hell no. The only thing I would consider other than what I'm doing now would be another form of law enforcement job."

"I like a man who knows who he is."

"You more than like me." He tipped her chin, then leaned closer. "And I'm falling in love with you," he whispered.

"Turn on the evening news," his father said as he barreled through the front door, his mother running right behind him.

"What? Why?" Tristan searched for his phone in the kitchen, but then realized he'd left it in the bedroom. Normally, when anything big broke, his phone would blow up before it hit the news.

"You're on the news," his mother said.

"No way." Tristan hated being interviewed for anything and avoided making statements to the press whenever possible. He tugged at Brooke's hand, pulling her into the family room, and stood behind the sofa where his parents had perched themselves as his father flipped through the channels.

"Do you have that thing where if you hit record, you can go back and watch the entire show?" his father asked, glancing over his shoulder.

"Give me that." Tristan took the controller. "Who told you I was on the news?"

"One of your brothers," his mother said, biting her fingernail.

He hit the record button, then rewound, seeing flashes of his picture from the Academy next to a picture of his father, followed by Brooke's mug shot and ending with a picture of Wendell giving a press conference last year. "You've got to be kidding me." He hit play before tossing the remote across the room.

Brooke squeezed his shoulder, only calming him a little bit. He didn't care that he'd been outed as one of the heirs to the self-made billionaire, except that it could potentially harm his father and family…because of his association with Brooke.

And that pissed him off even more because in a matter of a month, there'd be no criminal charges and her record would be expunged.

"Local State Trooper, Tristan Reid and the son of Albert Reid, the CEO of Highlands Pharmaceutical," the newscaster said, "has been named in a law suit filed by Wendell Knoll Ramsworth the III for defamation of character, sources close to the family say. The same sources also indicate that Sergeant Reid has been interfering in an investigation into property allegedly stolen years ago by Brooke Fowler's late grandmother, Ashley Fowler, while under the employment of the Ramsworth's. Brooke has a known history of violence, recently being arrested for assault. The Ramsworth's declined an interview and we have yet to hear from either Sergeant Reid or Brooke Fowler."

"Mother fucking asshole," Tristan said, not caring his mother gave him a disapproving glare. "I just got served this evening."

"You got what?" Brooke yelled, grabbing his arm and squeezing way too hard. Her eyes turned fire red.

"It happened while you were talking to Doug, then my parents showed up. I was going to show you the papers when we went to bed tonight. Will you please let go of my arm?" He didn't want to shrug it off, but he needed his phone and while he understood she was upset, it wasn't really because he hadn't had the chance to tell her yet.

She lifted her hand into the air, then pointed to the television. "You didn't think something like that would make the local news?"

"Nothing I can do to prevent it." Tristan stepped around her. "I need to find out if my boss, or internal has tried to contact me. When it comes to accusations against police officers, the higher ups tend to give a statement, even if it's to say they have no comment."

"I'm going to have to get on the horn with my legal team to see how we can fight back," his father said as he stood, hands on his hips. "I'm not taking this one standing down."

"Dad, yes you are, at least until I know what State is going to do. You come out swinging, it will just make it worse." Tristan stomped into his bedroom, snagged his phone just as his boss, Jared called, for the fifth time in the last three minutes.

"Did you know about this story?" Tristan didn't bother with a greeting.

"No. I did not. Nor has anyone in State been contacted for a statement. Were you really served?"

"Dinner time, then family things came up. I didn't think it would turn into a shit storm in four hours." He scanned his phone and other than messages from buddies coming in over the last ten minutes, nothing from anyone higher up. "This story stinks of Wendell and his petty games. This is the last thing my father needs, not to mention Brooke."

"Tristan," his mother snapped, standing in his doorway.

He held up his hand. "Stacey texted saying she's got a friend at the news station, so she's going to contact her."

"That's a start, but I'm going to have to make an official statement by morning. I'll be by shortly so we can go over things. Call Jillian too."

"On it," Tristan said, rolling his neck.

"Tristan!" His mother stood in front of him.

"Got to go boss, see you shortly." He tapped his phone. "What?"

"It's Brooke. She left."

"Shit," he muttered. "Did you try to stop her?"

"We tried," his father said, with a hand on his mother's shoulder. "But she said she needed to talk to someone by the name of Michelle."

"That is sooooo not good." Tristan retrieved his gun from the closet, hooking it to his belt along with his badge.

"Why?" his mother asked.

"Remember me about eighteen months after Tamara died?"

"Yes," his parents answered grimly.

"She's not far from hitting that boiling point. She'd been doing better, but really, this could easily send her over the edge."

His parents stepped to the side like the red sea parting.

He ran outside as a few clouds rolled across the moon. He tried calling Brooke, but she sent him straight to voice mail. So, he texted.

Nothing.

He took off jogging down the street, wondering how she planned on getting Michelle's attention. He just hoped it wasn't by tossing bricks over the gate. So far, he sensed frustration, but that tickle of rage was right behind it.

He slowed as he passed her house, seeing her under the street lights in front of the Ramsworth Manor, pacing, phone to her ear, yelling. He couldn't blame her for being royally pissed off and wanting to confront the source. Hell, he wanted to do the exact same thing, only he knew it was pointless and would cause more problems than it solved.

"Brooke," he said as he crossed the road. "Stop yelling."

She held her hand up.

"Michelle, you answered my phone call, which tells me you're willing to talk, so get your ass out here."

Tristan raised his finger to his lips, hoping she'd at least quiet down.

All she did was glare at him as she continued to pace, listening to whatever Michelle had to say.

"I don't want to talk to him," Brooke said, stopping in her tracks. "Come on Michelle, you said you wanted to start over, so let's talk."

"What are you doing?" Tristan asked quietly.

She held up her hand again. "Thank you," she said as she tapped her phone. "She's going to come out and talk to me."

"About what?"

"Everything, I thought I could chat with her and see if she'll let me know what the hell her husband is up too. But if I see Wendell, no telling what I'll do"

Headlights flashed from the north end of the street, blinding

Tristan momentarily. "I wish you hadn't stormed out of my house. My parents are worried."

"I am sorry about that."

He glanced over her shoulder at the oncoming car, traveling a little too fast for his liking. He took her by the elbow, moving her closer to the gate.

"I know you're a private man and didn't want the world to know everything about you, but also, your dad doesn't deserve this. He's quite remarkable, being self-made. I really admire him."

"I'm freaking out here a bit because I thought you went off half-cocked to string Wendell by his balls." Tristan tapped the butt of his gun.

"I'm not past crushing that man's nuts, but I also want to warn Michelle of what is to come. She's pregnant and that changes things. I texted Jillian that I want to go forward with claiming paternity. Mind you, I don't want their money, but if I can make that lawsuit go away, flip the house, get a job, I can move on."

"Fuck," Tristan muttered as Jared's truck rolled to a stop on the other side of the street. "My boss is here."

"Go home, you two," Jared said through the window. "They called 9-1-1 and a local is on the way."

"Are you serious?" Brooke tossed her arms up in the air.

"Come on." Tristan grabbed her hand, holding it tight. "Give us a ride to my place?"

"Yeah," Jared said waving his arm. "Because it's such a long walk."

"What was the complaint?" Tristan tried to help Brooke into the back of Jared's truck, but shrugged his hand off and climbed in.

"Man with a gun and a woman harassing them." Jared quickly rammed the truck into drive and took the corner a little sharp.

"Did they say it was us?" Brooke asked.

This up and down emotional rollercoaster the Ramsworth's had her on wasn't good for dealing with all the anger that still bubbled just under the surface.

"They did, but I wouldn't worry about it since I've been with you most of the time and there was no threat," Jared said looking in the rear-view mirror.

"That would be lying and I wouldn't want anyone to do that for me. I've put all of you through enough." Brooke stared out the window.

"It's not lie," Jared said. "I was on my way to Tristan's and saw you march across the street, phone in hand. I shut my lights off and sat at the marina, watching until I heard dispatch looking for a first responder."

The next fifteen minutes passed in silence as they entered Tristan's house and sat around the kitchen table waiting for local to show up, which didn't take as long as he thought and lucky for him, it was a local he'd worked with before.

"Sorry to bother," the officer said. "We had a call that you and your girlfriend were outside a neighbor's house threatening and waving a gun around."

Brooke stood, pushing the chair back, nearly knocking it over.

"Sit down," Jared said in deep tone.

Tristan glanced over his shoulder, eyeing her, cautiously.

She let out a huff of air before sitting down.

"We were there. I did have my weapon." Tristan tapped the butt of his gun. "But it remained holstered and Brooke was on the phone with Michelle, who is an old friend of hers, trying to mend broken fences."

"I need to talk to Brooke," the officer said. "Mrs. Ramsworth said you threatened her and her unborn child."

Tristan stepped back into the kitchen, pressing his hand on Brooke's shoulder.

"I never threatened her," Brooke said evenly. "I asked her to come outside and talk with me about a news story that broke and inform her of some of the details she doesn't know about."

"I watched the entire incident from my vehicle down the street," Jared said. "An inflammatory story on one of my troopers was misrepresented and we're just trying to get to the bottom of it."

"Thanks for your time," the officer said. "Though I'd recommend you keep your distance from the Ramsworth's."

Tristan closed the door, knowing he would not keep his distance, but he would play it smart. His phone buzzed. "Stacey's friend said the news anchor had been blindsided. The story wasn't supposed to air until everything had been verified, so now they're scrambling."

"That will make it easier to force a retraction," Jared said. "Can Stacey get her friend to sign an affidavit that the story was pushed through?"

"Stacey is already on it, but the only thing that was falsely reported was my interference and that there was even a new criminal case building." Tristan knew the system and in his case, he knew it would work for him, but for Brooke? She could end up royally screwed. "The bigger problem is the DA can rescind his offer to clear Brooke's name even after she completes classes and community service, which is why I suspect Wendell did this in the first place."

"You mean to tell me I could have to check yes to being convicted?" Brooke said slamming her hand on the table.

"Not necessarily," Jared said. "I'm sure Jillian can figure all that out. What I want to know is why out Tristan as a millionaire?"

"Makes me look like a liar and makes my integrity suspect. It's a simple deflection," Tristan said.

"If they know there is a question of paternity, why make this all public? Seems like they'd buy you off instead," Jared said.

"We're all forgetting something here." Tristan couldn't begin to understand Wendell's logic. But it didn't matter. "Wendell number one is still kicking and he's the one who gave the necklace to your grandmother in the first place."

"We have no reason to talk to him," Jared pointed out.

"But there is no reason why Brooke can't contact him." Tristan arched a brow.

"I don't like the sound of that, but I can't stop you." Jared shook his head. "Also, rumors milling about that the old man is losing his mind, so even if you get anything out of him, they will say it's gibberish from a dying man."

"I just got a text from Jillian." Brooke held up her phone. "She thinks because of the news tonight, that tomorrow I should prepare my own suit claiming to be an heir to the Ramsworth's fortune."

"You good with doing that? Making this thing even more public? We could go to them quietly," Tristan said.

"That's what Jillian is recommending. We go to them first with what we have and if they want to keep pursuing this, I file suit."

"Not to be a total dick, but I am going to enjoy making those people squirm." Tristan hated what it could do to Brooke, but if he got to take a few more jabs at Wendell and Brooke got her life back, it would all be worth it in the end.

CHAPTER 12

Brooke sat at the kitchen table in Tristan's home, scanning various job opportunities at a few dozen companies, including Highland Pharmaceutical. One in particular stood out as head of regional sales for all of New York. It appealed to her for various reasons, but the one that stuck out the most had been because she could stay close to Tristan.

I'm falling in love with you.

His words still echoed in her brain, sending her heart on a wild rampage. After he'd said the words, all hell broke loose. They'd gone to bed exhausted, both falling asleep as soon as their heads hit the pillow. This morning, he left before she awoke, leaving her a note that said he'd be sure to check his phone as often as he could.

They shared a few texts, but the day had been uneventful on her end, with the exception of setting in motion the confrontation about paternity.

Brooke glanced at her phone. It was nearly six in the evening and she figured at this point she wouldn't hear anything about Jillian's note to the Ramsworth's until tomorrow.

A tapping at the door startled Brooke, but she gasped when she saw Michelle standing at Tristan's front door. "What are you doing here?"

"Let me in, please." Michelle glanced over her shoulder, holding her middle. "Please. Wendell can't know I'm here."

As a young girl, Michelle had been shy and quiet. Mousey. At first, Brooke hadn't particularly liked Michelle, but it bothered Brooke that the other girls picked on her because of her shyness. Brooke had befriended Michelle and found out there had been a lot more to the girl than what appeared on the outside.

However today, Brooke stared at that same young, scared little girl she'd meet all those years ago. "Fine, come in." Brooke waved her hand.

Michelle stepped through the door, quickly shutting it behind her, pulling down the blind.

"What's going on?" Brooke asked.

"I don't have much time. Wendell thinks I went for a walk."

"Much time for what?" Brooke leaned back in her chair and folded her arms.

"They got the request for paternity and the entire family is flipping out." Michelle stood next to the door, constantly peeking out the window. "I think my husband's grandmother has always suspected her husband had an affair and produced a child, but I don't think they expected it could be your father."

"Not like it's something I suspected…or wanted." Brooke waved to the chair next to her. "I didn't want to go public with this entire fiasco. All I want is for the lawsuits to go away and to be left alone." Tension filled the air like a thick fog on a dark and creepy night.

"Grandmama doesn't like to be strong armed into anything and she's still holding on to the idea that your grandmother stole the necklace." Michelle sat at the opposite end of the table, one hand on her swollen belly, the other twirling her earring.

"I have proof she didn't, and once a paternity test is completed, she won't be able to deny it anymore." Brooke sensed an overall sadness filling the dense air.

"You need to stop. Wendell and his father are going to destroy you and your boyfriend if you don't."

"I didn't start this mess." Brooke leaned back folding her arms, doing her best not to go 'ballistic' on the woman who used to be her best friend. "But I'm not going to let them destroy Tristan. And their stunt last night, manipulating the news like that? What the hell do they have against Tristan's father anyway?"

Michelle glanced over her shoulder. "Wendell went nuts when he found out about Tristan. Figured he was the reason some deal with Albert Reid went south."

Brooke wasn't going to touch that one with a ten-foot pole. "Why are you here?"

"To ask you, for my sake, to let this go." Michelle looked everywhere but directly at Brooke.

"I told you, I'd be more than happy to when they drop all the lawsuits."

Michelle shook her head. "That's not going to happen. They know you don't have the money to fight them and they can drag this on forever." Michelle looked into Brooke's eyes for a long moment, then dropped her gaze to the floor. "They have the pictures."

Brooke narrowed her eyes. "You are a piece of work."

"I didn't know Wendell still had them."

"And that's supposed to make me feel better? You gave them to him in the first place. We were best friends. The only thing I ever did to you was point out that your husband is a cheating drunk."

"Wendell's changed." Michelle bobbed her head up and down. "The DUI forced his hand and then when I got pregnant, he really committed."

"So, you admit he's a cheater." Brooke chomped down on her lip. Her words had been harsher than she expected. Then again, the truth always hurt.

"Wendell isn't perfect, but I love him." She patted her belly. "Being a parent changes people."

Not Wendell, Brooke thought.

"He's been sober now for three months."

"Well, good for him," Brooke said, trying to be somewhat supportive, but failing miserably. "You don't look happy."

"You don't know me anymore." Michelle stiffened, squaring her shoulders. "You tossed our friendship out the window."

"No. I didn't." Brooke leaned in, staring at Michelle. Dark circles formed under her sad eyes. Her arms, covered with a light sweater, wrapped tightly around her middle.

The temperature had hit eighty-six in the late afternoon, and the humidity had been at an all-time high.

"Does he hurt you?" Brooke reached out, her hand hovering over Michelle's arm.

"Don't be so dramatic."

"You're wearing a sweater in the middle of summer." Gently, Brooke rested her hand on Michelle's arm.

Michelle jerked it away and that's when Brooke saw the bruise on Michelle's neck and shoulder, just near the top of her sweater.

Brooke swallowed a sob. "Oh sweetie," she said softly. "How long has this been going on?"

"You're crazy and have it in for my husband and his family." Michelle jerked back the chair and stood. "And now that you think you could be a Ramsworth, you're just trying to get your hands on their money."

"Do you hear yourself?" Brooke took a tentative step forward. "Let me help you. No one deserves to be hit."

"You don't know what you're talking about."

Tires squealed in the driveway, drawing Brooke's attention to the four-door black sedan that came to a screeching halt.

"Oh no," Michelle whispered. "That's Wendell."

"Go to the front bedroom. He'll never know you're here." Brooke grabbed Michelle by the arm, tugging at her, but she wouldn't move.

She just stood there frozen, staring into space with wide eyes.

"Go," Brooke pleaded. "I'll handle him."

But it was too late as he came barreling through the front door. "Get in the car, Michelle," Wendell barked.

Brooke stepped between him and his wife. "She's not going anywhere with you and I'm calling the police." Brooke yanked her cell phone from her back pocket, but he slapped her hand, sending the phone to the floor.

"Don't make me repeat myself, Michelle." Wendell shoved Brooke to the side, her back hitting the corner of the counter.

She groaned, feeling her skin tear.

Wendell took his wife by the hair.

"Get your fucking hands off her." Brooke lunged, forcing her way between Wendell and Michelle. "You're a pathetic excuse for a man."

Wendell raised his other hand and Brooke flung her arms in the air to protect her face, but he managed to backhand her right check. Her eyes blurred and the pain shot through her eyeball, sending a shock to her brain.

"You could never just mind your own fucking business." He still held Michelle by her hair.

Brooke held her cheek as she glanced up at Wendell. A small trickle of blood oozed from his right nostril.

"Let her go." Her resolve faltered. No telling what a man strung out on cocaine might do, especially when that man was Wendell Ramsworth. "You won't get away with hurting her and how will you explain hitting me, because I'm sure as shit not going to let this assault get wiped under a rug."

Wendell laughed, but it sounded more like a rabid dog. "I was never here. Isn't that right Michelle?"

She nodded with wide eyes. "It's going to be your word against mine." He released Michelle, before kneeling. "Those pictures, which by the way I've enjoyed looking at for years. I will say you have a very sexy body—"

"She's your cousin," Michelle said softly.

"Not by blood." Wendell sniffed a few times as more blood leaked from his nose. "My father was adopted."

"That's disgusting." Michelle covered her mouth.

Brooke's heart broke. All this time she'd been holding a grudge, Michelle had been a prisoner, trapped in a violent relationship.

"Shut up and go to the car," Wendell yelled, glancing over his shoulder.

Brooke looked around, eyeing her cell phone under the kitchen table. Quickly she reached for it. A crushing pain ricocheted from her fingers to her shoulder as Wendell's fist came down hard on her hand. The crackle of bones snapping, sent a cold shiver across her body.

She screamed as he yanked her to a standing position. She tried fisting her right hand to punch him, groaned when her fingers didn't bend properly.

Fisting her hair, he yanked her head and leaned in. His breath smelled of whiskey. "I was never here and you'll never be able to prove I was." He smiled wide.

"You're fingerprints are all over the place."

He frowned. "Guess I'll have to wipe them down." He yanked harder. "And make you disappear." He slammed her head against the wall.

Her temple burned on impact. Her vision blurred as her legs went weak. Nausea engulfed her. She blinked a few times, her hands gripping his wrists, trying to take the pressure of her scalp. Her mind fractured as her thoughts raced between how to get out of this predicament and what he meant by 'make you disappear'.

The intense throbbing boomeranged between her ears as he twisted her hair tighter. Out of the corner of her eye, she saw a shadow.

Tristan?

Then the world went black...

Tristan rubbed his throbbing temples as he sat at a light on the way home. The pain had come on suddenly about an hour ago. It had dulled since, but hadn't gone completely away. He checked his phone again and still nothing from Brooke.

Something was wrong.

Very wrong

He couldn't put a finger on it, but deep in the pit of his gut, he knew she was in some kind of trouble. A pang of anger swelled in his gut. Not his anger. Hers. Mixed with sorrow and the crushing pain in his head.

Where are you, Brooke?

As soon as the light turned green, he gunned the vehicle, making the turn tight, and raced up Cleverdale. He slowed as he drove past her house, her car nowhere to be found. He wanted to let out a sigh of relief when he saw her convertible parked under his carport, but something didn't feel right.

And he barely felt her.

Stepping from his vehicle, he secured his weapon. He noted his neighbors in the big house were pulling their boat into the boat house. The modular homes on the other side appeared to be empty and no cars in the driveway.

"Brooke?" He twisted the handle to his front door. It hadn't been locked. "Brooke," he yelled. The door hit something on the floor. He looked down to see a frying pan. "Where are you babe?" He retrieved his weapon, carefully stepping over the pan and other debris that seemed to have been knocked off the table. Next to one piece of paper, their appeared to be some blood. He peeked his head into the bathroom.

Nothing.

"Brooke?" he called out once more as he made his way through the family room and checking each of his bedrooms. "Damn it," he muttered. He pulled out his phone and called Jared, making his way back to the front door and out into the yard without touching anything.

"Jared Blake here."

"Brooke's missing and my house looks like foul play could be involved."

"Be there in five minutes."

Tristan quickly tried Brooke again.

Straight to voice mail.

He sent a text to Stacey, asking her to check in with Jillian, hoping they'd gone out to talk, except why would Jillian drive all the way here to go back toward the village?

For the next few minutes, he thought of all the places she could have gone on foot. If she'd walked to the corner store, he would have seen her. She wouldn't have gone to the Mason Jug alone. That left the Ramsworth's and he didn't have their number.

Jared parked his truck at the end of the driveway. Still in uniform, he waltzed down the pavement. "Why do you think something happened?"

"My door was unlocked, crap on the floor, possible blood, her car is here."

"Did you call it in?"

Tristan shook his head. "I've been trying to reach her and thought it might be prudent to wait for you to check things out."

"The new kid is on till midnight. I'll have him come out. Rather us control this if anything has gone wrong."

"The one place I haven't check yet is Ramsworth Manor."

"I thought we agreed she wouldn't contact the old man and let Jillian take care of everything." Jared scratched the back of his head.

"We did and I doubt she went there on her own. If she did, it was because something happened or Michelle asked her to, but she would have texted or called me."

Jared turned his back, phone to his ear.

Tristan paced. His heart raced wild and the dull head-ache turned to a stick of dynamite that exploded, coupled with an overwhelming sense of confusion.

"Get in my truck," Jared yelled as he jogged down the driveway.

Tristan raced behind him. "What's going on?"

"Michelle is at the Sherriff's office. It would appear Wendell hit her and she's saying he's got Brooke and that he's high as a kite on coke."

Tristan jumped into passenger seat, slamming the door just as Jared peeled out. "What else do you know?"

"An APB was put out on Wendell and Brooke with the vehicle information Michelle gave the police five minutes ago." Jared tossed his cell in the drink holder. "She thinks they are headed north on route 9. Possibly Lake Placid."

"Why there?"

"They have a condo there, I guess. We'll stop by the sheriff's department, talk with Michelle and go from there. Do you have her find my iPhone activated?"

"Not connected to my phone." Tristan sent Brooke another text.

"You really should. All of ours are connected. I really only did it so I know where the kids are."

"Caitlyn is going to hate you when she starts dating."

"She's not allowed to date. Ever."

The rest of the ride to the local sheriff's office had been done in silence. No matter what Tristan did, he couldn't calm his pulse, something he normally had some control over when adrenaline took over.

"I need to talk to Michelle," Tristan said he stepped into the station.

"She's in an office and it's already been arranged." Jared waved to a female officer who nodded, waiving back. "Follow her."

Tristan showed his badge, and followed the young female officer around a couple of corners before she pushed opened a door to a small interviewing room, not to be mistaken for an interrogation room.

She turned her head, showing off a bruised cheek, her eyes puffy and swollen. "I'm sorry," she whispered.

He clenched his hands, wanting to put them through the window. "It's not your fault." He pulled up a chair and sat across from the broken woman. "Did your husband do this to you?" He raised his hand, but she flinched, so he dropped it to his lap. "Does he hit you often."

"He didn't hit me for a long time until she came back in town and things went crazy."

"It's not her fault either."

Michelle nodded. "But it's easy for me to blame her. Otherwise, it means I allowed this to happen."

"You're a victim," Tristan said. He'd seen his share of battered women's cases and most were gas lighted into believing everything was their fault. A difficult cycle to break. "We can protect you from him."

"Now that I'm carrying his child, I won't be free of any of them." She blinked a few times, staring into his eyes. "I've never seen him like this before. He's always been a partier, but never this out of control. When I got pregnant, he promised he'd clean up his act. And he did. Until a couple of weeks ago."

"Are you sure he's only been using for the last few weeks?"

She shook her head.

"Why do you think he's headed to Lake Placid?"

Michelle gasped, covering her mouth. "He didn't think anyone would go looking for her there."

Tristan's lungs burned as he tried to suck in oxygen.

"He said he could make her disappear there."

"Thanks for your help." Tristan patted her leg, doing his best to remain calm, even when all he wanted was to race out of the room, not letting himself care one bit about this young woman who had the unfortunate fate of falling for a narcissistic asshole. "Don't go home to Ramsworth Manor. Let the police help you and your baby start over. You're better than they are and I think it's important you know and accept that." He tugged a tissue from the box on the windowsill and handed it to her, along with his card. "You can call me anytime if you need help with anything."

Her hands shook as she took both the tissue and the card, looking up at him. "Just save Brooke and tell her I'm sorry. I should have listened to her."

Tristan nodded, before heading out the door just as Jared rounded the corner.

"He's been spotted and we've got a tail on him."

"Give me your keys?" Tristan held his hand out.

Jared slapped him on the back. "I'll drive because you're not doing this on your own."

Brooke watched in horror as Wendell took a small vile from the center console and snorted more cocaine. That had been twice in the last hour. "I should drive," she said, holding up her bound hands. "You're going to get us in an accident."

"Relax. I'm doing forty-five in a forty-five zone and no one is around." He spoke fast and he constantly fidgeted in his seat. "Besides, you're not going to make it out alive."

"You're talking crazy shit." She swallowed. "You're not going to kill me."

He laughed. "You have done nothing but fuck with my life and if you think for one minute I'm going to allow you to waltz in and take what is rightfully mine because my grandfather couldn't keep his dick in his pants, you've got another thing coming."

"Looks like you take after him, considering you haven't been faithful to Michelle."

His hand crashed into the side of her face, hitting her already bruised cheek. "You have no idea what the fuck you are talking about."

"You won't get away with this."

He glanced in her direction with a sinister smile. "Did you know Tristan's family has a place in Lake Placid? A nice little, well actually, big cottage. Imagine if you were found dead there? And after I'm done making him out to be an out of control police officer with a thirst for violence, everyone will think he murdered you."

"That makes no sense." She stared out the window, palming her cheek. The sun had disappeared behind the mountains, only a faint glow shined above the tree lines. The blue sky slowly turned dark, stars began to form in the sky.

"Well, lucky for you it doesn't matter. You'll be dead."

"Where's Michelle?" Brooke had no idea how long she'd been unconscious, but she suspected maybe an hour or so based on the darkness of the sky. The piercing pain in her head had become a dull thud, but her vision still blurred.

"At home," Wendell said, his fingers tapping on the steering wheel. "And don't go getting your hopes up that she's going to mention anything to anyone about what happened. She's my wife. Loyal to me."

Brooke looked at the door, wondering what would happen if she pushed it open, letting herself roll out to the pavement. Visions of her head being squished like a bug, splattering her brains all over the road forced that idea right out of the realm of possibility.

"You're not a killer," Brooke said. "We can work this out and I can make sure nothing happens to you."

"You can't promise that." He laughed. "And who says I'm going to actually be the one killing you." He tapped the side of his head. "I'm a smart guy, so trust me when I say, my hands will be washed of you, free and clear."

She shivered. The sky darkened as the car's headlights beat through the low fog. If her calculations were correct, it was near nine at night, which meant they had to be close to Lake Placid, if that was indeed where he was taking her.

He turned a corner down a narrow road with a few log cabins. The lights flashed across a body of water. "Welcome to the Reid residence."

"Do you plan on breaking in?"

"Something like that."

Her heart pounded against her ribs. She sat very still in the front seat, watching Wendell waltz around the front of the car. He pulled opened the door, and yanked her out by her arm. "You don't want to do this. Think about your baby. How can you be a good father if you're behind bars?"

"Don't you worry your pretty little head about me." He dragged her down the long windy driveway, past five houses until he stopped in front of a massive log cabin overlooking the lake.

A shadow immerged from the porch. "It's unlocked," a deep dark voice said as the silhouette moved down the steps.

Wendell handed the man an envelope, then guided her up the stairs.

She wanted to scream, but thought that might cause a chain reaction that would actually land her dead.

Two scenarios raced through her brain. Either Wendell had really fallen off his rocker and planned on murdering her, in which case, if she played her cards right, she might survive. But if he managed to hire some kind of hit man in the last hour…well, that could be a different story.

Either way, she had to buy some time.

"I need to use the bathroom."

"Not sure that will be possible."

The wood creaked from their combined weight. She stumbled on the last step. The wind kicked up, sending moist, humid air across her skin. The sky darkened, as clouds covered the stars that normally light up the night sky. A clap of thunder rumbled in the background.

The front door clicked open and he shoved her inside.

"I can't see," she whispered.

A few seconds later, a small light glimmered.

Wendell pulled her into what appeared to be a family room. He pushed her onto the sofa.

"What now?" She breathed deeply through her nose, letting it out in a slow exhale through her mouth.

"We wait for the man who will be terminating you, making sure that Tristan is blamed, securing that both of you will get the fuck out of my way."

She swallowed a gasp. Even the sounds of crickets on a cool summer eve's couldn't calm her nerves.

Another roll of thunder as the night sky lit up with a few bolts of lightning. A tap at the door made her jump.

"Do you have the money?" a dark voice asked. It wasn't the same voice as the man who let them into the house.

"I do," Wendell said. "But how do I know you're going to go through with it and not just run off with my money?"

"You don't," the man said. His tall shadow hovering over Wendell. "Give me the money, leave, and never look back."

Brooke tried to swallow, but her dry throat made it impossible. She blinked, hoping she'd wake from this bad dream because no way could this be real. This shit happened in movies, not to her. She nearly laughed at the absurd thought.

Wendell handed the man something, then walked out the front door, slamming it shut.

"Hello there little lady. Ready to get this party started?"

Tristan eased from Jared's truck, quietly closing the car door, eyeing two unmarked cars parked at the top of the street, still a good three quarters of a mile from his parent's cottage.

He followed Jared toward the closest car, noticing a SWAT van further down the road. He swallowed his shock. SWAT didn't come out for a 'possible' abduction.

An officer from the Lake Placid Police Department greeted them. "Which one of you is Tristan?"

"That's me." Tristan held up his badge.

"I'm detective Holster. Everyone calls me Holes." The officer offered his hand. "We've got three people inside your house."

"Three?" Jared questioned.

Holes nodded.

"Why is SWAT here?" Tristan asked.

"We got a tip that Richie Rayburn was in the area," Holes said.

"He's suspected of being involved in a murder in Lake George," Jared added, scratching the back of his neck.

"He's a person of interest in at least a half a dozen murders in two states. Hired hit man for the rich. That's what the FBI calls him." Holes waved over another man.

"Wonderful," Tristan muttered. He stood at the top of the hill, staring down into the dark night, not even being able to see his parent's cabin. If it were a clear night, the moon and stars would glow across the lake, framing at least the porch.

But not tonight.

"We've got movement," Holes said, with one hand to his ear. "One person leaving the house."

"Who?" Tristan continued to stare down the street. "And did your men eye everyone that went in the house?"

"We don't know who just yet, but my men followed Rayburn to this area where he hung out in a patch of trees next to your house. They watched someone open the door for a man and a woman, who entered. Then Rayburn went in."

"Where'd the man go who opened the door?" Tristan tried to

recall everything about Rayburn and the crimes he was suspected of, which included rape and torture. Not your standard hit man. He liked to play with his victims before killing them. And that he liked to torture them slowly, watching them suffer.

"He went to a house on the next street over. I've got a man knocking on his door to question him," Holes said.

"That could be someone in the Bower family. They live here year-round and some people give them their keys. My parents used to, but then started using a service." Tristan realized how eerily calm his pulse had become in the last few moments. His mind laser focused. He also sensed Brooke's mind was too. That had to be a good sign. "I know that house inside and out. I can get in the back door off the kitchen."

"We'll send in our guys. You can explain the layout," Holes said.

Tristan shook his head. "We've got a better shot at saving Brooke if I go in with some of your team members as back-up." Tristan pointed down the road. "The cabin right next to mine has a high roof. From it, you get a bird's eye view of my family room and den. On the back side of the house, if you put a couple of snipers in the trees, you've got access to three of the five bedrooms."

"Still a lot of house that isn't covered." Holes put his hand to his ear. "Time to roll. Put people in the trees to the west and the house to the east. Sergeant Reid will explain the rest."

Tristan took two steps when Holes put his hand up.

"The neighbor was paid ten grand in cash to let Wendell in. Also, Wendell just got into his car."

Tristan rested his hand on the butt of his weapon. "I want a few words with the asshole."

"That I'm not signing off on." Holes pointed to the SWAT van. "You work with SWAT and get in there now. Jared and I'll talk to Wendell."

"I can live with that." Tristan jogged toward the SWAT team, who were already heading in different directions. Someone tossed him a wire and a bullet proof vest.

"We're on instructions to follow your lead."

Tristan removed his weapon from its holster. "Hold on babe, I'm coming."

CHAPTER 13

BROOKE SAT ON THE SOFA, hands bound in her lap, staring up into the eyes of a beast. He had to be over six-foot-four and the width of his shoulders the size of a small car. He smiled, which looked more like a sneer and not pleasant at all. Two prominent scars lined his right cheek just under his eye.

She swallowed the bile rising in her throat, forcing the sense of dread deep inside. She needed to hold onto hope. She made herself believe that she could feel Tristan close by and that he had a plan to save her from whatever vile creature Wendell had sent to kill her.

"I was paid extra not to toy with you too much."

She had no idea what that meant, and wasn't about to ask.

"It's going to be hard for me, especially with such a beautiful woman as yourself." He stepped closer, reaching toward her face.

She jerked back, feeling his sick, twisted desire to hurt people.

"I think it would be alright if I put a little cut right in that swollen cheek." He traced it with his thumb.

She tried to turn away, pushing her head all the way into the sofa cushions. His touch sent her stomach on a roll, churning up more bile. She gagged.

"Quiet one, aren't you?" He stepped back, lifting a box from the floor, and placed it on the coffee table. "That's okay, baby. I'm going to make you scream for daddy."

Overwhelming fear engulfed her body. Her pulse beat so fast she felt as though it might bust right out of her chest. Eyeing the door, she bolted up right. She had to try to run. Something hard circled her stomach, stopping her dead in her tracks. Gasping for air, she kicked and screamed as her body slammed against the sofa.

"Trying to run just gives me a hard on."

The beast grabbed his crotch and groaned.

Her eyes went wide as he held up a large knife. Drawing his forefinger across the sharp edge, he smiled. "Your friend didn't really care how I killed you, so long as I make this place look like a struggle went on, then dumped your body where no one could find it."

"How much did he pay you?" She adjusted herself to a sitting position, doing her best not to hyperventilate.

"Now why would I tell you that?" He reached into his pocket and pulled a lighter. Holding the knife over the flame, he heated the metal.

"Because whatever it was, I can double it if you let me go."

The beast laughed, tossing his back. The noise echoed across the room like a hyena.

"He's my cousin." Brooke thought maybe keeping the beast talking might at least slow down the process of death by hot knife long enough for Tristan to find her. "He wants me dead because he doesn't want to have to share the family fortune."

The beast let the flame flicker out. "As tempting as that is, you've seen my face."

"So, has he."

"Valid point, but he needs you gone and I don't need the money." He flicked the lighter and ran the blade through the flame as he stepped over the coffee table. "Besides, I'll enjoying killing you so much more than that little prick."

She scooted to the end of the sofa. "My boyfriend's a State Trooper. You won't get away with this."

"Oh, but sweetheart, I already have. More than once." He reached down and yanked her to her feet.

She tried to run again, but he held her neck, lifting her off the ground with one hand. Clutching his wrists, she kicked and squirmed, trying to breathe, but the crushing of his fingers against her neck made it impossible. The room spun in a vicious blur.

"Oh no, baby. Not yet."

"Put the knife down and step away from the lady," a voice that sounded like Tristan said.

Delusional. The lack of oxygen, even for a few seconds made her hallucinate. She blinked a few times, trying to gain focus. Her hands clutched the beast's massive forearm. A sharp sting slipped across her cheek.

"I will do no such thing," the beast said, pressing the knife into her neck, the hot metal sizzled against her skin. The smell of burning flesh filled the room like a barbeque.

A figure standing in front of her slowly came into focus.

"Tristan?" she whispered. Her knees buckled, but the beast held her up.

"This place is surrounded. If you want to walk out of this place alive, you'll put the knife down and step away from the lady." Tristan held a gun in both hands, pointing it at her and the Beast. His eyes didn't seem to look at her, but she knew she consumed his thoughts.

"I'm walking out of here alive, with her."

She let out a shrill as he pressed the knife harder, pinching her skin.

"That's not going to happen. We've got a dozen snipers with orders to shot to kill."

"You're not going to risk me killing her," the beast said, reaching in his pocket, he pulled out a small hand gun, pressing it at her temple.

Tristan cocked his head, drawing his lips in a tight line.

She sucked in a breath. They were going to let him walk out, using her as shield. Tears coated her eyes like a dense fog. Her feet scrambled on the floor. The knife still burned her neck. If she moved the wrong way, or if the beast moved the wrong way, the sharp blade would tear through her jugular.

Or a bullet through her brain.

The beast took small steps backward. "You're going to let me leave, or she dies."

The front door clicked open. The wind howled and a few large rain pellets smacked her face. "Please, just let me go," she whispered.

"No can do little lady."

"I let you leave, and she dies anyway." Tristan inched his way forward. "The only question is how badly do you want to live."

"Going to prison isn't living. So, if that's how you want to play this, I'll kill her right here right now."

Brooke gasped, eyes wide.

Tristan stopped, quickly raising his weapon to the sky. "Boss says you get to walk." He looked directly into her eyes. His thoughts and emotions flooding her body with the force of lightning. She swallowed her breath as the beast pulled her down the steps.

Trust me.

Not an easy thing to do in a situation like this, but she had to believe that the connection she had with Tristan was real. That her instincts about what he wanted her to do were real.

I love you, she thought, staring into his dark, warm eyes.

"You stay right there," the Beast yelled, pointing his gun at Tristan. "Take another step and I'll kill her."

The beast dragged her down the stairs. The rain hit her body sideways as the wind whipped her hair in front of her face, covering her eyes. She struggled to keep her legs from completely collapsing as he continued to pull her across the lawn, Tristan disappearing from sight.

Trust me.

"Open the door." The beast pushed her against a car door, arm still around her body, knife at her throat.

Her fingers trembled as she tried to lift door handle but failed. "It's locked."

"Fuck." The beast twisted. "Reach inside my pants pocket."

She held her hands up. "How do you think I will manage that with my hands tied?"

He dug the tip of the blade into her neck.

She bit down on her tongue to keep from screaming. The sharp pain rattled her teeth.

"You're going to regret being snippy with me." The pressure of the knife disappeared as he fisted her hair, yanking it back, twisting her body to the side.

A loud snap followed by a louder pop startled her, making her jump. She fell to the ground face first as she heard two more excruciating bangs that made her head feel as though a bomb had gone off inside. She tried to cover her ears, but couldn't with the way her hands were clasped together. Knowing she was no longer being held by the beast's thick arms, she dug her heels into the wet ground, crawling away, when two hands hoisted her to her feet.

"Let go of me!" She pounded her tied fists into a hard chest, trying to push away.

A constant ringing in her ears drowned out the voices around her. At least she thought she heard voices. She slammed her hands against whoever held her. The broken fingers in her hand throbbed as she continued to squirm, trying to break free. From the hardness of the chest she smacked, she had to be right back into the arms of the beast.

"Brooke!"

She froze as a hand pushed her hair out of her face. She blinked. Red and blue flashing lights lit up the sky. Men wearing dark suits ran across the yard yelling commands at each other.

"Look at me," Tristan said, cupping her cheeks. "Brooke?" His gaze shifted from her eyes, to her check as he tilted her head, groaning when he glanced at her neck. "I need a medic over here." He cut through the plastic that held her hands together.

The air burned her lungs as she heaved in harsh breaths. She turned her head and saw the beast, laying in the muddy grass.

"Is he dead?" she whispered.

"I believe so," Tristan said. "Let's get you someplace dry."

"I did not sign on for this." Heat raced up her body. She pounded the thick vest Tristan wore. "Where is Wendell?"

"In custody." Tristan tilted his head. "It's over."

"Over!? I didn't know it began. All I wanted to do was bury my grandfather and try to rebuild my life and that asshole tried to kill me." Her hands came down hard on Tristan's shoulders. "God only knows what he did to Michelle."

"Michelle is fine." Tristan curled his fingers over her wrists, but she yanked them free, groaning in pain.

"Where is he? I'm going to wring his neck." She took two steps around Tristan before he circled his arms around her middle, stopping her.

"Let me go," she said behind a tight jaw.

"Brooke, you need to relax."

"Don't tell me what to do!" Being held, even by Tristan, set off a rage so intense she felt no other recourse but to strike back, pounding at his chest as hard as she could. Her body so filled with fury, it's all she could see, feel, or taste.

Tristan's hands held her hips. "Get it out, babe," he whispered.

His soft voice slowly bringing her back to reality.

She looked up at him as she took her hands and hit his chest once more. The vest so thick and bulky it felt like she stood a mile away. Feverishly, she tried to find how to remove it.

"You're going to hurt yourself more than you already are," Tristan said as he gently took her by her wrists, letting her arms drop to her sides. The sound of Velcro zipped across the night air as he removed the vest, then pulled her into his loving arms. "It's going to be okay." His hot breath tickled her ear. He slid his arm under her knees and lifted her against his strong body. "You've a very brave woman, Brooke Fowler."

"I don't know about that," she whispered, nuzzling her face into his neck, letting her body relax, which brought on a guttural sob. "When will I wake up from this nightmare?"

"It's over." Tristan set her down in the back of an ambulance. Someone wrapped her in a blanket.

"Don't leave me." She reached for him and he leaned in, wrapping his arms around her.

"I'll never leave you," he whispered. "But right now, you need to let them check you over. You've got a couple of nasty cuts that need stitches, a few fingers that looked mangled, and a very large bump on the side of your head." He kissed her temple. "And yet, you manage to still be the most beautiful woman in the world."

"You're full of shit," she said softly, staring into his eyes.

"Ma'am," a paramedic said. "We need to run an IV and get some fluids in you."

The paramedic helped her onto the gurney. As he examined her wounds, the sharp throbbing pain of her injuries filled her body. She closed her eyes, sucking in a deep breath, trying to focus on anything but the pain.

"Tristan," she whispered.

"Right here, babe." His hand covered her good one. "I'll be right here the entire way to the hospital."

"I hate hospitals."

"Can't say they are my favorite place, either." Tristan patted her hand.

"I have something to tell you." She tilted her head, cringing at the tearing sensation in her neck.

"Not here. Not now," he said with a smile. "Save it for when you can show me you mean it."

CHAPTER 14

BROOKE HADN'T EXPECTED to spend five days in the hospital, but between needing minor surgery on her hand and a concussion that decided to make her talk gibberish for twenty-four hours, the doctors deemed it necessary.

She touched the side of her neck with her good hand. She fingered the bandage that covered twelve stitches from where the knife had sliced through her skin. The burns caused by the blade being heated, now itched. Her neck looked like crinkled paper. The swelling on her cheek had gone down, but the stitches would remain for another couple of days.

A tap at the door pulled her from her thoughts.

"Brooke?" Jillian asked as she peeked her head in the door. "I've got the paperwork."

"Come on in." Brooke had been surprised by how quickly Jillian was able to wrap up things with the Ramsworth family, but they had wanted to keep the paternity issue out of the public eye, and with everything that was going on with Wendell's arrest, she totally understood why. She felt bad for some members of the family, but she wanted nothing to do with them and the feeling was mutual.

Jillian rolled the food tray over the bed and placed a stack of papers on it. "This first document is the Non-disclosure agreement. They accepted all of our changes. But it's important for you to know that you can never admit to being a blood relative, even if asked."

"That's not a problem."

"You have no further claim to their assets both personal and professional."

"I don't want a claim to anything."

"If you break the agreement, you owe them half of the settlement." Jillian flipped a few pages and handed her a pen, tapping a line, awaiting her signature.

Brooke held up her left hand with a dark blue cast. "Thankfully, I'm right-handed." She signed the document.

"This next one is your hush money. They countered back at two million and I told them that you'd take it."

Brooke let out a long sigh. She hadn't wanted their money, but after everything that happened, and the fact they defended Wendell, speaking publicly about his innocence in regard to her abduction and the hiring of a hit man, she decided it was better if she did take it. "What about Michelle? Did they agree to release her and her baby?"

"I'm not Michelle's attorney, so I'm not privy to what that agreement states. All I know for sure is she's agreed to testify against her husband if the criminal charges go to trial."

"Will she be protected?" The biggest regret Brooke had was what had happened to Michelle and her baby during this entire ordeal.

"That's between her and law enforcement." Jillian flipped to the signature page. "I know that seems harsh, but the good news is not hearing from her probably means they put her in witness protection."

Poor Michelle. She didn't deserve the cards she'd been dealt. Nor did her unborn child.

"The second signature page of this document is also an NDA, stating you can't acknowledge they paid you a penny."

Brooke gladly sighed.

"The only contingency on this one is they get back anything you have in your possession that your grandmother indicated was given to her by Wendell Knoll Ramsworth the 1st."

"Tristan has everything ready to be returned."

Jillian took the stack of papers, setting them aside and pulled out one last set. "This is the offer we discussed from my husband and Doug. You can have an outside attorney look at, which I recommend."

Brooke flipped through the pages. The offer for the property was more than fair. Part of her wished she had a bigger attachment to the piece of land and the house, but even if she did, it was ruined by the fact the Ramsworth's were right down the street. "I'm good with this."

"I highly recommend you having an outside person check over the numbers."

Brooke shook her head. "I need to put an end to this part of my life, and start fresh." She signed the last set of papers.

Jillian nodded. "It's a cash deal, so you'll be able to close in thirty days or less."

"Thanks for taking care of all this for me."

"You might want to rescind that when you get my bill."

Brooke laughed.

"What are you going to do now?" Jillian asked.

"My community service and anger management classes are up here, so until those are done, Tristan said I could stay with him. After that, I need to find a job and move on."

Jillian smiled as she sat on the edge of the bed. "Things going well with Tristan I take it?"

"Honestly, right now they are a little awkward."

"Why?" Jillian had a motherly personality, but one without judgement.

"He seemed taken aback that I didn't want him staying here all day every day here with me and pushed him into finishing his recertification for SCUBA." Brooke ran her good hand across the yoga pants Tristan had dropped off last night for her to wear home today. "He's been so tired when he comes to visit, I feel bad, knowing he needs his sleep, so I sent him home."

"Tristan is a tough read sometimes." Jillian smiled sweetly. "I don't know Stacey's co-workers like Doug or Jim do, but I know enough about Tristan to know that almost losing you tore open some old wounds that will probably never heal completely."

Brooke nodded. Tamara's death would always be a part of who Tristan was as a man as much as the loss of her parents and grandparents would forever be a part of her physiological make-up "He's picking me up shortly. Technically, I was released hours ago, but he was adamant I not find another ride back to his place and I can give him that."

"You're very much in love with him," Jillian said with a smile and a twinkle in her eye. "It's quite obvious he loves you back."

The corners of Brooke's mouth tugged upward into a smile. Tears welled in her eyes. "That's what makes this awkwardness so difficult and the fact we've never really said it out loud to each other."

"Jim was so afraid of those three little words." Jillian fiddled with her wedding ring. "He'd dedicated his entire life to Stacey and Doug that letting a woman in felt selfish to him. I related to that because of my own situation with my kid. We avoided saying our feelings out loud for months until one morning, we were all sitting around the breakfast table."

"All?" Brooke asked, finding herself enjoying this tale of happily-ever-after.

"I'd spent the night at Jim's place and Doug and Stacey were still living there. They'd just gotten engaged." Jillian laughed quietly. "Jim looked at me and said, 'I know you love me, and I love you too, so move in with us.' Stacey spit out her coffee and Doug choked on a piece of bacon. I just smiled, and said it's about time."

"That's so sweet." Brooke remembered the first time Tristan had used the word love, but qualified it with 'I think'. Right after, all hell broke loose and it had been an emotional upheaval until now.

She had yet to say the words, and perhaps that was the problem.

"Take the time and stay with him while you finish out the necessary evils to get back on your feet. Enjoy each other and really get to know one another. The words will come when you're both ready."

"Thank you," Brooke said taking the older woman's hands in hers. "You've been such a good friend."

"I hope we can remain friends. I'm always here."

A tap at the door startled both women.

"Hi ladies," Tristan said as he waltzed in.

"I was just on my way out." Jillian leaned in, giving Brooke a warm embrace. "He's changed for the better because of you," she whispered.

Brooke watched Tristan hug Jillian before she glided out the door.

"Did you sign all the papers?" He sat down on the edge of the bed, gliding his hand up and down her thigh.

"I'm officially a rich bitch."

He laughed. "You can do anything you want, including starting your own business if you wanted."

She shook her head. "I don't think that is what I want, but I'm going to take the six weeks of community service and workshops to make sure I'm the person I want to be and then find the right job. There are a few at Highland that are promising."

"I hope the jobs are at least somewhat close to me, though I'm not opposed to relocating anywhere in New York."

She smiled. "Are you saying you'd move for me?"

He nodded, tugging at her arm. "Let's get out of here. I've got something to show you."

Tristan helped Brooke step from the dock onto his fishing boat. It was hard to believe he'd only known her less than a month. Every morning he woke up thinking about her and every night he went to bed wanting to hold her.

The last five days had been torture. Not only because he couldn't hold her in his arms all night, but he hadn't spent all his waking hours with her because of his recertification for SCUBA.

She'd been right when she told him to finish his training, which was the only reason he'd done it. He sensed her need for him to finish those things he was passionate about. He would have done the same thing had he'd been the one laying in the hospital bed.

"Where should I sit?" she asked.

"On the bench behind the steering wheel." He untied the boat, before jumping in and starting the engines, sitting down next the only woman in the world who understood him.

"Where are we going?"

"Nowhere in particular." A true statement. All he needed was for the sun to set, which should happen in the next ten minutes or so. "I thought a night in the fresh air would do you some good."

She snuggled up against him, resting her good hand on his thigh.

He navigated the boat up the shoreline, keeping the throttle just in gear. No need for speed. Just a leisurely ride toward the wide-open space just south of Dome Island. Lucky for him, there was no breeze and the only waves he had to deal with were those made by other boats.

She shivered, wrapping her sweater tighter around her body.

"Cold?" he asked, hugging her closer.

"I can't believe how much the temperature has dropped in the last week."

He kissed her temple, careful not to rub against her cheek. Her scream the night Rayburn intended to kill her still haunted his dreams. "I'm sorry that I didn't get to you sooner," he whispered in her ear.

"You need to stop apologizing for that. None of it was your fault, and you did find me before he could inflict real damage."

Tristan growled right before he gently kissed her neck, making sure he didn't touch where she'd been burned or cut. "He hurt you. That right there is too much damage."

She shifted, facing him. Her eyes a mix of red and orange, only the red lacked any anger at all. "That night." She palmed her neck. "You held me and told me it was over and it is. The beast is dead. Wendell is in jail and hopefully going to prison for a very long time."

She kissed his cheek. "I'm alive, and thanks to you and your friends, I have the chance to reboot my life."

"Hopefully that reboot includes me." He kissed her lips before she had a chance to say anything.

The light from the sun disappeared as the night sky took over. Tristan put the boat in neutral and shut off the engine, letting the watercraft float in the calm water. He stood up, making his way to the bow of the boat and arranged the cushions before spreading out a blanket. He could feel her calmness, but that didn't help his nerves. He wanted to spend the rest of his life loving her like there was no such thing as a broken heart. "Come here." He held out his hand, thankful it didn't tremble like the rest of his body.

She smiled sweetly, which warmed his heart, but the cuts and bruises affected him to the core. At times, he felt like he had failed her somehow, as if he'd been the one that had caused her cuts and bruises. He'd felt the same way the day Tamara died. Intellectually, he understood it wasn't his fault, but emotionally, it was impossible to shed the guilt completely.

"Lay down with me." He helped her to the floor of the boat, pulling her head to his chest. "The first night we met."

"Must you remind me? I was so toasted it's embarrassing."

"You never have to be embarrassed with me. Remember, I'm the guy who made the comment about your breasts not being too far apart."

"But they are." She laughed.

"Far apart? Yes. But that's the way I like them."

She looped her arm around his middle. "What are we doing out here?"

He held her hand, using her pointer finger and touched different stars in the sky. "That night, when I was trying to tell you that you'd had too much to drink, you managed to fall into my lap."

"Orion's belt," she whispered. "I see it now."

"You remember." He turned his head, catching his gaze.

"There are parts of that night I'm glad I have little recognition of, but I'm glad you picked up the phone when a stranger called."

He cupped her chin, pressing his lips gently against hers. "Do you remember sitting in the front lawn of your grandfather's place, discussing my inability to talk to women?"

She laughed. "You do realize that was never really a problem, right?"

"It was, but never with you." He dropped his forehead to hers, locking gazes. "I had a weird thought about wanting to take you out on the boat, lay under the stars, and just hold you. No woman has ever made me think to do something like this. And honestly, it's not about being romantic, because we both know that's not my strong suit."

"I don't know, you're doing an awfully good job right now."

"Wait ten minutes, I'll blow it."

She rubbed her nose against his. "But I adore your idiosyncrasies."

He groaned. "Are you going to let me get through this?"

She nodded.

"The night we had dinner with my parents I said something to you that has been hanging between us ever since." He traced a path from her earlobe down to her cleavage. The necklace she'd been wearing when he'd met her gone, and the space felt bare. He dug deep in his pocket, pulling out a small velvet bag.

He sat up, and pulling her with him. He tugged at the strings on the pouch. "My family has no heirlooms or anything we passed down from generation to generation. But when Tamara died, my mother took all the pieces of jewelry my sister owned and made one necklace, a matching bracelet, and earrings out of it. I had no idea she'd done that until I called to tell her what happened to you." He paused to wipe his eyes. "You'd been in and out of consciousness the entire ride to the hospital. It had been hard enough to see that animal hurt you, but sitting in that waiting room, waiting to find out if you were okay, was one of the worst days of my life."

His hands trembled as he dumped the contents of the bag into his hands.

"Tristan." She cupped his face.

"Please let me finish." It would be so easy to let her do or say whatever, versus him spilling is guts.

She needed to deal with her anger and move forward.

He needed to break down a few more walls.

"My mother handed me these." Carefully, he wrapped the necklace around her neck, fumbling at the clasp for what seemed like an eternity. Next, he wrapped the bracelet around her wrist, but couldn't fasten it. "Will you please help me?"

She laughed as she easily secured the silver chain around her sexy wrist.

"And these?" He held up the earrings.

She smiled, taking them in her good hand, admiring them for a moment before sliding them into the holes in her ears.

He shook out his hands before resting them on her slender hips. "My mother told me she had no idea why she had these made until the night she met you, which was the same night I told you I was falling in love with you."

She cupped his face. "Are you still falling?"

"No," he said. "I'm totally, madly, head over heels in love with you."

"Good." She pressed her lips against his. "I'm madly in love with you too."

He smiled, fingering the new locket that dangled between her breasts. Right now, it was empty and he looked forward to seeing what she put in it.

"So, are we going to get naked out here under the stars, or do I have to wait until we get home?" she asked.

"How about here, and then again at home?"

"You don't have to offer that twice."

Tristan tapped his chest with her forefinger. "You might have been a stranger when you called, but I was in love with you long before that."

Thank you for reading When A Stranger Calls. Please feel free to leave an honest review on Amazon and/or Goodreads.

Sign up for my Newsletter (https://dl.bookfunnel.com/6atcf7g1be) where I often give away free books before publication.

Join my private Facebook group (https://www.facebook.com/groups/191706547909047/) where she posts exclusive excerpts and discuss all things murder and love!

Never miss a new release. Follow me on
Amazon:amazon.com/author/jentalty
And on Bookbub: bookbub.com/authors/jen-talty

READ AN EXCERPT FROM THE LIGHTHOUSE

Logan Sarich dumped his rucksack in the lobby of The Aegis Network main building, well aware he hadn't showered in forty-eight hours and the Orlando summer humidity clung to his pores like flies on shit. "Hey Ashley." He leaned against her desk and smiled. Normally, he'd go clean up after an op, but Ashely's message said it was urgent. "Where's Asher and Decker?" He bit back a chuckle. He always wanted to say black n' decker when discussing his bosses, and the co-founders of The Aegis Network.

"Talking with a client," Ashely said, plugging her nose. "What's that smell?"

"A combination of two days of surveillance, stale coffee, fish tacos, a hot dog, and something I can't pronounce," Logan said, smiling. "You told me, and I quote, to get my ass to the office."

She shook her head. "No, I said to get your cute little tush in here as soon as you can. Next time wash that ripe smell off before you enter my space."

"Yes, ma'am." Logan had only been working for The Aegis Network for six months, after spending six years in the Special Forces, and before that, six years in the infantry. "I can leave and come back, if you'd prefer."

READ AN EXCERPT FROM THE LIGHTHOUSE

"I've smelled worse." She pushed a file toward the end of the table. "You've been assigned a new case."

He'd been hoping for a couple of days off, but he'd taken this job under the premise that all he wanted to do was work.

Be careful what you ask for.

He picked up the file.

"In Jupiter, Florida," she said.

He didn't open the file, just peered over the top. "The bosses want me to go to my hometown for a job?"

"Open it." Ashely crossed her legs, swiveling the chair.

Logan did as asked, but frowned the moment he saw a picture of Mia Vanderlin and her twin brother Markus. "My mother works for the Vanderlin's. I can't take this job."

"I was told you'd say that." Ashley waggled her brow. "And I was told to inform you that you have no choice. You the layout, the people, so you're the best man for the job."

Logan had learned his first week on the job not to argue with Ashley. She might not be the boss, but she ran this place for the bosses and she was a force to be reckoned with. "What's the assignment?"

"Bodyguard."

"Of the twins?" He flipped through the pages, ignoring the childhood memories of skinny dipping with the smartest and sexiest girl in school. "Why?"

"Mia and Markus are ethical hackers. Mia was hired to do a security check for DANA Corp."

"The defense contractor?"

Ashley nodded. "While doing the check, Mia found some sort of virus that swapped out good specs with bad ones."

"So, stealing information from DANA Corp?"

"Decker believes an organization known as STEALTH was behind the attack, but it hasn't been confirmed."

"I take it she blew the whistle?"

"Not at first."

"Please don't tell me she messed with the A-Hole's in

STEALTH." But Logan knew the answer. When messed with, Mia tended to fight back.

"She created a program that would spit out false information to STEALTH regarding various defense contracts and designs on some top-secret material. She also managed to send a message to the CIA, who were able to trace the origin of the original hack back to an abandoned warehouse. The CIA have people in custody. None of them are talking."

"Where?"

"Like the CIA is going to tell us that." She held her hand up. "Not that Asher and Decker didn't try, so let's focus on the assignment."

Logan still knew a few people at the Agency, and he suspected his boss knew that he'd use his contacts. "If she's the one who ratted out STEALTH, why does Markus need protection?"

"STEALTH threatened Mia directly, but since they are business partners, she thinks he could be a target as well."

Logan should dump the file back on Ashley's desk and inform his bosses this was on job he'd have to say no to. While it would be good to see Mia and her brother again, no way would he be setting foot on that property. "Why isn't the CIA protecting them?"

"They have bigger issues to deal with, like a breach in security, so when Mia was threatened, her family called us."

"We are the best." Logan tried not to wince at the memory of the last time he'd been at Mia's house. "I'm grateful for the work, but seriously, someone else has to take this one and I'll need your help to convinces the bosses. I know for a fact that Mr. and Mrs. Vanderlin will take one look at me and slam the door in my face."

"Dressed like that." She pointed at his muddy T-shirt that used to be white. "And smelling like a cow pasture, I'm sure they would, but I'm guessing that's not why you want to going running for the hills."

"My skill set is better suited for other ops. I'm not cut out to be a baby sitter for a bunch of rich people."

"Asher and Decker won't see that as a good reason to reassign."

READ AN EXCERPT FROM THE LIGHTHOUSE

She leaned back in her chair, crossing her arms, almost daring him to continue arguing with her.

"There might be a little bad history there," Logan admitted.

"Such as?"

The corners of his mouth tugged upward into a smile. The incident had been both part of the best times of his life, and the most embarrassing. "The Vanderlin's think I deflowered Mia."

"Deflowered? Really?" Ashley laughed, tossing her long hair behind her shoulder. "I never thought a word like that would come out of your mouth," she said.

"It's the word they used when they told my mother they caught me in Mia's bedroom with my pants down."

"So, it's true?" Ashley cocked her head, her face turned serious.

"Let's just say we deflowered each other." He covered his mouth, gliding his hand down to his chin, trying to wipe off the grin. There hasn't been a time in his adult life where remembering Mia didn't make him smile. He often wondered if she thought of him the same way.

"Well, It was the family who requested you personally, so I think you're screwed."

"Yes ma'am." He picked up his rucksack, flinging it over his shoulder. "When?"

"Right after you shower. It's only a two-hour drive."

"I've done it in less," he said as he turned toward the door.

"And Logan," Ashely said. Her words laced with humor. "Don't sleep with the client."

Available on Amazon!

ALSO BY JEN TALTY

THE NEW YORK STATE TROOPER SERIES

In Two Weeks

Dark Water

Deadly Secrets

Murder in Paradise Bay

To Protect His Own

Deadly Seduction

When a Stranger Calls

FEDERAL INVESTIGATOR SERIES

Jane Doe's Return

The Butterfly Murders

THE MEN OF THEIF LAKE

Rekindled

THE AEGIS NETWORK: THE SARICH BROTHERS

The Lighthouse

Her Last Hope

The Last Flight

The Return Home

Coming Soon:

The Matriarch

THE COLLECTIVE ORDER: THE RAVEN SISTERS

The Lost Sister

The Lost Solider

Coming Soon:

The Lost Soul

The Lost Connection

SPECIAL FORCES: FIRE PROTECTION SPECIALISTS

Burning Desire

Burning Kiss

Burning Skies

Burning Lies

Burning Heart

Burning Bed

Coming soon:

Crash and Burn

THE BROTHERHOOD PROTECTORS: OUT OF THE WILD

Rough Justice

Rough Around the Edges

Coming Soon:

Rough Ride

ABOUT JEN TALTY

Welcome to my World! I'm a USA Today Bestseller of Romantic Suspense, Contemporary Romance, and Paranormal Romance.

    I first started writing while carting my kids to one hockey rink after the other, averaging 170 games per year between 3 kids in 2 countries and 5 states. My first book, IN TWO WEEKS was originally published in 2007. In 2010 I helped form a publishing company (Cool Gus Publishing) with NY Times Bestselling Author Bob Mayer where I ran the technical side of the business through 2016.

    I'm currently enjoying the next phase of my life...the empty NESTER! My husband and I spend our winters in Jupiter, Florida and our summers in Rochester, NY. We have three amazing children who have all gone off to carve out their places in the world, while I continue to craft stories that I hope will make you readers feel good and put a smile on your face.

    Sign up for my Newsletter (https://dl.bookfunnel.com/6atcf7g1be) where I often give away free books before publication.

Join my private Facebook group (https://www.facebook.com/groups/191706547909047/) where she posts exclusive excerpts and discuss all things murder and love!

Never miss a new release. Follow me on Amazon:amazon.com/author/jentalty
    And on Bookbub: bookbub.com/authors/jen-talty

facebook.com/JenTaltyRomanceAuthor

instagram.com/jen_talty

amazon.com/author/jentalty

Made in the USA
Columbia, SC
17 March 2019